Lady Chatterley's Confession

Also by Elaine Feinstein

NOVELS

The Circle
The Amberstone Exit
Children of the Rose
The Ecstasy of Dr Miriam Garner
The Shadow Master
The Survivors
The Border
Mother's Girl
All You Need
Loving Brecht
Dreamers

POETRY

In a Green Eye
The Celebrants
The Magic Apple Tree
Some Unease and Angels
Badlands
City Music
The Selected Poems of Marina Tsvetayeva
Three Russian Poets
Selected Poems

BIOGRAPHY

Bessie Smith
A Captive Lion: The Life of Marina Tsvetayeva
Lawrence's Women: The Intimate Life of D. H. Lawrence

Elaine Feinstein

Lady Chatterley's Confession

MACMILLAN

First published 1995 by Macmillan

an imprint of Macmillan General Books
25 Eccleston Place London SW1W 9NF
and Basingstoke

Associated companies throughout the world

ISBN 0–333–63235–4

1 3 5 7 9 8 6 4 2

A CIP catalogue record for this book is available from
the British Library

Phototypeset by Intype, London
Printed by Mackays of Chatham PLC, Chatham, Kent

The author would like to thank the estate of Frieda Lawrence Ravagli.

One

It is October. The beech trees are red; there is leaf dust in the air. A new war stretches across the whole of Europe. And here I sit in the sunshine, waiting for a letter from the man I love.

As I try to make sense of everything that has happened to me, my thoughts go back to the woods of Wragby, and the gamekeeper's hut where I first lay in Mellors' rough bed. Even if I have lived wrongly and foolishly, I cannot regret the happiness I found then.

People were sorry for my husband, Sir Clifford Chatterley, because he had been paralysed in the Great War. And so was I, but when I think of those years of his convalescence, I chiefly remember my own stunned blankness. No resentment. There were so many dead. No bad temper between us. We lived as peaceably and quietly together as if all our emotions had been destroyed at one moment, in the same explosion that wrecked Clifford's body.

People were sorry for me, I knew, as another casualty of war. I was so young a wife. Even his friends would have winked at a discreet infidelity. Clifford himself encouraged me to take a lover who might give us a child he could pretend was his own. He wanted an heir to Wragby Hall. He wanted that more than he wanted anything other than our quiet companionship. And for a long time I, too, believed that our friendship might be enough.

When I married Clifford Chatterley I liked him, or liked talking to him, which in those days seemed the most important part of any relationship. We were good friends. Enjoyed the same music. The same literature. He'd studied in Germany, as I had, and come rushing back to England in the same way when war began. I met him in the uniform of a first lieutenant, with blue eyes, an open face and sturdy English bearing, and found him the most natural man to marry in my whole world. I didn't care about his position. Clifford wasn't rich, even though he was a baronet and heir to Wragby Hall. And our honeymoon was happy enough: we were both young and passionate. Who knows how things would have gone? I mean if he hadn't been sent back from France smashed and gallant in a wheelchair, to make a marriage without sex or the hope of children.

All I wanted was to love and be loved. Nothing else gave me the strength to leave my husband's house when I was carrying Mellors' child. It was after my beautiful daughter Emily was born that the doubts began. I listened to a great deal of advice then. From my father, for one, usually so indulgent to me, and now exasperated by my indolence and indecision.

It was a day in late March, a month or so after Emily's birth, that he arrived to take me for lunch at the Café Royal in Regent Street. I was staying with my sister Hilda in the Kensington house my mother left us. The magnolia in the garden was in bud, the sun brilliant, when he came to collect me. And I knew he wanted to give me a good talking to.

Now my father wasn't a moralist. He'd had a few affairs himself, and reckoned he was entitled to them, because he was an artist. A good one; celebrated even; a member of the Royal Academy. I'd always forgiven him his peccadilloes. Partly because I was proud of him: Sir Malcolm Reid RA. Partly because I was his favourite daughter. And partly because my mother was long dead, and far less vivid to me.

Old, bluff, hearty, my father brought me into the quiet mahogany rooms of the Café Royal like a prized possession, explaining to the waiter that I was his daughter, smiling at some of his cronies at the neighbouring table. He was always rather full of himself, but I didn't mind that. I knew what he had on his mind, though he got to it a bit slowly. He'd been in New York when I went into the nursing home to give birth and I guessed he had not been travelling with my stepmother. Now he felt a bit sheepish about broaching the subject of my future.

For my part, I was pleased to have him order an excellent meal. Hilda was going through a period of being very pernickety about vegetarianism: there was far too much nut and yoghurt in her cook's repertoire. So my father amused me, as we ate a dozen oysters each, with his tales of New York art dealers. At last he came to the point.

'You must look after yourself, my dear. It's very important. If your poor mother were alive, she would have known how you should do it.'

I was a little put off by this invocation of my dead mother. 'I'm rather glad not to have her clucking over me, if you want to know.'

'You never understood one another,' he said. 'Fine woman. Fabian, that kind of thing. She'd have been concerned. Of course she would. About your health, you see.'

Now I'd never had to worry about my health. What I saw every day in the mirror was a good-looking, country face with russet colouring and a fresh complexion. When I was at school, I'd found my robust milkmaid appearance decidedly unromantic; I can even remember drinking vinegar to give me the fashionable, drawn cheeks which made Hilda so glamorous. So I knew it wasn't my health he was worrying about.

'I'm perfectly well,' I said.

'You must rest. Build yourself up,' he insisted, pouring me another glass of red wine. 'And we must talk seriously. About your plans. Will you go back to Clifford?'

'No,' I said.

That at least I was sure of, whatever else.

'I suppose not,' he said, nodding. 'I can't say I'm surprised. Never really liked the man. Not my kind. Not even when he was all in one piece. Never liked his writing. What makes a man suddenly decide he wants to be a writer?'

I shook my head.

'Still less now that he fancies himself as a mining magnate. But what are your plans exactly?'

'I've made none,' I said. 'I don't know what I shall do. Except look after my daughter.'

'Yes. Pretty child. Very happy for you, my dear,' he said. 'But we'll have to sort something out. Investments and so on. Can't have you going short because of a marital row, can we?'

I said that I thought I would have enough to live on.

'True enough, or would be in ordinary times. Still, if you've been reading the papers lately, there's rather a nasty drop on the old stock market.'

The waiter had brought a rare fillet steak, which I began to eat with an enormous appetite. My father watched me with approval.

'Good. Good. You'll just have to make sure you

behave sensibly. When did you last see the other fellow?
Your gamekeeper?'

'You mean Mellors,' I said quietly.

Saying his name gave me an odd pang. In the echo
of that shock I realized I was living in a kind of sleep,
from which only the thought of him had the power to
wake me. It was as if I had forgotten the man himself,
and yet there was a small part of me still alive which
could be reached by his name.

'Comes up to London, does he? From time to time?
Yes, I suppose he must.'

'He visited me once in the nursing home,' I said.

He laid down his knife and fork carefully and took
my hand.

'Do nothing foolish,' he begged me.

I was still bewildered by the numbness that had so
recently yielded.

'I thought you liked him,' I said.

'Well, he is a decent enough fellow. Never blamed
you for taking up with him. Now have I?'

I agreed he had not.

'Or seeing him now. Father of your child and all
that. I can understand how it would be. Yet, when all is
said and done—' He shook his head. 'When I think of
the education you've had, I'm a bit surprised. That it's
still going on, I mean. I know you've never been an
intellectual, Connie. No matter for that.'

He laughed, and I did not argue with him. I was

trying to understand myself and what I felt. He saw my remoteness and frowned, as if guessing its cause.

'I *do* worry sometimes, worry about your common sense, Connie,' he said.

I looked up at him wonderingly. All I wanted was to love and be loved.

It must have been a little over a month later that I had a letter from Mellors to tell me his divorce from Bertha Coutts had at last gone through. I'd never set eyes on his wife, but I knew they'd lived apart for many years before Mellors and I met, and she was said to be a drunken slut of a woman. His was a cool note, matter of fact, as if he were refusing to put any pressure upon me. Yet the sight of his writing was enough to remind me of his voice and presence. For the first time since the birth of my child I let myself think of being with him as a wife. And I knew what I must do. I would have to visit Clifford and persuade him to give me my freedom. So I left my baby daughter in the care of Hilda's housekeeper and hired a car to take me to the Midlands.

As I was driven once again through the fine parkland that surrounded Wragby Hall, that ugly old warren of a house, my optimism faded. There was something so blind about the windows, as though no one ever looked out of them; and I was a little afraid to approach the heavy wooden door. It was only a year since I had left my husband, and there was no reason to think he had forgiven me.

Clifford was waiting for me in the morning room, sitting in his wheelchair, more red-faced than I remembered but still impeccably dressed, with a deliberately chosen, rather garish, hand-painted tie. He received me with a show of civility, manoeuvring his chair with great dexterity to open the drinks cabinet, and setting out glasses for us without the assistance of a servant. I saw his pride, and his hurt. His courage touched me.

'Gin and tonic?'

'No, thank you.'

'Perhaps not,' he agreed. 'Fruit juice? Mineral water?'

I accepted the last.

'Better for a new mother,' he said, his eyes very bright, his whole face shining with his ironic sense of the situation. We talked of the landscape and the mines and the journey up from London. Yet, for all the courtesy of his words, his eyes frightened me: they glinted with malice. In my letter I had mentioned my need to talk to him about something urgent and serious and, whatever he guessed, he was not going to help me by raising that before I did. At length, I approached the purpose of my visit.

'So my former gamekeeper Mellors is now a free man, and *this* is the important matter you wanted to discuss with me! I'm very disappointed, Connie. Such news is of no interest whatsoever.'

'But perhaps it is to me,' I began.

'Does it really concern you? I don't think so. It may be important to *Mellors* that his squalid marriage is at an end, I grant you that. But do you seriously expect me to release you so you can marry him?'

'I hoped—'

'Did you hope I would do so?' he repeated, almost gleefully.

'I did. Yes. You know I have a child.'

I could see from the alarming lines that now bit into his face that he must have had hopes of his own in relation to this meeting, and that his disappointment was unlikely to make him charitable.

'At the moment the child has the protection of my name. Nothing wrong with that, is there?' he said presently.

'Except that she is Mellors' child.'

'Do you want to bring disgrace on the whole family? Declare the scandal, my inadequacy, your disloyalty? Is that what you want?'

'I simply want to marry Mellors,' I explained.

'I'm doing you a favour, Connie. You don't see it now, but you will. What you think of doing could only be a disaster. I know you and your sister have some fancy socialist beliefs you picked up as students, but do be sensible.' He paused. 'I haven't been following

Mellors' career since he left my employment. What is he doing now?' He gave a bark of laughter. 'An agricultural labourer, isn't he? Can you imagine what life is like in those tied cottages, Connie? How could that be a fit place for your daughter?'

'We can buy a farmhouse,' I said. 'A pretty stone house, in Derbyshire. And some land.'

He stared.

'With your money, I suppose?'

'Why not? He will have to work hard to keep us. It seems fair enough.'

'I imagine you would be providing a good deal of the income as well as the capital.' He laughed. 'Times are hard, as you'd know if you read the newspapers.' His face had twisted into a worldly leer: he always prided himself on his knowledge of financial matters. 'I don't really understand you, Connie,' he admitted. 'If you are still so passionate, why don't you simply take weekends away together?'

'We want a whole life together, not a few weekends.'

Clifford looked sceptical.

'A whole life? With a man like that? You'll find it isn't possible. There's too wide a gap between you.'

'What's the gap? I don't feel it,' I cried. 'I don't believe in the class system. Nobody does. It has no meaning these days. Why should it prevent me doing what I want?'

He smiled at my sudden vehemence.

'Put it out of your mind, Connie. What *you* want is quite irrelevant in law. I suppose you have seen a lawyer? You understand the possible grounds for divorce, do you? In an English court?'

'I know I have given you ample grounds,' I said.

'If I choose to make use of them. But I do not. Sorry. Do you expect me to behave like a gentleman and take the blame on myself?' His smile made him look like a wolf. 'I can hardly do that, can I?' he said, with amusement. 'It's medically impossible to pretend, so you need not ask it. In the nature of things, you cannot divorce me. And I'm glad to be able to prevent you making such a horrible mistake.'

He smiled in triumph, as if that wartime wound, which had left him incapable of sexual intercourse, had at last found its justification.

On the way out of Wragby Hall, I met Sir Clifford's housekeeper, Mrs Bolton. She was a village woman who had lost her own man in a mining disaster. When I had begun to find caring for Clifford was running down my health, she'd been employed to nurse him. She attended to all his most intimate needs. And she had grown very close to her patient. Even before I left Wragby, she was answering his bell when he woke in the night, and staying awake to play chess and cards with him in the small hours. There was a time when I'd leant on the kindness of this woman, her complicity even, when I first began to visit Mellors in his game-keeper's hut.

Mrs Bolton was greyer now, and looked tired, as if the year since I left Wragby had not been easy. Yet there was a curious air of triumph in her, too, as if she was proud of taking care of Sir Clifford through all his rages. I paused for a moment in answer to her greeting, and tried to read her expression.

'I do so hope you'll be happy, my lady,' she said.

I wondered if she gave me my title with some malice.

'Don't call me that,' I flashed. 'My family were never aristocracy. My England is Kensington or the Scottish hills. Nothing grander.'

'I meant no harm, I'm sure,' said Mrs Bolton. 'How is the baby? A girl, isn't it? Where did you leave her?'

'My sister's housekeeper is looking after her for a few days, but I usually like to look after her myself.'

'Quite right.'

There was always something sly about Mrs Bolton. I imagined her in the early hours of the morning, smiling as she smoothed the pillows under Clifford's head when he wished to sleep. She enjoyed looking after him. Her nursing always had a sensual element in it, as if stroking Clifford's poor paralysed body gave her the pleasure a mother takes in her child. I had always been repelled by the delight she took in the service she gave him; it was an undignified, almost obscene pleasure.

'But I wish you could have brought her to give us a sight of the little creature,' she went on. 'It might have softened Sir Clifford's heart.'

It was as I suspected: Clifford had guessed what I might have in mind. He had talked it over with Mrs Bolton. She was privy now to all his thoughts.

'Emily has nothing to do with Sir Clifford,' I said coolly.

'I don't suppose you think to be coming back here, do you?' asked Mrs Bolton.

'I don't,' I said, giving the woman a wry smile. If Mrs Bolton feared to be replaced from her strange eminence in Wragby Hall, she had nothing to worry about from me.

That night I stayed at a small hotel in a nearby town, and my spirits were low as I returned to London the next day. It was a cold afternoon as my cab drew up outside the Kensington house. In the central gardens of the pretty square a magnolia tree was in flower, and the first apple blossom hung over the door, but the pavements were wet and the wind had an edge to it. As the maid let me in Hilda came towards the door wearing a pale green housecoat.

'You *do* look exhausted, Connie,' she observed, her tone more impatient than anxious.

'Well, I am rather cold,' I admitted, with a shaky laugh.

'Travelling is so uncomfortable these days. I'll get Maria to light a fire.'

I followed her along the white and gilt corridor into a sitting room with huge windows.

'Where's Emily?' I asked.

'She's absolutely fine. Don't fuss. Maria took her to the park this morning and now she's having her bottle in the kitchen. Would you like coffee?'

'I think I'll have a bath first.'

Hilda paused, her eyes alight with curiosity.

'Aren't you going to tell me what Clifford *said*?'

'There's nothing to tell. He said no. He's quite adamant.'

I drew a very hot bath, and put some of my sister's bath salts from Harrods in the water. Then I lay back in the huge bath tub to savour the heavy perfume. Remotely, I admired the impudent mermaids flirting on the green-tiled walls. Then I sat, soaping myself and looking down at my swelling breasts and the fine brown line that ran from my navel to the triangle of thick red hair between my legs. That line was a reminder of giving birth to Emily. As I thought of the child I was soon going to hold in my arms, my weariness melted from me.

Once out of the bath, I looked at myself for a time in Hilda's long mirror. My body was rich and full and still firm even after the pregnancy; my waist sloped gently down into rounded thighs. For a moment, in my imagination, I felt a loving hand on my buttocks. I shook away the memory. I would not let myself think about Mellors. Not yet. Not until I knew for certain what I was going to do. And what seemed best. For myself. And the child, too.

'I suppose Clifford wants you to go back and play nurse to him,' said Hilda, as she poured coffee after I was bathed and dressed.

'He didn't suggest it. It doesn't matter. The important thing is he won't give me a divorce.'

Hilda set down her cup and saucer thoughtfully.

'Don't snap my head off,' she said, 'but is that so terrible? Mellors can always visit you in London.'

'He hates doing it,' I said. 'He's too proud.'

'So, what will you do now?'

'I don't know.'

'No sense in brooding,' said Hilda briskly. 'Come with me to the Skeffingtons' tonight.'

'I don't think so.'

'Do. There'll be interesting people to talk to.'

'There's nothing I want to say to them.'

'You can flirt and be irresponsible, can't you? Remember how we enjoyed ourselves long ago with the students in Dresden? And some of the people at the Skeffingtons' are a good deal more glamorous.'

'Who *are* the Skeffingtons?' I asked. 'I don't think I know them.'

'I met Geoffrey through my first husband,' said Hilda, colouring a little so that I knew immediately they had once had a more intimate relationship. 'He was part of a Cambridge group of friends then. Married and divorced since. Knows everybody. The Prime Minister, T. S. Eliot, George Gershwin. All the fashionable people. Maria will look after Emily.'

'I suppose I must try and cheer myself up,' I said, frowning, 'whatever I decide.'

The Skeffingtons lived in Bloomsbury in a house with high Georgian windows and brilliant white furniture. Whatever Skeffington did these days to earn his money, he clearly had a great deal of it. Wragby Hall was dowdy and unpainted, while the Skeffingtons' house glittered with lights and mirrors and shining floors. The guests, too, glittered: the women were like birds, feathery and brilliant; the men well-groomed and shining with the attention they lavished on themselves.

For all their gloss and colour though, in my bewilderment the people seemed insubstantial to me: living ghosts, as they whirled through the morning room into the ballroom. Hilda knew how to float into such a room, from hostess to illustrious guest in a wave of perfumed ease. In contrast, my thoughts made me heavy, almost bovine. It was not that I knew no one, but that I could not bring myself to feel concern for any of them. It was like one of the dreariest parties in the old days at Wragby Hall. And my conviction that it had been a mistake to come was confirmed as I recognized the flat, pale face of the successful Irish playwright Michaelis, with whom I had once had a short affair. I turned my face away; I hoped he was sufficiently occupied with the admiring young woman at his side to pay me no attention, but instead he came over towards me. He still had that awkwardness of a stray dog which had attracted me when he came to visit Clifford and me in Wragby Hall. For all his success, he never seemed comfortable in English society.

'Didn't expect to see you here,' he said.

'I don't know why I've come,' I replied.

He looked at me sadly, and I recognized that loneliness in his eyes which had once moved me.

'You have a child now, I hear.'

'A daughter.'

'I was glad for you,' he said.

I saw he was curious, too, and determined to give him no further information. As I looked at his soft, boyish face, I remembered, with a little revulsion, how his lips had once pressed into my breasts.

'And now you are in town,' he was saying. 'A good thing. I can never understand why the landed gentry put up with being bored in the country. Are you doing lots of interesting things here?'

I tried to remember the last exhibition I had visited

with Hilda. 'Sometimes I go to the National Gallery,' I said at length.

'We have a fine show of celebrities tonight,' he said, staring around with satisfaction, as if simply being in the same room with famous people enhanced his own precarious sense of worth. 'Noël Coward. Did you see *Hay Fever* last year? So witty and wicked.'

'Do you know him personally?' I asked.

'Well enough to introduce you, if you would like that.'

He seemed, however, to need to brace himself for the task. I smiled.

'I mean, do you see these people as friends, apart from such occasions?'

'I suppose these *are* the kind of occasions we meet,' he said, a little puzzled. 'We are all very busy. We exchange a few words. Catch up with one another's lives. As you and I are doing now, I suppose.'

The thought of a life made up of such distant encounters appalled me. Michaelis continued to chatter.

'Do you like these new films – the talkies, I mean?'

'I don't often go,' I admitted.

'I can't understand the passion for Al Jolson,' he continued. 'I've tried to, but I don't see it. Greta Garbo, on the other hand—'

I did not attempt to take in all he said. I wasn't really listening. I was remembering how I had once liked this

18

man, for his melancholy perhaps, or the impudence with which he manipulated a world that terrified him. I could see his face pressed down in my lap and pleading; I could remember him as a lover. Trembling. Always trembling. And then sobbing. Always too eager. All the while he talked, I found myself imagining his little shamed boy's face as he came to a climax of pleasure. I still felt some attraction towards him, but I did not want to be moved by such memories: his presence seemed to point up rather painfully how meaningless so much of my life had been.

Unbidden, a memory of Mellors came back to me. He was standing very straight under a streetlight, on the pavement outside a cheap London hotel. He was refusing to come back with me to Hilda's house. It must have been while I was still pregnant. As he turned, he smiled at me; an ironic glint of a smile; his blue eyes looking at me directly. He was saying goodbye.

As I thought of that goodbye, a great emptiness filled me. I did not want to flirt and have fun as Hilda did. I did not want to be moving around with shadowy people who had no substance for me. Mellors was the only person I knew who had any solidity, and I wanted to be with him.

'I must go now,' I said to Michaelis suddenly. 'Will you find me a taxi?'

For a moment he misunderstood me, and then saw my pallor and determination.

'Are you quite *well*?' he asked, with a measure of concern in his voice.

'Perfectly,' I said.

Indeed, for the first time that year I felt a strange kind of serenity.

Over breakfast, Hilda tried to dissuade me, but my mind was made up.

'It's not a question of morals, Connie. You know me better than that. Think of the talk there's bound to be.'

'There won't be any talk. I shall give myself his name.'

'Are you taking Emily?'

'Of course.'

'And whose name will the child have?'

'The same, naturally,' I said impatiently. Now that my mind was made up, I was eager for the arrangements to be made. 'I can't imagine why I have been making myself so unhappy about such trivial legalities.'

Hilda shook her head, but she could see I was determined.

'I'm sending a wire straight away to the cottage, so that he will be at home when we arrive,' I said. 'Can you arrange a car? I shall have to spend the next few days shopping.'

Mellors' cottage lay south of the Peak District, at the outer edge of a mining village called Plomford. After about an hour and a half, the hired car crossed naked railway lines into a long street of blackened brick dwellings, flush on the pavement. The light was going as the car made its way between about a mile of grimy brick houses. There was a stink of sulphur in the air, and smuts on the spring flowers. There was a little shop selling rhubarb, lemons and soap; a chapel with panes of purple glass; a draper's shop and a huge hoarding in garish colours advertising Al Jolson. And then, just as the hedges began again, in the first green of the countryside, there was a group of cottages, with Mellors' at the end of it.

I could see him through the window. He was alone. He looked like a fox, I thought: nervous, thin, almost sly. He had made a life for himself without female help. Then I tapped on the glass and he swung round to see who was there. He smiled as he saw the child in my arms.

'Shall I wait with the car?' asked the chauffeur smoothly.

'No. I haven't come on a visit. I've come to stay. Unload the cases and the cradle.'

I tapped on the window again and Mellors came out to take the child from me. It was more than three months since I had set eyes upon him, and I smiled radiantly, but he did not respond. His face was closed, as if he did not trust me. He took the child inside and then helped the chauffeur take in the packages. He watched me pull out money to pay the man and send him on his way. He looked almost angry.

The interior of the cottage was a living room, ten or fifteen square feet, with an open kitchen range in the scullery, with a sink and a copper. The floor was waxed linoleum.

'Who keeps this so clean?' I asked, a little put out at the way he had received me.

'I do. It's small,' he said.

'We could do a great deal with it,' I said brightly. 'Perhaps we could sand the floors?' I looked out of the back window. 'And the garden is lovely.'

He did not altogether like my enthusiasm or my energy.

'What will the child have?' he asked.

'I've prepared a bottle. It only needs warming,' I said. 'And then I'll put her to bed. She's tired.'

He watched me quietly as I moved about arranging the child's clothes. We were uneasy together, and I was vexed that he showed so little welcome.

'You seem in doubt about my coming here,' I said at last.

To my alarm, he nodded.

'I am,' he replied.

'Isn't it what we arranged?'

'Yes. But what can I offer you, really?' He frowned. 'I know what I want,' he said slowly, 'but I don't know if I can have it. I don't even know if we can live side by side.'

It was not how I had imagined my arrival. A little answering frown formed between my eyes.

'What do you do in the evenings?' I asked him.

'Oh, I read.' He smiled.

I had thought of him as having quite a different appetite for life. Yet what had I expected? Would I have felt more at ease if he had spent all his evenings at the cinema or the pub?

He set up the cot and I began to prepare Emily for sleep. I undressed her completely, then washed and wiped her and put powder under her buttocks before putting her in thick sleeping garments. She was behaving well, perhaps enjoying this concentration of my efforts upon her. And then, as I buttoned her into her sleeping suit and at last bent over to put her into the cot, I became aware of a change in the way he was looking down at me. I kissed the child's soft feet before tucking them under the little eiderdown. Perhaps he was sorry for his curmudgeonly reception. As I turned, he put a hand on my neck. It was the first time he had touched me since I arrived, and the tenderness and warmth of his big hand almost brought tears to my eyes.

'There,' he said.

My mouth dried. All the moisture in my body seemed to flow downwards to the centre of my being as he lifted me to my feet and towards him so that I could feel his body pressing against my own.

Two

An hour before dawn, I woke briefly to the sound of a bird's call rising to a piercing cascade of notes. Mellors was lying awake beside me, and I put my lips against his shoulder.

'A robin,' he murmured.

Blackbird, thrush, robin and wren, I thought drowsily, without speaking. I was at the heart of England, and I was happier than I had been in years. Everything was going to be easy. The night before we had made love, the first time since the birth of my child, and the pleasure of it still filled me. His face beside me on the pillow was finely drawn; his hand on my breast was long, narrow and capable. And if when he opened his eyes there was something unrelenting in them, it only added to his attraction.

I woke again, much later, to find him looking down at me with amusement. He was fully dressed. I sat up at once, in the mid-morning sunshine.

'Where's Emily? What time is it?'

'Emily's been up since five with me. I showed her

the pigs, then I put her back for a sleep. I've made you some breakfast. Would you like it in bed? It's Sunday.'

A smell of country sweetness reached me from the open windows; a dangle of yellow barberry framed them. I lay back on the pillows.

'You'll make me lazy,' I smiled. 'Don't spoil me.'

'I only do what I like,' he said, watching me. 'There's toast and sweet jam made from last year's quince. Fresh eggs. And a pot of tea.'

'Sounds lovely.'

He sat watching me while I ate.

'Does Clifford know you're here?'

'Not his business where I am.'

'What does he say about the child?'

'He didn't seem to care much about her. Might have been different if she'd been a boy.'

'Of course. He'd have minded then,' he agreed.

'What do they think about your divorce around here?' I asked.

'Nobody's talked to me about it,' he replied. 'I'm not sure they know I was ever married.'

'Good. Then I can call myself Mrs Mellors,' I announced. 'You can say your wife and child have come from London. The south anyway. There won't be a problem.'

For a moment he looked sombre. And then he grinned and spoke in the local accent.

'Happen we should have gone to British Columbia an' all. There'd have been no talk there.'

I felt a little twitch of a frown between my eyebrows at that. I'd never fancied the idea of life as a woman pioneer, and feared we might be destitute and far from friends.

'I like it here,' I said. 'It's so pretty. Do you always get up so early?'

'Five? That's not early. This is a mining village. A miner gets up at quarter to four in the morning.'

'And the women?'

'They say it's bad luck to meet a woman before going to work on the morning shift.'

After lunch, we carried Emily to inspect the duck-pond and the village green. There were great oaks and a magnificent horse chestnut; hawthorn and apple blossom everywhere. I came back full of plans, hardly registering the mean houses flat against the pavement of the main street.

'We'll buy a farmhouse. And a few fields. Why should you work for someone else? What you do now for your employer, you can do for yourself. I'll investigate tomorrow. Go to an estate agent for you. Find somewhere that's not been on the market too long. Then you can come and look at what I've found when you're free.'

'And how will I find the capital for the land, let alone the livestock?'

His blue eyes met mine directly.

'Please don't be difficult,' I said. 'You know I have the money. Why shouldn't I help to make things better? You'll have to work all hours to keep the three of us. It seems only fair to make my contribution.'

He had not dropped his blue gaze and, for all my rapid words, he seemed unconvinced. Emily had begun to cry and I took the child from him.

'Don't think I want to drag you down to my level, Connie. Nor the baby,' he said at last. 'But we'll have to talk about it more thoroughly. There's more to running a farm than looking after animals. I don't have the experience.'

'Well, I must feed the child now,' I said, rather crossly.

As he opened the door at the side of the cottage, I felt the measure of his resistance, but I was convinced it was an obvious move. Farmers lived well, and labourers worked for a pittance.

'It's a risk, you know,' he said, as I mixed the milk for Emily's bottle.

To my mind, his natural capacity for organization made it a risk well worth taking. I'd never had to worry about money myself, and was determined he should learn to be less anxious about it. So I set myself to persuade him.

After a few months we found a stone farmhouse, about twenty-five miles to the east, outside a mining village. It was cheaper than I'd expected and, though

Mellors sucked in his lips and hummed and hahed about it, I pushed the deal through. He gave notice to the farmer he'd been working for and, once in our new home, I could see he enjoyed having property to care for. He never said as much, but he worked at whitewashing walls and making shelves. We were both happy. I had rugs brought from London, and a piano, some paintings and some furniture but, apart from these expenses, I used no more of my income than I had in London. There were no animals ready for market that first year, but we had a fine Christmas all the same.

Hilda's letters teased me for playing house like a wife in the suburbs:

'What on earth do you find to do in the evenings, Connie? Or do you and Mellors go straight to it after supper like animals in rut? Aren't you bored yet? Or has Mellors discovered some new erogenous zone?'

I don't remember what I replied. Something about the way he taught me to make berries into jam, perhaps, or to braise a hare that he caught in the back field. Hard to explain the happiness of those first years. Just sharing the ordinary business of being alive, the pleasures of sunshine and the hot smell of flowers seemed to be enough. Together we watched Emily learn to crawl and then, soon after her first birthday, begin to totter between us. I was determined to look after her myself, unlike my own mother, who left me in the care of nannies. And Emily's fearlessness pleased Mellors, and he was amused by the embraces she liked to shower on his old dog Flossie. He liked to lift the child high on his shoulders, while she held on to his hair, laughing.

I thought it would be fun to do my own housework, but my old spoiled life hadn't prepared me for it. Mellors was kind about my mistakes at first. He didn't complain when I burnt a rabbit he brought in as a treat, and when I found it impossible to unwind the sheets boiling in the copper, he helped me get them out. But my relationship with Mellors was never as peaceful as Hilda imagined.

Even in the earliest months of being together, we had violent arguments. Once he shouted at me for throwing out all his socks rather than darning them. I was shaken to the core by his fury, which seemed altogether unreasonable when I was prepared to buy new socks as he needed them. It was as if my refusal to operate the frugal code of his childhood was a form of rebellion. No one had ever spoken to me in such a voice before. And the note of my own voice rose in response. But when we made love that evening, I remember, the sex was particularly sweet and intense.

He never liked saying he loved me when I asked him to.

'Nay, what does that *mean*, woman? When all's said and done? I can't mouth the words.'

'It means something to me,' I said, taken aback. 'It's the reason I'm here. Because I love you.'

'I know why you're here,' he said slyly.

I was incensed by the sexual confidence of his grin.

'I must find a local woman to clean up,' I said some time in our second summer together. 'Or you'll end up looking after me as well as the farm.'

'You are untidy,' he agreed. 'You leave your stockings and bits everywhere. Well, you'll be able to pick and choose women to help. There aren't many jobs going locally.'

Mary was a fresh-faced village girl, good-natured and hardworking, and taciturn by temperament. She disappeared back into the village street as soon as she had worked her hours. From her departure after lunch to the time Mellors returned for his tea, I was alone. I usually played the piano, with Emily at my feet pushing on the pedals and sometimes singing.

One afternoon later that year I went shopping in Tatterwell, taking Emily wrapped up warmly against a brisk wind. Coming back in the trap, we drove through a crowd of men in hobnailed pit boots and few women in clogs, standing about the main street. Our trim appearance drew their attention but they didn't touch their caps. They looked rather hostile, I thought, and instinctively put an arm round my daughter to reassure her, though she showed no sign of alarm.

'They are only miners and their wives,' I told her calmly. 'I believe there is no work for them.'

When we returned home, Mellors came out to help me unload the parcels, and to lead the horse away to the stable. After that, he came in to build up the fire. Emily sat in front of it, humming contentedly, while I waited for a chance to ask about the men standing around the village street. Mellors frowned when I did.

'Things are bad,' he said. 'The mine was working two days a week until this month, but now even that is stopping.'

'Why?'

I was genuinely puzzled. Not only Clifford but many of the families we knew had taken so much of their income out of mining. Didn't people need coal? He saw my face.

'Did the men frighten you?'

'Why are their teeth so bad?' I asked, shuddering. 'There's hardly anyone in the village with a full set of teeth, and some just mumble.'

'They can't afford good food,' he said, amused. 'That's what it is.'

I was ashamed of my spoilt ignorance.

'What do they live on?' I asked curiously. 'If they have no work, I mean?'

'Some have the dole. 'Bout thirty bob a week. Till their stamps run out.'

'But . . . how do they live on that with families?'

'Most of their money goes on rent,' he answered levelly. 'They have potatoes and dripping, and a bit of bacon if they're lucky. It'll be worse in winter.'

'And those men standing around? What are they doing? Are they Bolsheviks?'

'They won't have thought that far,' he said, grinning.

'They hate me anyway,' I said, wanting for all my certainty to be persuaded otherwise.

'Why shouldn't they?'

'It's nothing to do with *me* that the colliery has stopped working,' I said, startled by his reply. 'Who are their masters? They should hate them.'

'They recognize you,' he said.

'How do they?'

I thought I'd been dressing so carefully, with so little sign of superiority.

'Your skin and your hair,' he said. 'They can see what you are, easily enough.'

A faint smile came to his narrow face.

'And they hate me for that?' I asked.

'They imagine you live in luxury.'

The word stung me.

'*Here?* What can they mean?'

'Space, for a start,' he said.

I had never asked myself how they lived in the houses along the village street.

Seeing my dismay, he put an arm round my

shoulders. He didn't feel guilty. He worked hard in all weathers. Ours was a smallholding; even in good times it was too small for easy profits; and these days the margins were tight.

'I ought to try and get to know some of our neighbours,' I said over supper one evening.

'The local farmers, you mean?'

'I mean in the village. If they *knew* me, they wouldn't look at me with such hostility.'

'They're friendly enough folk,' he said. 'But you won't find it easy. They'll not be much interested in books and music.'

Mary usually came in to help in the mornings, but when the builders came to install a new bath and a modern hot-water system, I decided she ought to come in all day. I could easily have waited till Monday to say so, but decided instead to take the opportunity to visit her at home. Mary lived with her coalminer father and a truculent-looking mother with several younger children. Approaching the cottage nervously, I saw Mary's mother at the door, in a sacking apron and with a brush in her hand.

She said nothing as I approached.

'It's a fine day,' I said, with an agreeable smile.

The face was closed to me. Angry. The child that was clutching the woman's hand had a dirty, tear-stained face, and a torn blue cardigan. She began to whimper.

'Shut up your noise,' said the woman.

'Would you like a sweetie?' I asked the child.

The child looked up doubtfully, with the light of a little hope in her eyes.

'No, she wouldn't,' said the woman. 'She doesn't take sweets from strangers.'

'But I'm not a stranger,' I said. 'Your Mary works for me. Is she in?'

'She's not,' said the woman. 'What shall I tell her?'

When I explained about the builder, the sardonic expression on the woman's face deepened. She rubbed her hands on her apron.

'She'll be glad of the money,' she said.

From indoors, I could hear the growling voice of Mary's father; a short man with thick arms, and blue scars over his nose and forehead which had once alarmed Emily in the village street.

'I'm meant to be black-leading the stove,' said the woman with the ghost of a smile.

My own smile recognized the claims of female solidarity, however inappropriate.

'Will you come in for a cup of tea?' asked Mrs Allen hesitantly.

I had been hoping for just such an invitation, and followed her willingly into the crowded little cottage. There on a table covered with an oilcloth was a tub full of water and crocks waiting to be washed. Under the table was what looked like a pile of dirty clothes, mixed up with socks to be darned. A line of washing hung overhead. There were several children pushing and squabbling in the same room. As the woman fussed to set a kettle on the fire amid the confusion, I marvelled at her amazing equanimity; it was difficult to imagine remaining calm under such pressure. When I took a cup of tea from her, I was surprised at how clean it was. As I drank the tea I tried desperately to find some topic to interest us both, but Mrs Allen was drawn away by the voice of her husband, and I soon gave up the attempt at conversation.

'How *can* they all sleep in that house? How many bedrooms can there be?' I wondered aloud to Mellors later that evening.

'When I was a child,' said Mellors, 'we slept eleven to a room.'

'*You* lived in a house like that?'

'It wasn't a bad life. Coal fire, kippers, strong tea. Father was usually in work. That's what makes the difference.'

I thought of the grim miner and the blue scars on his face. I described them, and the fear they engendered.

'They're like tattooing,' I said.

'That's exactly what they're like,' he said. 'The coal dust enters the cuts. And then the skin grows over it.'

'What was your father like?'

'A brute. Didn't like me, of course, because he thought I was mardy, and he didn't read much himself so he didn't approve of it. He used to sit in his shirt-sleeves looking at the racing finals while Mam did all the work. But it wasn't so bad. I don't remember feeling poor. Things were different before the war. It's a long time ago.'

As winter came on that year, I often saw dumpy, shawled figures of women in heavy black clogs kneeling in the cindery mud near the old mines, and searching eagerly for chips of coal. On every side there were slag heaps and hoisting gear but none of the pits was working.

'Are they stealing the coal?' I asked Mellors one dark evening.

'The colliery don't prosecute very often,' he said abstractedly.

It was a new remoteness. With the beginning of autumn, I had observed a change in his spirits. At first I was unsure what the cause might be. He had begun to work out our yearly accounts, and I watched him all through one long, dark evening, and knew he was anxious.

'I'm failing you, Connie,' he said at last. 'It's not working out.'

I had never seen him look so ashamed, and it hurt me.

'We don't have to worry about money, do we?'

'Yes,' he said. 'If the farm doesn't pay, you haven't the money to keep it going.'

I hadn't thought of that.

'I suppose not,' I said doubtfully. 'We only have to pay our way, though.'

'A man has to provide for his family.'

'I can easily provide for Emily and me,' I said.

A little darkness crossed his face. And he stood up away from me.

'I should never have let you in if I couldn't look after you. I can't just live on you. It's not dignified.'

'Well, you don't,' I said quickly. 'You've your army pension.'

He laughed drily.

'We'd not get far on it.'

'You work every day, all weathers. Where's the indignity in that?'

'I can't master the situation.' He shook his head. 'I don't know what to do.'

But somebody must, I thought.

A little while after this, I met Tommy Bruce, who owned the large farm adjacent to Mellors' smallholding. He drove through the gate one afternoon in a land truck, to deliver some machinery Mellors had bought from him.

'You'll be Mellors' wife,' he said, intrigued, I could see, by my appearance. I flushed under his stare. 'Are you happy here?' he asked me. He was a big man, six feet four, with broad shoulders, a heavy-featured face and the confidently physical air of a boxer. His voice was tinged with a Derbyshire accent and his face was reddened with too much beer. I couldn't think of him as a gentleman, but he looked me closely in the face like an equal. 'I don't know as I should care to live so close to the village.'

'It isn't easy,' I admitted.

'The farm was a snip, though,' he said. 'He bought it at the right time. If he ever wants to sell, he'll be all right.'

'Why should he want to sell?'

'Well,' he chuckled, 'people are poor these days. There's not much meat getting eaten. And it'll get worse when the other mine closes.'

'Why should it close?'

'It doesn't make money.'

'Can't they modernize it?'

In those days, I often felt impatient at the way men just accepted what was happening all round them. I remembered Clifford talking about a new German engine, with a feeder that didn't need a man to stand over it. I think I said something of the sort, and Tommy Bruce's eyes began to glisten with interest. It was not the way many wives talked in Tatterwell.

'Mellors is a lucky fellow,' he chuckled appreciatively, 'to have such a sharp little wife. Good-looking, too.

What do you think to a Charleston now and then at the Pally?'

'Not for me,' I said.

'Then maybe an afternoon at the pictures? There's talk of bringing a cinema to Bakewell. What should you think to that?'

I stared at him. There was a mixture of sexual interest and another kind of curiosity in his voice.

'It doesn't seem a good time for a cinema,' I said slowly, dodging his invitation. 'Will people be interested? Have they got the money, if they're as poor as you say?'

'Not for a new coat.' His eyes went up and down my own modest costume. 'Or hats for their children. But they'll spend it on a bit of dreaming. Especially the women.'

'What about the men?' I asked tartly. 'I suppose anything they have goes on drink.'

'Well, you're an oddity round here, and no mistake,' he said.

He was on to something. It was obvious. I didn't like the insolence in his face, but it came to me that a local farmer could be helpful to us. He would know what to do.

'All the farmers are worried,' I said to Mellors, fresh from my conversation with Bruce.

He stared at me.

'What do you know about that?'

'You should talk to them,' I said. 'They know the market place.'

'Tommy Bruce,' he said, with an edge of venom in his voice.

'You don't like him?'

'No.' He hesitated. 'I saw you talking to him when he brought the machinery round.'

'And that's why you don't like him?'

I smiled at what I took to be jealousy.

'I don't like his style. His conceit.'

'Wasn't he in the army, too?'

'Can't you see the kind he is? A mingy, arse-licking prig. He doesn't want to work with his hands, just to buy and sell.'

'But that's exactly what we need to know about,' I cried. 'Talk to him.'

'Maybe,' said Mellors. He was angry. 'But I'll not be managed like a baby.'

A few days later, Tommy Bruce saw Mellors in Tatterwell and asked us round for Sunday lunch.

'Should have invited you long ago,' he told him. 'No wife, you see. Can't be neighbourly. But I'll get my cleaning woman to put a haunch of meat in the oven and potatoes round it if you'll come. She makes a good apple pie, too.'

The invitation did not altogether please me, though

I knew any friends I made must be easier to find among the gentry than the haggard villagers whose livelihoods were bring stripped away. Yet I had seen the way Bruce sized me up and guessed at my background. There would be questions, and I should have to invent plausible answers. I didn't like the idea of thinking up a whole new family background for myself. The thought of it made me feel tentative and embarrassed. Mellors had more straightforward anxieties.

'He knew my old employer,' he said.

'And how does that signify?' I said, with a boldness I was far from feeling.

We had been living as if on a protected island out of society, and I was afraid that discovery and exposure might be at hand. In the event, the explosion was quite other. Mellors knew, as I did not, how bad things were, and his resentment at the way things were going on the farm made his temper as ready to flare as tinder.

Tommy Bruce had inherited land from his father, and knew everything there was to know about sheep and Derbyshire. His farmhouse was far larger than ours; with rather vulgar wall lights and a good deal of shiny furniture. The other guests were from further away: Freddie Saunders, Bruce's cousin, who farmed 800 acres in Wiltshire and had a wife with a flat, blank face and a passion for hunting. The conversation over drinks mainly concerned the hunt of the previous week-end and there was a good deal of hilarity at the expense of a friend who had failed to take a gate as he should.

'Do you ride?' we were asked.

'I've no time to spend jogging round the country-side,' Mellors replied quietly. 'Nor money to spend on keeping a horse that can't work on the farm.'

As we sat down to the meal he was taciturn, but I could see there were fires of anger underneath. For my part, though I disliked Bruce's country heartiness, I let the alcohol loosen my tongue and began to chatter, not much attending to the darkness in Mellors' face, or the conversation he was having.

It was Freddie Saunders who made confrontation inevitable.

'Well, I had a good war,' he said. 'And the men did, too. Most of them.'

'Did they now?' said Mellors softly. 'Were you in France?'

'India,' said Freddie. 'I'm not ashamed of that.'

'I should think not,' said his wife. 'Went where you were sent.'

'It was all a lie, though, wasn't it?' said Mellors, quietly. 'What they fed us in the war.'

I tried to send him a warning with my eyes, but it was no use.

'You have to defend your country, I suppose,' said Tommy Bruce, good-humouredly enough, and urging additional roast potatoes on to my plate. But I was suddenly not hungry in the least.

'The whole thing will have to go,' said Mellors. 'It'll have to be blown up. And then maybe we can build a decent society on the ruins.'

'Things are bad,' Bruce temporized. 'But you wouldn't want the poor to take to the streets with their pitchforks, would you?'

'They'll not do it here. It isn't Russia,' said Freddie Saunders.

'I should hope not,' said his wife. 'This is a democracy.'

I saw Mellors lay down his knife and fork. The woman was a little discomfited by him, had been throughout the meal, though for my sake he had used the English of his army days. I hoped now he would not lapse into dialect speech, as he sometimes did when he was angry.

'They haven't the spunk,' he said. 'Unfortunately. Look at the people in the streets of Tatterwell. Grey and drab. Willing to give up the whole culture of the island for an American song and a glass of beer. Democracy? That's just one of the words used to get us poor sods out to fight.'

'That's a bit extreme, don't you think?' said Tommy Bruce. 'We can vote and say what we think here. Doesn't that make any difference?'

'*Voting?*' said Mellors. 'What difference could it make? None to me. Who could we vote for? We choose one lot of crooks or another.'

'Yes, but the point is, in a democracy you can change the crooks. So they have to worry a bit about what you think of them.'

'*Do* they?' countered Mellors. 'Is there any sign of that? They don't give a bugger what they do to people. They know we're too beaten down. Does it help me make a living to vote?'

I could see that Tommy Bruce was annoyed by what he saw as Mellors' arrogance quite as much as by his political opinions, and I can't remember what he said after that, except that it was heated and loud for a time until Mellors fell silent. I couldn't taste the apple pie, and we left soon after, with an excuse about a babysitter, though in fact we had arranged for Mary to stay overnight.

After we got home, I tried to explain that the others were just chattering and hadn't expected to be taken so seriously, and we began to quarrel.

'It was just a lunch party. People don't expect to have to defend what they say so passionately.'

The hostility I saw in his face made me flinch.

'Don't your lot *care* about what's true, then? No, I suppose not,' he said. 'If they know what they think. Which I doubt.'

'It's a question of courtesy,' I cried. 'Manners. And they aren't my lot.'

'And how about what is *true*? You treacherous bitch

45

– I was arguing over something *important* and all you can think about is manners.'

I was near to tears as we went up the stairs, and his face was closed to me. First I checked that Emily was comfortably asleep, and shut the door of her bedroom. Then we went into our own. The anger still darkened his face and I was a little afraid of him. I put on my white nightdress in silence. If I had been alone, I should have thrust my face into my pillow and sobbed; instead, I stifled the tears that pricked the back of my throat.

'Will you get into bed?'

'In a moment,' I said.

Was it possible to make friends? There seemed to be nothing I could say that would make things better between us. I shivered as I got under the sheet.

Then, as we lay side by side, he put a hand on my shoulder. To my astonishment, my flesh, which had been quivering with cold and anxiety, seemed now to be charged with a strange electricity. The whole of my skin was alive to his lightest touch. As his fingers felt for my breast and squeezed my nipples, I was suffused with a sensuality so fierce that I almost cried out with the intensity of it. My mouth was dry; my body streamed with desire. He, too, I could feel, was already thick and heavy. The touch of his flesh against me was so disturbing, I longed for him to take me at once, without the least preliminary gesture. And when his body

46

plunged inside me, I came almost immediately in a single blinding orgasm that left me exhausted. We both fell asleep almost at once in the wake of that pleasure.

Three

Mellors went off to market in the company of Tommy Bruce. He returned in a black mood.

'What happened?' I begged him to tell me.

'Those bastards,' he said. 'They all stick together. You can't expect anything else.'

I went over to him and put my arms round his neck.

'We needn't mind.'

'Yes, we must. We do. They cheat me, and I can't do anything about it.'

He lay on his back and looked at the ceiling. His bitterness was overwhelming.

'It was better being a gamekeeper,' he said. 'There was nothing to worry about then but wild things that could look after themselves if some poaching sod didn't creep up on them. I never wanted to go into business on my own. That was your idea, and I shouldn't have fallen in with it. It wasn't what I wanted.'

I felt his reproach at the very centre of my being.

'I'm sorry,' I said, 'if the farm has been a mistake for you.'

He turned restlessly away from me.

'It's my own fault. Any man's fault if he starts listening to women.'

Meanwhile, Emily was growing up. She was a precocious child. As she grew, I marvelled at her. The wide blue eyes were my own, and the glints of red in her hair, but there was a sharpness in her expression I could not recognize in my own childhood photographs. She had learned to speak very early, and her wonderings had an adult alertness.

We had little contact with the village children. A few days after Emily's third birthday, I looked through the front window. I saw three boys with tough, pasty faces and red hair sticking up around their heads. They had come through the open gate and were pushing Emily on the swing Mellors had set up for her. As one of them clambered on the seat with her and began to swing with wild abandon, I ran out in panic to protect her. But Emily was enjoying herself.

'Pushed me very high,' she said complacently.

'You mustn't—' I began. And then stopped, uncertain what to forbid.

The boys looked hardly human to me, and I was afraid of them. I was ashamed of such feelings, and I could well imagine what Mellors would say if I forbade his daughter to play with the common children. The boys seemed friendly enough, even a bit scared to be somewhere unfamiliar, and eager to be away from the whole situation. Cravenly, I offered them all a sweet, to mollify them; to conceal, I suppose, my sense they were enemies and that I wanted to keep my pretty, golden-haired child separate from them.

It was for her healthy, open face, apple cheeks and broad face that I had chosen Mary to help me, hoping above all for good nature, and I'd worked hard to establish a good relationship with the girl. I gave her roasted chickens and apple pies from Bakewell to take back to her family. I thrust discarded summer clothes into the girl's hands. And, after a year or so of monosyl-lables and caution, Mary had at last seemed to be warm-ing into a kind of friendship. She had begun to confide her anxieties about her own sweetheart, who lived in the next village. She complained how her father always quarrelled with her mother when he came back from the pub, and sometimes beat her. Once she gave a graphic description of what happened when a flat iron thrown by her mother broke the kitchen window.

'Took him by surprise, that did,' she said with a certain relish. 'But it missed him. He wor that mad after, I thought he'd kill us all. My mam has a bruise the size of a goose egg on her forehead this morning.'

In my turn, I talked cheerfully of the plans we had for refurbishing the farmhouse. In my conversations with Mary, I learnt all the village gossip I would otherwise have missed. If it did not quite make up for the spice of the conversation I had once enjoyed with Hilda, at least I heard some interesting tales. Tommy Bruce was always after the young girls of the neighbourhood, it seemed, and people said he kept a woman in Bakewell.

'Well, he's a handsome old rake,' I said, not entirely disapproving.

Mary was very shocked at rumours of sexual misconduct, and anticipated no sexual pleasure for herself.

'Men like it, I know,' she said darkly, 'but there's not much in it for women, except carrying children.'

When I teased her about her feelings for her own young man, Mary was not to be persuaded.

'No man'll get the better of me till he's put a ring on my finger,' she told me proudly.

I was delighted to have provoked so much animation.

'You're a good girl, Mary,' I said.

'If we get a machine, I could sew curtains,' I suggested to Mellors. 'I've got some pretty material.'

'Where did that come from?' he asked.

He had spent all night lambing, and was very tired.

'My sister sent it.'

He frowned.

'You can't *mind*.'

'No. I've won the war, haven't I? I can let a few battles go,' he agreed.

After the sewing machine was delivered from London, I busied myself making new damask curtains for the sitting room. And then, a little after Easter, Mary's behaviour changed inexplicably. She returned to her earlier taciturn self, her manner coloured now with a resentment that I could not understand. It was almost as if the girl felt betrayed.

'Will you help me hang the curtains, Mary?'

'If I've time when I've cleaned the kitchen.'

'Of course you have the time if I say you are to do it,' I said. 'We could have a cup of tea first, if you like.'

'I've the fires to lay,' said Mary sullenly.

'Is something the matter, Mary?'

'Nothing.'

'Did you have a good Easter?'

'I was at my auntie's for a day. It was all right.'

'*Something* must be wrong,' I said, meeting the full, brooding unhappiness of the girl's expression. 'You must have worries at home. Is that it? Is your father being difficult again?'

'We manage,' said Mary shortly.

'Is it your boyfriend?'

As Mary did not reply to this, other than ducking her head into the fireplace, I shrugged and went off to find Emily.

Emily was kneeling on the piano stool. She had been

trying to pick out a tune and, failing, had begun to bang on the keys in exasperation. As I lifted her gently on to the floor and sat down at the piano myself, I didn't rebuke her. The sunshine came in at the long windows.

Falteringly, I began to play a little early piece of Mozart which I had once known by heart. The child sat composedly on the carpet, looking up, her blue eyes intent and wide, the golden hair lit by the sun.

'Pretty,' she said.

Encouraged, I began to rustle through some sheet music which Hilda had sent me when the piano first arrived.

'I don't sight-read very well,' I confessed, while the child waited impatiently. 'What about this?'

Emily listened, frowning, while I played a simple, old-fashioned jig.

'No. The other one.'

'What, you prefer Mozart, do you?'

I laughed, but the child nodded seriously. Not for the first time, I wondered if she did not have a pronounced musical talent.

'Look,' I said. 'Give me your hand.'

The child willingly stretched her fingers wide.

'When you are big enough to push down the keys, you can learn to play yourself. As long as you don't just bang the piano.'

Then I found a picture book she liked with coloured

paintings of animals, cuddled her to me, and explained the noises they made and the letters that began their names. She responded eagerly, her delicate lips whispering the words after me with great concentration.

Returning to the kitchen, I found Mary washing the stone floor and, having no one else to tell, began to discuss Emily's precocious eagerness to learn. Mary gave a strange, brooding look from under her lids. A little baffled by this, and conscious that I must have sounded vain, I went on gaily, 'No thanks to me. I've no particular musical skills. And yet these things are supposed to run in families.'

'I never had much time for all that myself,' said Mary.

Her obvious reluctance to chatter was beginning to exasperate me.

'I'm told people like to sing round a piano in the evening. In the cottages.'

'Happen so,' said Mary, phlegmatically.

Just before Mary was to leave for the evening, I said, 'I'm going through my wardrobe tomorrow. Would you like to see if anything would suit you? I've a lot of things I don't need.'

Rather to my disgust, I could hear the wish to be liked in the pleading tones of my voice.

Mary said, 'I don't need much.'

'But you're going to get married soon, aren't you?'

'Next August,' said Mary.

'Wouldn't *he* like you to have a few nice clothes for your honeymoon?'

'I don't know. He's very low Church,' said Mary. 'And I don't want to upset him with anything fancy.'

'Please yourself,' I said, shaking my head. 'And the curtains?'

Mary followed me into the living room, and I began to unfold the new curtains.

'Aren't they a lovely colour? So heavy. I've put the rings in but I need another pair of arms to help me put the curtains in place. Could you?'

Mary helped with the first pair of curtains but when the operation was concluded I put my hands on the girl's shoulders so that I could look into her eyes.

'Mary,' I said, 'tell me the truth. Don't you want to work for me any more?'

The girl looked scared, and did not reply.

'Is that it?'

'No, mum.'

'Are you sure?'

'Yes, mum.' The girl spoke in a rush. 'We couldn't manage at home without my working. But . . .'

'What is it?'

'I don't want to be late home.'

At this, I lost my temper.

'What use are you if you won't do what I ask? What's *changed* since you came here eighteen months ago? You were willing enough then.'

'Don't shout at me,' said Mary. 'I do my job, don't I? And I know you, missus. The whole village knows what you are.'

'*What* do they know?' I asked carefully, furious with myself for provoking the conversation.

'You needn't give yourself airs with me,' said Mary, her voice shaking. 'At least I'll be a respectable married woman when I set up home.'

I understood now. And that understanding made sense of all the shrugging and turning away I had observed in the preceding weeks.

'It's true, isn't it?' said Mary. 'You aren't married to Mr Mellors.'

'What makes you say that?'

I sat down on the square white chair, heedless of the curtains piled on it.

'My auntie told me all about it.'

'And how does your auntie know?'

'She's related to someone who works at Wragby Hall. You're that wicked Lady Chatterley that ran off, aren't you?' Mary spoke with a kind of awe. 'I never thought to work for someone living in sin.'

'So that's what it is,' I said dully.

The girl seemed already sorry she'd said so much. She looked meek and unhappy.

'Will you give me my cards now, mum?'

'No, Mary. I did ask you,' I said. 'It wouldn't be fair.'

Nevertheless, when the girl had gone, I sat miserably where I was until Mellors returned.

'You could get another girl easily enough,' he said, as if the story did not surprise him.

'But what difference could that make?' I asked him.

I began to wake at three in the morning, lonely and unhappy in the moonlight, and listen to the noise of lorries climbing the steep road to Bakewell. Mellors slept deeply, his hand cupping the warm flesh of my belly, but I knew he was equally troubled. I puzzled over where we could go. Was it certain there would be work in British Columbia? I dreaded the idea of finding myself alone and helpless so far from home. I had six hundred a year. Surely we could find somewhere closer.

Four

The chestnut candles were at their fullest in the early May sunshine when Hilda drove down to see us in her open, low-slung Sunbeam Talbot. She was still in town clothes: a low-waisted beige coat and a head-hugging hat, I remember. As she got out of the car outside Mellors' farmhouse, hands must have lifted net curtains all down the village street. She was seemingly unaware of those eyes as her court shoes clicked neatly over the Derbyshire stones.

As we embraced in the hallway, I could smell the perfume of her skin.

'How lovely you look,' I said.

She had matched the honey tones of her silk scarf and the amber of the beads trailing to her waist perfectly. Hilda accepted the compliment and held me at arm's length to study my own appearance.

'Well,' she said. 'Well, let me look at you.'

I was wearing a simple print dress without ornament; my hair full at the neck.

'Hmm,' she said. 'You must cut your hair, Connie. Look.'

She took off her hat to show me her own hair, which had been elegantly cropped at the nape. Her eyes darted everywhere, alight with curiosity. The hallway with its stone floor and freshly painted walls seemed to please her.

'You really are amazing,' she said softly.

Following me into the kitchen, she found Mellors dressed in dungaree trousers and a torn grey jumper, standing in front of the stove. A pleasant smell of roasting meat filled the air. The kitchen looked neat enough, because Mellors insisted on that, but he looked up in sardonic surprise to see Hilda there.

'Take Hilda in the parlour,' he advised. 'She won't want to slum in here.'

We had furnished the front room with square arm-chairs in flowered washable covers, and there were drawings of Father's on the walls. Hilda kicked off her shoes and sat down comfortably.

'I like your curtains,' she said at once. 'Are all the floors stone? Duncan Forbes has a weekend perch in the Cotswolds not half so pretty as this.'

I'd quite forgotten how readily Hilda talked. She rattled on now eagerly, while I only half attended. Mellors and I rarely spoke to one another with such careless cheerfulness; indeed, the last few weeks had been spent in near silence. I'd almost lost the habit of quick and idle replies; but Hilda did not seem to notice my inability to join in.

'Let me see Emily,' she demanded.

'She's upstairs. I'll call her.'

The child looked demure enough as she came down the stairs. 'How do you do, Aunt Hilda?' she said, as I had instructed her. Hilda was delighted.

'Connie, how sweet she is! Can she really remember me? How polite. How old is she now?'

'Three and a bit,' I said.

Hilda had brought the little girl a straw hat, some silky ribbons and a white party dress which the child held daintily against herself with delight.

'She looks like a ballerina, doesn't she?'

Hilda's eyes took in the girl's steady blue gaze and the perfection of her skin.

Mellors came in from the kitchen and studied his daughter carefully.

'Plumper than those skinny creatures,' he said.

His daughter ran to him and he lifted her up in the air high above his head, while she squealed with delight.

'She takes after Connie,' Hilda decided.

'Except that Emily's more precocious,' I said proudly.

'She'll have to learn not to be so clever if we stop round here,' said Mellors. 'Set the table now, Connie.'

At once I rose to my feet, but Hilda frowned at the

authority in Mellors' voice and I could tell she did not approve of the meekness with which I obeyed.

'I'll need a *wash* before I eat,' Hilda said, as if to establish her own choice of timing.

Mellors gave an ironic grin and, when she had gone to find the bathroom, remarked, 'She's still a good-looking woman, your sister. Haughty, though. No one's ever broken her in, I don't suppose.'

The note of admiration surprised me more than the criticism.

'Women aren't horses,' I said, with a little show of resistance.

'They need mastering, though,' he insisted, with a crooked smile, giving me a friendly slap on my buttocks.

Over lunch, Hilda and Mellors did most of the talking.

'They look so menacing,' Hilda said of the crowd of men in the market town.

'They're too bewildered to be dangerous,' he said contemptuously.

'Someone might organize them, nevertheless. They need something to believe in. Do you see things getting back to normal round here?'

He stopped eating for a moment.

'Do you mean will things get back to the life your kind had before the war? No, they won't. There's too much hatred for that. The pits are idle and the people are starving.'

'In the Midlands, do you mean?' Hilda wondered.

'The whole country is finished,' he said.

'Then it's the strikes finished it.'

'Perhaps. But I don't notice things getting any better now the strikes are over. Something else is rotten.'

'You must agree. The men brought industry to its knees.'

'Maybe it isn't industry we want.'

'What, then? How else can there be jobs for those poor creatures? I expect you're a Bolshevik,' said Hilda.

'Sometimes I think they have the answers.'

'Those murderous Russians?'

'Might be better than here, whatever they did. I don't mean for your lot,' he acknowledged her point. 'But for people like us.'

'Is that what you think now, Connie?' asked Hilda, suddenly conscious that I'd said very little.

'I don't know what to think,' I said, an unaccustomed stammer on my tongue.

Hilda frowned.

'You used to have ideas of your own,' she said sharply.

'I never understood politics.' I shrugged.

'Women don't,' said Mellors comfortably.

Hilda began to reply, but changed her mind. Thereafter they spoke of the problems of local farming, and the price of young lambs.

As I stood up to clear away, I fretted a little at the way the conversation had gone, disliking both the way Hilda had spoken and the way Mellors seemed to listen. There had always been a little edge between Hilda and me. A little rivalry. More men had fallen in love with me, perhaps, but Hilda had always been the more articulate, and the more confident, ever since our student days in Germany. At the end of the meal, Hilda lit a cigarette and, even though I felt the ripple of antagonism between her and Mellors, I felt a flicker of jealousy.

That evening, as I was sorting my embroidery silks, I overheard Hilda say to Mellors, 'I hope there will be no more at least.'

He looked startled, and I guessed he did not know what she meant.

'Children,' she explained. 'One is enough for Connie.'

'Oh, when people are in love,' he said, 'I don't believe in taking any action that way.'

'Isn't that rather selfish?'

He looked at her jeeringly, uncowed by the note of reproach.

'Don't you think Connie looks tired?' she continued, as if I were not in the room.

'She's well enough,' he said.

'Pale, though. Subdued.'

'She doesn't paint her face,' he said.

Hilda stood up, perhaps wondering whether to find her room, but instead she lit another cigarette, tapped it on her cigarette case and began to fit it into her long holder.

'You don't approve of me, do you?' she asked Mellors provocatively.

'You're like all modern women,' he said at last. 'Nothing special to you. All opinion and no real feeling.'

She was indignant.

'You know nothing about my feelings.'

'Anyone can see what they are. What matters most to you is getting your own way.'

He smiled, without hostility.

'I suppose you *don't* like your own way?' she scoffed.

'It's natural in a man.'

'Isn't that rather an out of date prejudice?'

'It's not out of date round here.'

'Well, maybe that's what's wrong with round here. All those men with nothing to do but wait for the pubs to open, while their women work themselves into the ground.'

'I'd have said one sex earning the money and the

other doing the domestic chores is a good enough way to organize things,' said Mellors, mildly enough.

'Yes, but there may be better ways.'

'Jobs for women, you mean?'

'Education, anyway. Maybe that's the future: to share out the work differently.'

'Society shares things out well enough, unless it's sick. The cobbler does one kind of thing, and the farmer does another. Anyway,' he smiled, 'if you're thinking of Connie, she has a girl to help her. And I don't think she wants a job.'

Hilda was far from mollified.

'Of course I *didn't* mean Connie should work. But Connie is worth more than the women round here. You know that. That's why you fancied her. She's entitled to more of a life.'

He looked at Hilda broodingly.

'I know what you think makes a good life,' he said.

'How do you?'

'It's written on your body.'

She flushed at his impudence and did not reply. Instead she took out a powder compact from her handbag and renewed her bold red lipstick.

'Do you have a man of your own at the moment?' he inquired.

'As it happens, I have. A film director.'

'Where is he now?'

'He's staying with his own friends in Derbyshire. I

didn't think he'd enjoy it here. I'll join him after a day or two.'

'At your choice, I suppose.'

'Yes.'

Mellors' eyes narrowed with amusement.

'And what's wrong with that?' she demanded. 'Why shouldn't I decide what happens to me?'

'Your kind make any man into a toy.'

She didn't mind his rudeness. She was almost flirting with him. 'Don't you like my clothes, is that it?' she teased.

As she stood up, the soft beige material accentuated the angularity of her body. Her pale face was lit by those brightly painted lips which curved mockingly. There was something quicksilver about her.

'No, I don't like the style,' he said. 'Women aren't boys. A woman should have a waist.'

The words should have pleased me, but they did not. His eyes were gleaming and I wondered if he was attracted to the very qualities he so censured. So I bundled Emily into her sleeping bag and took her upstairs to her cot. When I came back, they were still disagreeing about women and fashion.

'Hilda looks absolutely beautiful,' I said rather wistfully.

'Well, don't think to go off and look the same,' said Mellors.

'Next to you, Hilda, I feel slow and heavy. Like a cow,' I laughed, but I was hardly joking.

'Well,' she said, a little patronizingly, 'you always had a different shape from mine, but there's a way of following fashion for everyone.'

Mellors seemed all at once to lose interest in the argument.

'I'll go to bed,' he said.

It suited me. I wanted a chance to talk to Hilda on her own: it was so long since we had spoken intimately.

'Don't be long, then,' said Mellors, and rose.

As soon as he had left the room, Hilda came over to me and sat at my feet.

'Look at me,' she commanded.

I raised my eyes slowly.

'Connie, *how* can you live like this?'

'I like it,' I said.

'But the man is an opinionated bully. And his ideas are from the stone age.'

'I don't care about his ideas.'

'You don't have any fun.'

'And what do you call fun, exactly?' I asked. 'Grand houses? Staying up late? Dancing to jazz?'

'All those things,' said Hilda.

'I can do without them quite cheerfully,' I said. 'I was bored and half dead having what you call fun.'

67

There was an edge of contempt in my voice.

'You think you have something better?' asked Hilda.

'I know I do.'

'Well, whatever it is, you look exhausted by it,' said Hilda, with a gleam of spite. 'Connie, listen to me – you'll be old soon—'

'Everyone gets old.'

'Not in the same way. Look at the women round here. They're old because they are overworked and bullied.'

'Don't exaggerate,' I said patiently. 'My life isn't like theirs.'

'But, Connie, you don't have any life of your own,' said Hilda. 'That's the only thing that lasts. Have this Mellors if you must. If he pleases you. Why not? But don't let him boss you about.'

'He's very gentle with me,' I said.

Hilda raised her eyebrows.

'I've *seen* the way he treats you.'

'He helps me in all kinds of ways,' I said. 'He's a very kind man.'

'That may be. But you do everything he says. For a woman, freedom is nothing to do with *kindness*,' said Hilda. 'It's about not letting a man tell you what to do.'

'I don't mind that.'

'Yes, but you *should*. You must think for yourself.'

'I've never wanted to much,' I said. 'Not really. What

do you want me to be thinking about? I'm a very simple person. Tell me some gossip. You've said nothing about yourself.'

Hilda looked mutinous.

'I have no news, if what you mean is *men*. Men aren't news. I don't need them. I go where I like, eat and drink as I like, and if I want to fuck, I don't need to live with any man.'

'Still, in your letter you said something about a Giorgio,' I tempted.

'Yes. He's a film director. I think he understands what I want out of life.'

'What *is* that?' I asked, genuinely curious.

'Some kind of excitement. Something to make me feel I'm young and alive. You know, the bones in my face could have made me an actress when I was younger.'

'I remember you used to play at acting.'

'Connie!' Mellors called from upstairs.

I began to rise to my feet, but Hilda checked me, genuinely outraged that I should respond to so ungracious a summons.

'Connie, I'm ashamed of you. I thought you had more spirit. If you let yourself be treated like a servant, you'll dwindle into one. In the end you'll turn into his *mother*. That's what happens to women in his class. It's what he expects. But you—'

'Connie!'

The voice sounded angrier now. I moved her hand away.

'He *needs* me,' I tried to explain.

Hilda shook her head.

'Modern women don't just go off when they're called like that. They have more pride.'

'I *must*. Don't worry. We are really very happy together. He does love me, Hilda. And I love him.'

Hilda's noise of scepticism and indignation pursued me as I left the room.

I checked that Emily was safely asleep as I passed the child's room. Then I turned towards our bedroom, my heart beating rather faster than I liked. There had been a harsh note in Mellors' voice and, though I hadn't confessed as much to Hilda, I guessed why.

Mellors was lying in bed. His eyes were small and hard as pebbles.

'Did you have your gossip?'

'Not a very lengthy gossip.'

'About me, was it? Bound to be.'

'Not exactly,' I said.

'What is that supposed to mean?'

'It was more about what has happened to me.'

I began to undress. He snapped the light on from the dangling button over the bed, but I continued to undress quietly, the yellow light of the lamp making my flesh glow warm and rich as butter.

'It's the same thing. She despises me, and she despises you for staying with me,' he hissed.

'She didn't say that,' I protested, alarmed at the expression of torment on his face.

'I'm not talking about what she *said*. I'm not stupid. Come here.'

I went uncertainly. The expression on his face was far from loving, but I was obedient nevertheless. I couldn't be anything else. I had thrown in my lot with this man with my whole being. Everything was committed to him. If he summoned me, I had to obey.

'Lie down.'

I did as he asked, and he raised himself on his elbow to look at me. There was no tenderness in his face, even though he put out one hand and stroked the curve of my waist.

'What else did you talk about?' he asked.

'I can't remember,' I said evasively. 'Her new man, I suppose.'

He eased himself across the bed so that he could look down on me.

'I know better,' he said.

'She *can't* understand us,' I admitted. 'Please, don't be unhappy, or angry with me because of that.'

'I'll be what I like,' he said.

His eyes were cold, and he stopped caressing my body.

'Very well,' I said, making to rise from the bed. 'I've things to do if you don't want to be friendly.'

He gave a savage bark of laughter.

'How's that again? My lady,' he mocked me. 'Friend-liness, is it? Lie where I want you.'

He pulled me roughly back towards him. His unfa-miliar awkwardness frightened me.

'Here, do you mean?' I asked.

'No,' he said, snatching the pillows away from me. 'Like this.'

There was a kind of desperation in his grip on my shoulders, and I could feel his fingers bruising my flesh. His clutch felt as much like hostility as desire. Then he pulled up my nightdress and parted my legs with one hand. The other found my left breast and squeezed the delicate flesh.

'You're hurting me,' I said, with surprise.

'Am I? Open your legs wider,' he said thickly.

And, as I did so, he thrust himself into me without the least affection, without preparing my body for his own in any way. The suddenness bruised me, but I made no resistance: indeed, the violence of his thrust excited me. And I fancied he seemed to take some pleasure in my gasp of pain.

'There,' he said. 'There.'

He was hard inside me for a long pumping moment,

and then, satisfied, he lay back against the pillows, seemingly indifferent to whether I had shared his excitement or not.

'That's it,' he said, with a kind of exultation as he fell away from me.

As I lay there, my body still streaming, my heart thudding, I kept my hold on him, pushing against his thigh until I had achieved my own satisfaction. Then I clung on to him to prolong the lovely moment, which had an unexpected intensity for all the selfishness of Mellors' performance. I could feel his naked flesh against my own, and could sense the enmity had gone out of him.

'Aye,' he said, queerly. 'Aye.'

It was as if he was dreaming.

'My love,' I whispered in his ear. But, although he fondled my hair briefly and moved his rough skin against my cheek, he made no comment on the quality of the experience. I puzzled why the violence of his lovemaking had so delighted me, even as my body clung to his. Then he turned on his back and fell deeply into sleep.

The next morning, Hilda eyed me oddly.

'He's at work, then?'

'He goes off very early,' I said, serenely.

'Good. I want to talk to you. Where's Emily?'

'Outside. In the garden.'

'Can we make some coffee?'

'I don't think there is any.'

In the morning light, the kitchen looked shabby and, as Hilda looked around, she said, 'I don't know much about farming, but I remember my ex-husband saying you can't farm less than three hundred acres except as a hobby.'

'Was he an economist?' I asked her.

She laughed.

'Do you *know* how much land you have?'

I didn't, but in any case it was not what she wished to be discussing.

Over a pot of tea, she said, firmly, 'The man is an animal.'

Against my will, my face must have shown some memory of the preceding night.

'Luckily, you aren't married to him,' said Hilda. 'You can take Emily and leave whenever you like.'

'But I've no intention of leaving him,' I said. 'What do you mean?'

'You said there were difficulties. I imagine they are financial?'

'Not only. I explained in my letter,' I said. 'The people round here think us immoral. Because we can't marry.'

'Of course,' said Hilda impatiently. 'How could it be any different? I suppose Clifford is adamant?'

'He thinks his refusal must force me back.' I looked

at her fiercely. 'But I've no intention of being forced to do anything.'

'And what about money?' she asked.

'You know I have my own. It's harder for him,' I said. 'It hurts him to be dependent on me.'

Hilda made a noise of rude incredulity.

'Rubbish. Without you he'd be struggling. This farm has no future. Let's be practical,' said Hilda. 'You can't go on living here. Not like this. Would you ever want to? Surely you won't send Emily to school round here?'

'I don't know,' I said. 'It's a problem.'

'Listen,' said Hilda. 'If you insist on continuing this love affair, you will have to leave the country.'

'I hate the thought of it,' I said. 'He used to talk of life in British Columbia. But it's so far from everyone.'

'I have another and better suggestion,' said Hilda. 'Somewhere in Europe.'

I lifted my head and listened with the first flicker of a new hope.

'I told you about my friend Giorgio. He's related to the Italian nobility. They have several grand houses in Tuscany, with acres of land around them. One of those must surely need a gamekeeper. It would take you away from this mean, pinched life. And Mellors might like it too.'

'He might,' I said. 'But he would never agree.'

Hilda made an impatient face.

'He would refuse anything that came through you,'
I explained.

'Stubborn men have to be handled indirectly,' said
Hilda. 'We must go about it in a subtler way.'

'Deceive him? I don't want to do that.'

'It's up to you,' said Hilda. 'But Giorgio is staying
with some friends outside Derby. We could easily
arrange for him to meet Mellors. Just casually. Doesn't
Mellors drink in the local pub?'

'I don't like the idea,' I said, uncertainly.

That afternoon, Hilda drove off to meet her friend,
with a promise to return at the weekend if the weather
remained fine. I walked round the garden with Emily
after Hilda had gone. There were the beginnings of
apples where the blossom had fallen from the trees,
and I lifted up the child to look at them. The garden
was small and pretty, and a huge blue and white
clematis was in flower all up the side of the cottage,
but Hilda's visit had made me restless. I longed to
stride through the fields.

'Let's go for a walk,' I said to the child.

Obediently, Emily took my hand and we walked
towards the opening in the dry-stone wall which led
down to the local stream. She romped at my side contentedly, and we clambered carefully under the bridge
until we were in open country. Then we walked along
the sedgy river bank away from the village, with sunshine flickering on the leaves.

As we rounded a bend in the river, I saw a group of young boys, a little older than Emily and probably truants, sitting with string and pins, hoping to catch fish. Emily ran up to them cheerfully and the boys responded off-handedly; then, as they seemed quite friendly, she sat on a tree stump and watched them. The river was shallow enough to paddle in at this point and the lads' chance of fish seemed remote. The sun was warm on my back. I had never, I knew, loved the landscape of the English Midlands as well as Mellors. There were beauties in the Peak District: Matlock, perhaps, with its banks of houses and shining river on stones, but here everything was too gentle and flat. I found my thoughts wandering back longingly to holidays in Italian hill towns in Tuscany, remembering Italian foods and wines, and the whole, open cheerfulness of the place in comparison with the gloom of the society around me.

Emily's bewildered cry roused me to my present surroundings, and I rose instinctively to see what was wrong. Nothing physically threatening seemed to have occurred, but Emily was red-faced and tearful and I hurried along to rescue her. At my approach, the boys seized their sticks and jars of tiddlers and flew down the path with taunts and cries. Among these, I made out the word 'bastard'.

'They went *horrid*,' said Emily. 'Horrid.'

And she burst into more tears.

'They don't know what they mean,' I said, as quietly as I could. There was a new sickness in my heart. Something had to be done.

Hilda did not return that weekend to visit us as she had promised, so I wrote her a letter and we arranged to meet in an hotel on the far side of Derby. Her friend Giorgio came too; an inordinately good-looking young Italian, wearing a black silk shirt and a brilliant green tie, who hung on Hilda's every word. I believed in the nobility of his family connections easily enough, but was more sceptical about his future as a film director. At any rate, the three of us enjoyed a quiet summer tea in the hotel gardens, and Giorgio declared himself very willing to help us.

Mellors went off to the Dog and Duck some evenings. He did not stay late and he never drank excessively but usually I was left alone, sewing, after the child went to bed. He took the dog with him, for company on the walk. It was a male world, in which I knew there was no place for women.

The Dog and Duck had once been a miners' pub, but these days people motoring through on the way to London often called in. Tommy Bruce occasionally used it. The landlord let Mellors' dog lie in front of the fire of the public bar in winter. Mellors enjoyed the beer and didn't particularly want to talk to the men there, though he liked them well enough. If they joked with one another about his fancy woman and bastard child when he wasn't there, they kept the smirk off their faces when he was. There was often a bit of a tune on the piano from one of the customers. This pub was where we had arranged for Giorgio to meet him. Mellors set off in sombre mood, almost as if he intuited something was afoot. But when he returned that evening, he was jubilant. He could see a way out of our difficulties, and in the flush of new hope, he gave me a full account of his meeting with Giorgio, doing all the voices in turn for me like the clever mimic he was.

He'd spotted the stranger as soon as he arrived in the pub. A Welshman, he conjectured at first, or a Cornish man, well-dressed in the London fashion, with a narrow, dark face. As he crossed the public bar to take his drink outside into the evening sun, Mellors had watched him and saw he had little to say to the men who stood around him.

'But I wasn't very curious about the fellow at first. There was Tommy Bruce, half drunk and pleading to be friends. Well, I told him, too late for that. And in no time we were at it, hammer and tongs. That's when this foreigner came over to listen. And he liked what I said.'

'Did he?' I asked, as neutrally as possible.

'Yes. Said they'd had the same troubles in Italy, but found a way to cure them.'

I bit off the thread of my embroidering silk and looked up at him as directly as I could. Luckily, he was too involved in his story to be searching my expression.

'An Italian, then.'

'Yes. Asked me what I did. So I told him. And I mentioned we were thinking of giving the colonies a try. Well, he was very interested in all of it.'

'Was he?'

'Asked me if I knew about horses.'

'*What* a strange thing,' I said, lowering my eyes again.

'I told him I'd worked in the cavalry during the war. *Connie*—' He grasped my arm so hard that it hurt. 'Do you know what happened then?'

I looked up doubtfully.

'He said his cousin had an estate in Tuscany and might have a job for me if I wanted it. What do you think to that?'

I was trying to look as if the suggestion was altogether new to me, but as he took my hands in his own I could see he found my odd expression entirely natural.

'I know what you're thinking, Connie. I can see it in your face. You'll be wondering, like I did, *why for me?* Well, this fellow said he liked my attitude. My politics.'

'Would you want to go?' I asked him.

'Aye,' he said softly. 'I would an' all. I could take you and the baby out of this.'

His blue eyes were alight with hope and I felt a stab of guilt at the deception that Hilda and I had practised.

'But is his offer *certain?*' I asked, feeling it appropriate to show some hesitation.

'There'll be a letter. He promised,' said Mellors, suddenly agitated with the fear of disappointment. 'Are you willing to give it a go?'

I said I was. My deceit in the arrangement still worried me but he seemed in no doubt that the plan was entirely his own.

'We'd have to sell the farm,' I pointed out.

'Let's worry about that when the letter comes,' said Mellors.

That night I soothed his suspense, and later in the week a letter duly arrived confirming the terms of a job on the Bellaggri estate. It wasn't difficult to sell the farm, either. Tommy Bruce was right: we had bought it at a very low price.

Five

Things, as such, were no longer important to me: I knew they did not protect me, and they did not comfort me. Some china I sent to Hilda; some I sold. Aside from clothes for myself and Emily, material for curtains and coverlets, and three Dresden figurines I kept from my father's home in Scotland, I had few possessions I wanted to take. And certainly I had no regrets about leaving the village street, and the mean faces behind their lace curtains.

Emily cried a little before we set off, because we were leaving the animals behind.

'There'll be wild animals,' said Mellors with a good deal of satisfaction.

'And you will *love* Italy,' I told the child. 'It will be sunny and the people are beautiful.'

'You can help me with the horses,' Mellors tempted. The child responded to his low voice as she never did to mine, and soon she was smiling and prattling again. On board the cross-channel ferry, she perked up altogether, as if the excitement of the change became

another reality as she watched the English cliffs dis-
appear into the sea. Mellors held her firmly so she
could stand on the rails while he explained about the
curve of the earth. She leant against him happily.

'You aren't worried yourself?' Mellors asked me ten-
tatively as we stood at the rail, the light salt wind in
our hair. I smiled and shook my head at the concern
in his voice. It was the first time he had voiced any
anxiety about how I felt, and throughout our preparations my main emotion had been relief that he never
once doubted the choice of an Italian life was his own
idea.

We took the train to Florence, and then a car to
Gaioli, where we were to be met by Mellors' employer.
The air tasted of sunlight, hot dust and some aromatic
herb as we travelled through the landscape of a Renaissance painting: shimmering olives, tufty cypresses and
neatly arranged vines.

We were making for the vine-covered hills north of
Siena, dotted with farmhouses, villas and baronial cas-
tles; the area of Chianti Classico, where some of Italy's
best wines are harvested. The steep hills were farmed
by cutting terraces into them; the soil held in place by
stone walls; the earth was the colour of clay, infused
with reds and browns. There were cypress trees planted
along the roadside for windbreaks.

Emily slept until it was time to unload our belong-
ings in the little square of Gaioli-in-Chianti. Dazed and

yawning then, she stood up and stretched in the sunshine. There was a wicker-covered *damigiane* transporting the local Chianti wine and wild boar ham, and I pointed out a stall of aubergines, courgettes, figs and olives.

'What *are* they?' Emily marvelled.

A shawled woman was carefully feeling and prodding vegetables, before gathering up what she needed into her apron. She looked up sharply at the word of English, but smiled readily enough at the child. Her warmth confirmed my sense of Italy.

'It's like paradise,' I said.

Mellors asked our driver to bring the cases towards a café where we were to be met. He knew no more than the few phrases of Italian learnt on the train as we approached; nevertheless his military bearing gave him a natural authority.

On the wall of pitted yellow stone, I saw there were coats of arms belonging to councillors and magistrates, among them those of the Bellaggri family.

Since there were no tables outside the café, the three of us went a little uncertainly into the bar, and Mellors lifted Emily on to a high stool. A few whiskery men in shirtsleeves looked up without much interest, rather like peasants from a Breughel painting.

'The men here haven't had the guts knocked out of them like the English,' Mellors told me approvingly.

'They haven't been broken. I like that. They're still fierce.'

'Shall we have a strega?' I asked.

Mellors frowned. He did not like me to drink, and was unsure whether women did so in these parts.

'We count as tourists,' I reassured him.

Our new employer did not collect us in person. Instead, about ten minutes later, his sun-browned servant in a straw hat helped us into a cart and we set off up a steep dusty slope above the village.

The track curved round a lake partly hidden by trees; behind the trees we could make out glimpses of a great house, with a stone Palladian front.

'Whose house is that?' I asked.

The peasant shrugged deeply, not understanding. Mellors hesitantly translated the question into Italian. A rattle of explanation followed, from which I made out that it was the house of our new employer. Mellors gathered rather more than I did, however.

'He says the Count has several houses, and that he only lives here in the spring and early summer.'

'That must be very pleasant.'

The pale walls caught the sunlight. The house looked much less austere than Wragby Hall in which I had once lived with Clifford, in what felt like another world.

Beyond the curve of the trees, the cart took an abrupt turn down a track pitted with ruts and stones, little more than a gap between the vegetation. We made our way downwards in a flurry of white dust and loose pebbles, with huge potholes at every turn in the track, arriving at last at a collection of outbuildings and a stone house.

'*Ecco*,' nodded the driver.

'I think we are here,' said Mellors.

Our new home looked surprisingly large. It had a square entrance and four doors opening on to other rooms, each with large windows overlooking the olive groves. There was, I soon discovered, neither tap water nor electricity, but Mellors explained that connections in the hills were being made and there would be electricity before the winter set in. Cooking was to be on charcoal or pine cones. The furniture was home-made, unpainted and plain; there was a mirror in the entrance, and a dining table with four straw-bottomed chairs in the kitchen. The kitchen was floored in red tile, and had a high ceiling, roofed with chestnut beams. There was a huge fireplace, too. It was cool indoors and Mellors murmured, 'We'll need that in winter, I reckon.'

His eyes were alight as I had not seen them for months, and my own spirits rose to match his.

'It's lovely,' I said.

He saw my happiness and was proud of it because he thought he had organized this for us and that I had trusted him enough to follow. He felt altogether a man again as a result.

'Come here,' he said.

So I went into his arms, as Emily looked up curiously while he held me and I felt his body stir against my own.

Those first months in Tuscany passed in an enchanted glow. We had been released from the grey landscape of slump and gloom, and I felt life taking on the sensual freshness of our first days together. He saw me again as he had seen me in the woods at Wragby and I felt calm and beauty return to my limbs. When I looked in the mirror, my short upper lip made my mouth like a delicious fruit, and once again I took pleasure in my face.

That first year in Italy brought back the happiness of the early days in Derbyshire, when we were so elated to find ourselves together and found tenderness and desire welling up within us whenever we touched. And I understood myself better now. I did not attempt to manage the house without help: there were so many cheerful Italian women round about who wanted to scrub my floors and help me with the fires. I took on Gina, a married woman with children of her own; her bustling energy left me time to teach Emily, who at four was eager to learn to read.

Mellors was delighted with the work he had to do. There were wild boars for the Count's hunt, and poachers to be deterred, but he also spent hours every day with the Count's horses. Once he had learnt to know them, he liked to bring Emily to the stables with him.

He and Emily were growing closer. He had begun to confide in Emily thoughts he expressed to no one else: how he found animals superior to man, in their enjoyment of the sun, the absurdity of their courage and the things they didn't know about, like dying and being sad for no reason. She didn't always understand what he told her, but she always listened and his thoughts went into her. She anchored him in a human world.

I knew she loved to watch the brutes calmed by his hand.

'Will you teach me to ride?' she asked her father.

'Maybe the Count will let us have the loan of a small pony one day,' he said, as he unsaddled a horse that stamped in his stall and laid back his ears when he heard an unfamiliar voice.

'Why can't I ride the golden horse? It's so beautiful.'

'It's a stallion,' he said, 'and not for little girls.'

I saw the horse was damp where the saddle had been removed, and there was a quiver of muscle under the belly. His great eyes glowed, and Mellors had to stroke him into acquiescence. Sometimes I wondered whether he would not prefer to make a life among animals: he found their ways so much sweeter.

'What about you? Can you ride him?' the child asked.

'I can master him,' said Mellors quietly. 'He's too much spirit, that's all. There's nothing bad in him.'

'I want to learn to ride a horse, too,' she said.

'And so you shall. But this one'd panic if he felt your weak hands on him.'

'Is he dangerous for the Count?'

'No. The Count can manage him,' Mellors answered.

It was fortunate that he did not see too much of his employer. He didn't like the Count's amused, contemptuous manner. But it couldn't spoil his pleasure in the new life.

When he walked in the high meadows up the stony parts of the hills, he sometimes took Emily there, carrying her when she got tired. He enjoyed the soft, warm weight of the child, the tenderness of her flesh and her blue, trusting eyes.

And, in her turn, Emily adored him. She loved the gentle way he treated the animals that were caught in snares. He didn't mind if she got her clothes dirty. When she fell in the mud, he picked her up and cuddled her just the same, and she could feel the whipcord strength of his muscles under his thin shirt in summer, and liked the sharp, clean odour of fresh perspiration.

Close to the cottage, she sat on the dry grass to

watch him fell a tree, and he sat on the stump of it afterwards while she brought him cold wine and prattled about her daydreams.

'I'm not as strong as you think, little Emily,' I heard him say once, troubled by her admiration.

She didn't care. He was her hero. Her loyal protector.

Late in our second summer, I received a letter from Duncan Forbes. Duncan was an old friend, a Cubist painter who had known me since childhood and loved me at a distance without ever being my lover. When I was wondering how best to persuade Clifford to agree to a divorce he had even offered to pretend to be the father of my child.

'What can *he* want?' asked Mellors.

He was in a hurry that morning.

'He has friends round here. He thought he would visit us.'

'And who told him where we are?' demanded Mellors.

Whatever came from England, even letters from his own family, made him suspicious. It was as if he had hoped to throw away everything from the England that defined us.

'I suppose Hilda may have mentioned it,' I confessed hesitantly.

I knew that Mellors found everything to do with Hilda infuriating, but he was in too much of a hurry to quarrel about it, and I failed to mention that Duncan was due to show up that very day.

Just after two, Duncan came down our bumpy, rutted road in his two-seater, and got out of the vehicle to look back ruefully along the way he had come.

'I don't think my old banger will make it back up again,' he said. Then he examined my face, with its hint of golden tan, and bent to kiss me.

'You're looking well these days. Hilda will be relieved. Is Mellors okay?'

'He likes it here.'

'And do you both speak Italian yet?'

'Mellors can. He's *frightfully* quick with languages. And he studies every evening. My Italian was never as good as my German, but I'm picking it up.'

'You must find it hard to get to know your neighbours.'

'They're friendly enough.'

I led him into the kitchen.

'But you can't exactly gossip, can you now? And you used to enjoy a gossip, didn't you? In the old days.'

'That's all I *did* enjoy in the old days.' I laughed. 'Shall we open a bottle of wine?'

He nodded.

'I gather you're enjoying an illicit honeymoon. After all this time. It's quite a tribute to your lover.'

He lifted his glass as if to honour my pleasure.

'I never think of it as illicit.' I frowned.

'Do you hear from Clifford?' he asked me.

'No.' I hesitated. 'How is he?'

'No worse,' he said. 'He isn't going to die conveniently.'

'Is he still very angry with me?'

'He speaks of you in a hushed voice, as if you were incurably ill.'

'Well—' I tried to laugh. 'Nobody seems to question our marriage here, so the divorce no longer seems important.'

'And Mellors is happy, you say?'

'Yes.'

'He's wasted, of course.'

I was startled at this.

'I mean his intelligence. People don't always find a way to use themselves.'

'I don't think he's ever wanted anything else,' I said.

'Wouldn't you like him to grow and expand himself?'

'Do you know, I don't think I would,' I said. 'I like things as they are.'

'Now then, you mustn't be possessive, Connie,' he chided me, picking up, I suppose, my wish for Mellors to remain my own private passion. 'It's dangerous.'

'I thought that was what true marriage was supposed to be.' I smiled. 'Cleaving to one another, and so forth.'

'It is,' said Duncan. 'That's why there are so many domestic murders.'

I caught my breath at that.

'At any rate, you aren't bored?'

'Not yet.'

'You won't need to be. Not round here. There's plenty of amusement. Do you know who lives over that hill?'

I shook my head.

'A painter friend of mine. From SW7. I'm staying with him for a week or two ... Hughie Williams. He's not five miles from here. Near Raddo-in-Chianti. He knows all the expat English.'

I shook my head again.

'We've come here to get away from all that.'

'That's what Hilda said you would feel. You think they'll know the scandal about you?'

'Of course they will.'

'But they wouldn't care,' he cried. 'They're artists. And Emily? Doesn't she need friends?'

'She isn't lonely. She plays with the children of the woman who comes to clean. They are very gentle. And she's learning the piano.'

He stared at me incredulously.

'How old is she now? Nearly five, I imagine?'

'Oh, I know, I know,' I said. 'She'll have to go away to school. But not yet.'

When Mellors came back from the stables, he was

surprised to see Duncan, but he received him with good enough grace. If he remembered with some resentment the suggestion that Duncan should pretend to have fathered Emily, he did not feel invaded by Duncan's presence. The space around him in these Tuscan hills made him feel he could afford to let people into his home. When Duncan suggested we might like to visit his friend Hughie Williams, he smiled at the idea. Even less than I did he want any contact with his expatriate neighbours.

'What are they? Let me guess. Young men just down from university, trying to live the life of artists?'

'Pretty well. But older, you know. As I am.'

'They might do as much in London,' said Mellors contemptuously.

'But not in the sunshine. Or so cheaply,' said Duncan.

'The last thing I want is to suck around their kind,' said Mellors. 'I don't much care about people, not most people. Certainly not any of that lot.'

'If you don't like people,' puzzled Duncan, 'what *do* you care about?'

Mellors' face was craggy and his eyes unreadable.

'Animals. Trees. The whole lovely natural world that man hasn't ruined.'

'You might find a common cause with my poor friends,' said Duncan mildly. 'As fellow exiles.'

'They aren't exiled,' said Mellors contemptuously. 'They're no more than tourists.'

'Still, they are trying to make a home of sorts here, rather as you and Connie are.'

'They don't belong here,' said Mellors.

'People belong where they work,' said Duncan. 'Don't they?'

'A nation is more than a family business,' said Mellors.

'What else is it? Or do you believe the kind of rubbish these local Fascists spout?' demanded Duncan.

'They are *patriots*,' said Mellors. 'No bad thing.'

'What about the war?' I cried. 'Wasn't that all misguided patriotism?'

'What do *you* know about war?' Mellors jeered at me. 'In your own person, I mean.'

I flushed at his rudeness.

'They justify some terrible things,' said Duncan sharply, 'these patriots of yours.' But I knew he was really annoyed at the way I had accepted Mellors' snub. When I made an excuse and went off to dress Emily, I overheard him say quietly to Mellors, 'You *are* happy here with Connie, aren't you? It's what you wanted, isn't it?'

'Why do you ask?' Probably Mellors knew very well, I thought, but he wasn't disposed to excuse his own behaviour.

When I returned, the conversation had moved on

and Duncan was asking, 'Does it bother you not to be your own master here?'

'Not at all. I *like* working for someone,' Mellors said. 'I never enjoyed all the hustle of working for myself. It *sounds* grand, but it makes you into a kind of commercial traveller. Here, it's like being in the army. I do what has to be done, and I don't have to be trying to please apart from that. I suppose England is in much the same mess as it was when we left?'

'Industrially, do you mean? Worse, I think. Don't you get the English papers here?'

'The local ones are good for my Italian,' said Mellors. 'And they write about what's wrong and what's needed.'

'A strong *leader*, you mean?' said Duncan sceptically. 'There was always a reformer in you; I suppose that's why you see things so simply.'

'Reform England? We'd have to blow her apart,' said Mellors savagely.

'I suppose something must be done about people out of work,' admitted Duncan. 'They wouldn't much like being blown up, though.'

'I suppose you think it'll be Communism has the answers.'

'I don't know,' said Duncan. 'Who do *you* see of an evening?'

'Men who work in the olive fields or on the vines,' said Mellors.

'Do they speak English?'

'A few words. They learn them from the tourists. Come and meet them. Connie doesn't care to know them, do you, Connie?'

There was an odd note of rejection, almost spite, in his voice as he said that, which surprised me. Mellors sometimes walked down in the moonlight to the café in Gaioli and talked to the men there. He explained the pleasures of it to Duncan, ignoring my expression. It was almost as if he wanted to establish that he had another life apart from mine, I thought unhappily. Yet I had no wish for anything apart from him. My thoughts raced. I knew his friendship with the villagers was important to him, but why did he give Duncan that sly gleam of a smile as if he were proud to have found a life separate from me? What would become of me if he did?

Later that evening the men set off together, and I put Emily to bed before trying to concentrate on the cushion cover I was embroidering. When Emily called out, I went readily enough, with a glass of squeezed orange.

'When will I go to school?' asked Emily.

'Soon,' I replied, without really listening.

I went to bed before Mellors returned, and found myself lying awake in the moonlight waiting for the sound of their returning footsteps on the stony road. Even when I heard the heavy front door shut, the voices continued downstairs. Perhaps I fell asleep. When Mellors appeared in the bedroom it was past two in the morning. I watched him approach the bed, lost in his own thoughts, complete in his own strength and confidence, and the electricity of that stirred me.

I was wearing a simple loose nightdress. He preferred me not to get into bed naked, as I had in our first days together. Now I felt him looking down at me as I lay there with my eyes closed. I felt altogether his to do with as he liked. He got into bed beside me and lay on his back.

'I am awake,' I whispered.

He did not reply.

'Are you tired?'

He turned to me then, and I saw the same quiet, uncanny smile on his face I had seen before he set off with Duncan.

Presently he shifted his weight in the bed and said, very coldly, 'I don't want Duncan's friends trailing over here, filling this house with their chatter.'

'Of course not,' I said.

'They're your kind, not mine.'

'I don't know what kind they are. As for Duncan—'

'Oh, Duncan's a decent enough bloke,' he said.

He was looking at me ironically now, and made out easily enough that I wanted him to make love to me. He pushed up my nightdress and began to stroke my body, and my belly. I felt the strokes of his hand with impatience, longing for them to reach between my legs, but he seemed reluctant to caress me there. At length I reached for his hand and brought the fingers towards my bush of hair.

'Don't do that,' he said sharply.

I stopped at once, snubbed. With a sudden shift of weight, he lifted me so that he could enter more easily. We were barely together before he found his own satisfaction. It came to me unhappily that he no longer wanted or needed my response, and that he possibly disliked my wish for pleasure. I didn't understand how that could be, since he had taught me all I knew of desire and once delighted in the fulfilment of it. I hated his new separateness. In my frustration, I almost hated him. And yet another part was hurt with the love I continued to feel.

'What did you find?' I asked Duncan the following day, when Mellors had gone out early.

'My Italian isn't fluent,' he admitted. 'They seemed an interesting lot of men.'

'Followers of Il Duce?'

'Not all of them. There was a lot of argument.' He hesitated, observing me narrowly. 'You don't look so cheerful today. Why don't you let me drive you over to Hughie Williams? Nothing conventional or boring there, I promise you. He's not a great artist, but decent enough.'

'Some day perhaps,' I said.

We normally left our door unlocked. One day, when Emily and I had been picking herbs in the fields behind the house, relishing the hot savour of the huge rosemary bushes, we came back to find an Italian I did not know sitting in our kitchen, waiting for Mellors. He explained haltingly that he wanted to learn English, and that Mellors had offered to help him practise his conversation. He seemed shy and had little to say for himself, beyond the sentences he had rehearsed to explain his presence, but when Mellors came in the two men both burst into voluble Italian.

Later that evening I watched Mellors thoughtfully as he tidied the kitchen, standing at the stone sink to rinse the food from the plates.

'No need to do that,' I said. 'Gina will do it in the morning.'

'I don't like to let the flies get at it,' he said.

I approached then to give him some help, still lost in my own considerations.

'I really must try harder to learn Italian.'

'If you can,' he said.

'Why should I find it particularly difficult?' I said, stung by the implication.

'Not difficult,' he said. 'But a nuisance. And probably unrewarding. I don't suppose you particularly want to get close to the local peasantry.'

'Well, but I must talk to someone apart from you and Emily,' I said smilingly.

'You won't be interested in them, and they won't be interested in you,' he said.

His quiet conviction exasperated me.

'You always think you know everything about me.'

'Let me make a prediction,' he said, quite amiably. 'In a few days you will remember there are some English people living over the hill and find that an easier proposition.'

His certainty struck me as altogether smug.

'No reason why I should *not* visit them,' I said slowly. 'But you're wrong. I have absolutely no such inclination.'

'Well, we'll see,' he said.

'You think you are so clever,' I flared suddenly. 'Now I *can't* go without proving you know me better than I know myself.'

He burst out laughing at my fury.

'You mustn't mock me,' I said.

'*Mustn't* I?' His eyes danced with amusement. 'Why, what will you do if you don't like it?'

My blood pounded in my ears. It seemed to me for a moment there was nothing I could do. Then I set the dishes I was holding carefully on the table.

'Perhaps I'll just go for a walk,' I said.

He made no attempt to prevent me.

Outside, the air was still warm but unexpectedly humid; there was a ring of vaporous cloud round the moon. I walked down the path to the rosemary bushes and took a handful of their leaves into my palm, crushing them as I tried to recapture the pleasure their hot smell had given me earlier that day. But it was no good. Nothing reached me.

Then I heard his steps crunching on the stones outside the kitchen door. He was coming towards me in the darkness.

The moon had emerged briefly from the clouds, and I stood where I was until he came up to me. His face looked white and thin in the moonlight.

'Are you coming in?'

'Not yet,' I said, distantly.

He walked at my side for a time and then put an arm around me casually, as if nothing had happened. I stiffened for a moment. I wanted him to understand how badly he was treating me. It wasn't a question of women's rights, as Hilda might have claimed, but a question of kindness. He seemed to *need* to hurt me, and I wanted him to know that I minded that. After a moment he took his hand away, as if he understood the snub and accepted it.

'Don't be angry with me, Connie,' he said. 'Don't

let's fight. Sometimes I can see so clearly what's bound
to happen to us and it makes me angry.'

'Nothing is *bound* to happen.'

We both stopped walking. He felt the curve of my
body against his own. Then he turned me towards him
and his fingers moved slowly over my clothed body. I
began to shiver as I let my body melt against his.

'Let's go back,' I said.

'No,' he said. 'No.'

His hands went over me. He kissed my open mouth,
tasting the hotness of it with excitement. Then he
began to pull me down to the wet ground.

'Don't—' I said. 'Not here.'

His face gleamed in the moonlight. He kissed me
again, feeling how his caresses softened my resistance.

He pressed me backwards. He no longer cared about
my torn clothes. He pulled roughly at me, and we
collapsed on the earth together.

He has become a stranger, I thought. But at that
moment I did not mind the strangeness. On the con-
trary, I delighted in it. He felt for the bare flesh of my
thighs, where the dress had torn open below the waist;
it still clung round my breasts. Then he pulled at the
chiffon of my underwear. Now he could reach me, and
lay with his head on my belly. He did not often caress
me so intimately with his mouth, but now he did so
wantonly. I felt it was almost a way of making up to me
for his earlier behaviour, that he was showing me how

much he wanted to please me. And I gave myself up to the delight of that. I could feel the lick of his rough, lascivious tongue on the skin of my thighs and the hair between my legs. I arched backwards in pleasure. Then he lifted himself up to me and, in doing so, saw the sensuality in my face. My enjoyment was something apart from him. Perhaps he did not like that separateness. But he had gone too far to deny himself now. In an abandon of sexual frenzy he thrust himself into me. Together we took our own gratification. And, as I found my own pleasure again and again, I forgot everything else apart from that extremity of sensation.

For all the passion of our reconciliation, something soon changed between us once again. Mellors began to give English lessons. The man he taught worked on the Bellaggri family land; he was a handsome fellow, brown as a nut, with sun-bleached hair, and not poor, though he could not afford to study as he wanted. Most evenings after work had ended in the fields, Bernardo came up to the stone farmhouse, and Mellors took him out to a table in the shade of a cypress tree where the olive groves began. At first Bernardo was most interested in learning English but, as that improved, Mellors began to pass on some of the mathematics he had learned in the army. And Mellors learnt something himself. He explained: 'He knows the poetry of Dante and d'Annunzio by heart.' All I saw was that he liked to be close to the boy, that he enjoyed the intimacy his teaching brought him. It seemed to me that his relationship with Bernardo was far more intimate than any pair of Englishmen allowed themselves to enter, at least after they had left school. They put their arms around one another's shoulders. They laughed at shared jokes. It was almost as if Mellors had fallen in love. I was jealous. And not only of his time, though it was hard not to be galled by the evenings Mellors spent instructing him.

Sometimes I leant out of the window of Emily's room and looked across the dark ruts in the grass to where the two of them were sitting under the cypresses. Bernardo was about medium height; strong, dark-skinned and about my own age. I could make out the movements of his muscles under the blue cloth of his shirt, the thickness of his neck. I could not hear everything Mellors was saying, but Bernardo was listening to every word. It seemed peculiarly unjust that, after our recent quarrel, Mellors had so easily found someone to turn to, while I still had no one else; Duncan didn't count in the least, even though I knew he was waiting in Tuscany for months with the hope that I might turn to him. Even as a friend he was too boringly familiar, too much part of everything I had known all my life.

As I gazed and pondered, I couldn't tell if Mellors

knew I was watching him, and decided he could not; he did not even glance in my direction. He was impatient with what he saw as my possessiveness. After all, his new friendship took nothing away from me. And he liked the authority it gave him. When Bernardo puzzled over a piece of English, he corrected the man carefully.

'*Sicuro*,' I heard him say one evening. 'Now, let us have a glass of wine and you can run off to your wife.'

'I don't have a wife,' said Bernardo.

Mellors watched the man open a bottle against his thigh, and then pour out the wine, with his head lowered. He seemed in no hurry to leave.

'You should find one,' said Mellors.

Bernardo shook his head.

'No, I don't want. My two brothers give my mother her grandchildren. She has enough. I want to do something for myself. *Something.*'

He shrugged at such an indefinite desire, then smiled, and questioned Mellors: 'Are you happy looking after horses?'

'I am,' said Mellors.

'And were you never wanting more?' asked Bernardo. 'To be a thinker, make something beautiful?'

'No,' said Mellors, smiling. 'It's life I want, not art.'

Bernardo made an impatient movement of his head. 'Not enough for me.'

Mellors nodded, as if he, too, wanted something

outside the domestic and the uxorious. I wondered if he hoped Bernardo could give it to him, or the comradeship of the Party to which he belonged.

'Are you a Catholic?' asked Mellors.

'My family, of course. But me, I don't believe. And I can tell you why,' said Bernardo. 'Il Duce proved to me. Have you heard him?'

'No,' said Mellors. 'I don't like political rallies.'

'Oh, he is not just politician,' said Bernardo.

'What was his proof?' Mellors humoured him.

'He took a watch from his pocket,' said Bernardo. 'Then he put it on the table and said to God to strike him dead within five minutes.'

'Nothing happened, of course?'

'Nothing,' said Bernardo. 'I was young man, but I understood. Years ago. Now I take no notice of the Church or what the Church says.'

'Has it occurred to you there could be a God who *chooses* not to take notice?'

'Then I take no notice of him,' said Bernardo.

Mellors laughed. The man's faith was not his concern. Nor was his enthusiasm for the Fascist Party, though he often questioned Bernardo closely about it.

'You English,' said Bernardo contemptuously. 'You are so proud of this Parliament. But what does it do? We had one here. It talked and talked and the people were still hungry. Strikes every week.'

'What about those who don't agree with you? It's

not possible everyone feels the same way.'

Mellors had to repeat his thought more simply, but when he did Bernardo nodded vehemently.

'The man in the gutter, he must kill the man who holds him down.'

'As to that,' said Mellors, amused, 'there are bound to be two opinions.'

Six

Duncan had gone back to England in the autumn, but the following year he came to call on me again, and, as luck would have it, found me in some distress. I had been quarrelling with Emily: an absurd thing to happen with a child who was barely six. Over that winter Emily had been growing up. Her direct gaze often seemed to judge me, and sometimes to mock me when I tried to discipline her behaviour. I can't recall the particular naughtiness that maddened me, but I gave her far harsher words than I intended, and found myself bursting into tears immediately afterwards. She was stunned at such a display of emotion, and I was ashamed of it myself. I went over to put my arms round her and said I was sorry, holding her delicate child's body close to me, and smelling her freshly washed hair. After a moment, her gentle arms went up round my neck. Then she ran off to play with Gina's family without giving me a backward glance.

Some part of my ill temper was no doubt attributable to Mellors. He had spent three evenings in succession with Bernardo and his friends. Altogether, Duncan's invitation to visit his friends over the hill was far from unattractive, though I was uncertain that meeting the local expatriate English was a clever thing to do.

'You see how it is,' I tried to explain. 'We don't want to have people know our story here.'

'I can promise you,' said Duncan, 'it will never come up.'

'And what will Emily do?'

'Isn't she being looked after by Gina in any case?'

I agreed that she was. And so I went.

It was early June, and the flowers were in bloom everywhere. Bougainvillaea climbed up the stone walls. In Hughie's garden there were blue chicory and flowering mallows, and white roses growing carelessly among clumps of weeds. Hughie himself was a bearded, muscularly thin Englishman with a voice that suggested Oxford, a good family and no need to do anything for money. Lavatory seats had made a lot of money for his father, so he could afford to live on the income from that and learn to be a painter.

He showed little interest in me once I was introduced as Mrs Mellors, whose husband worked for the Count.

'What do you do yourself?' asked Hughie Williams, pausing at my side for a moment with a plate of figs and a bottle of Chianti.

'I look after my daughter,' I said pleasantly.

How I hated this habit of defining people by occupations, I thought. It was as bad as any other kind of snobbery.

Something in my manner made Hughie pause speculatively for a moment, as if doubting the social description Duncan had given him. The wife of an English servant? But there was nothing in my face to encourage further inquiry.

Idly, I watched a green lizard.

'What does it feed on?' I asked Duncan.

'Grasshoppers, probably.'

Hughie's beautiful wife Cynthia was serving *bruschetta*: that delicious toasted bread with garlic and oil which I had learnt to enjoy since living in Tuscany. I admired the plates of brightly coloured local pottery. Hughie poured everyone glasses of Gallo Nero. No doubt of it; these people were enjoying Tuscany with gaiety.

'Tuscany has always a certain *campanilismo*,' I overheard Hughie remark to one of the guests.

'*What* does he mean by that?' I whispered to Duncan.

'He is patronizing the Tuscan peasantry. He likes to think their values are those of the parish,' he replied. 'Unlike his own, I suppose.'

We both smiled at that: the ambience was so altogether that of an English country tea party, for all the wine and *bruschetta* and the sound of cicadas. And the conversation too.

Elaine Feinstein

For all the comfort, I did not like Hughie Williams or his guests. I was repelled by the quality of their animation: the promotional eagerness that went along with it. It reminded me of the old days with Clifford at Wragby Hall, when he was so excited at the thought of becoming a well-known writer of short stories. These young people were even more flagrantly ambitious than the writers and artists who had visited us in those days; the excitement ran across the sexes, was far more important to them than the pursuit of sex itself, I guessed. And the women were as much involved as the men in explaining their particular means of expression.

A very slightly built girl called Myra was talking about the way forward for the novel. She was not as young as she looked, but very charming. She was wearing several strands of beads of black mineral and they hung between her small breasts, which had vigorous thrusting nipples that could be seen through the slight shift of her dress. Her hair was as short as Hilda's but thickly black and wavy. For all the charm, I detected something hard and aspirant in her; something I guessed Mellors would not like. Still her whole face lit up when she opened her mouth in a smile. She was talking to a man who lay on the rug at her feet. He had brown, curly hair, a spade beard and bright eyes that crinkled over his healthy cheeks. He was built so powerfully, he looked as if he could fell an ox.

'A butcher's son,' Duncan advised me in a whisper.

112

'Do you know his name? David Worth. People think highly of his books these days.'

The name was unknown to me but, listening, I made out his Yorkshire accent as he began to tell Myra the story of his most recent novel.

'She also wants to be a writer,' said Duncan, frowning. 'I don't know if she has published anything yet. Over there is her husband.'

He nodded towards a bland, comfortable-looking man, possibly of similar age but looking very much older. Myra's husband was in an open-necked shirt, khaki shorts and sandals, and his face had the curious, blind look of a short-sighted man not wearing glasses; his eyes were a pale, defenceless green and his teeth were yellowed with the smoke of his pipe. I disliked his air of measured kindness.

'He is some kind of Oxford don,' said Duncan.

'What you say is marvellous,' Myra breathed, her eyes fixed the while earnestly on David Worth. 'It's the *politics* that count, though. We have a duty to make people see. That's what we must all do. Something to make people see the insanity of this arms race. Europe must not pull itself apart again.'

At a little remove sat David Worth's wife, in a neat dress.

'She's another academic,' said Duncan helpfully. 'Brilliant, they say.'

There was a lively amusement in her face, for all her

spectacles and emaciated body. She had pretty, pointed cheekbones, a cat-like charm and cornflower eyes. Of all the women, she was the most elegantly dressed.

'Isn't this a pleasant party?' said Duncan.

I did not think so. I was quite sorry I had come. There seemed really no point, since no one was taking any notice of me. And Duncan's presence could not make me feel less lonely.

Presently, however, a handsome young man came to sit down next to me on the grass, and my gloom lifted a little. He had dark grey eyes and thick brows.

'Kurt Lehmann. From Germany,' he introduced himself at once. 'On the run, I'm afraid.'

He had a thin, engaging smile which I found myself returning, though I couldn't imagine what he meant. I liked the warm quick grip of his hand, but the freshness of his face made me feel rather old, though I was only in my mid-thirties. When our eyes met, I observed his were fringed with dark lashes. There was a strange contrast between the sun-gold of his hair and the darkness of his eyes. He seemed both eager and earnest.

'I suppose you are an artist?' I said.

He was amused.

'I sketch a little. Sometimes. But I don't have the right temperament for any kind of artist. I'm too curious about how things really are; I don't want to make them up. I prefer to find out how the world actually works.'

I was intrigued.

'How do you do that?'

'I'm a biologist.'

'*That* doesn't sound much fun,' I said, disappointed with his answer, though still taken with his enthusiasm.

'That's because you imagine a schoolmaster drawing on a blackboard. Real biologists are curious about the human body. All our impulses and their chemical source.'

His eyes wandered over me, and I felt myself flushing.

'You make us sound like machines.'

'Not in the least. Machines feel no emotions. They have no responses or wishes of their own. They can only do what we tell them to do. Bodies are endlessly *surprising*. And that's why science fascinates me. Especially physiology. Natural functions are far more surprising than anything human beings could invent for themselves.'

I had never taken much interest in the matter, and certainly never perceived it as in the least glamorous. Kurt himself, however, pleased me. I studied him covertly. He seemed very sure of himself, even arrogant. I coloured a little when our eyes met, afraid he had noticed the intensity of my gaze, but he was unaware of my attention.

'You speak good English,' I said.

'Well, I studied it with a motive,' he confessed. 'I'd

like to continue my work in Cambridge. If my friends can arrange it. The English are good biologists.'

'Are we noted for science?' I asked doubtfully, since I'd never given the matter any thought.

'You produced Darwin,' he reminded me. He could see I was uncertain about Darwin's importance. 'The arts please more people than science, I admit,' he said restlessly, responding to my evident bewilderment. 'I like to make music myself. And to sketch, as I said.'

'He even has some talent,' said Duncan wryly.

Kurt looked impatient, as if such praise were altogether irrelevant to his image of himself.

'Schoolboy facility,' he said. 'Still, would you sit for me? I'd like to draw you.'

I knew Mellors would hate the idea. He had already said as much to Duncan: 'I don't like other men gawping at my wife.'

'I don't think so,' I said. 'In any case—' I stopped, not wanting to fish for a compliment, but genuinely feeling too heavy these days.

'I would only draw your face,' he said.

'It would be an excellent piece of draughtsmanship, I can assure you,' said Duncan.

I said I would certainly think about it, and felt confused and distracted by the unexpected flattery of the request. Meanwhile, the conversation grew general and began to range about the work of Ezra Pound, an

American poet Hughie had been entertaining the previous evening.

'Come to live in Italy for good, or so he said. Talked all the time. I couldn't understand a word of most of it,' Hughie was saying. 'Pretentious rhetoric, probably.'

'I like his Chinese translations,' said David Worth thoughtfully.

I saw the young German at my side looked impatient, but he said nothing until Hughie invited him to comment.

'Come on, Kurt. You might venture an opinion or two.'

'Ezra Pound is a fine poet, but I don't like his opinions,' he said shortly.

Then he flushed, hearing the apparent rudeness in his response.

'Know the poems *well*, do you?' demanded Hughie, with an edge of irony in his voice.

'I read some of his early cantos,' said Lehmann. His vehemence made him look vulnerable. 'You can't expect me to pretend to like his politics.'

'There's no need to be so *serious*. We're just throwing ideas about. It's not a university seminar,' grumbled Hughie.

Soon after this, the young German made his excuses and left. Before doing so, his eyes met mine and I experienced an odd flash of recognition. Afterwards I puzzled at what resemblance I could have identified, and decided that, for all the difference in age and sex, what I had seen in his direct gaze was the innocence and honesty of my own child. I was touched by him.

'Lehmann *always* does that,' complained Hughie Williams, irritably. 'Says nothing for most of an afternoon sometimes, and then with one sentence focuses the whole attention of the party on himself. But he isn't as clever as he thinks he is.'

'What did he mean by saying he's on the run?'

'He's Jewish, poor fellow. When Hitler got into power this year, he thought he should leave Germany.'

'Was it necessary?'

'There are some pretty horrible things reported from there,' said Hughie.

'So there are here,' said his stringy-haired consort. 'But I've never seen any sign of them. Have you? I expect it's all exaggerated. Like the Belgian atrocities in the Great War.'

A political discussion about the direction Europe ought to take broke into violent animation.

'Do you think he may have talent?' I asked Duncan. 'He seems very sure of himself.'

'I don't know about *talent*. He certainly must be pretty *bright*,' said Duncan. 'Hughie met him at the Huxleys'. In Switzerland, you know.'

'Anyone feel like a swim?' asked Hughie, moving round his guests hospitably. 'Sometimes we drive into the mountains. Use the old reservoir. I think it's too cold for the mountain pools today.'

'The old reservoir is filled with weeds,' said Duncan, turning to me. 'Are you a strong swimmer?'

'I haven't got a costume,' I said.

'Let's go and sit with our feet in the water. At least it will be cool.'

From the side of the reservoir I watched Hughie, whose long, thin, ungainly English body was in fact enormously strong and muscled, as he swam halfway across the weedy reservoir like an arrow. I thought he had been unfair to Lehmann: I was convinced the young man was not in the least showing off his knowledge, or concerned to try to make people admire him. Only *shy*, for all his seeming confidence.

We hadn't told Mellors where I was going, but as we came down the bumpy track in Duncan's car I saw him in an upper window. As he turned away, I knew he guessed where I had been.

'I won't come in,' said Duncan, perhaps making the same deduction. 'I promised to be back for supper and I'm already late.'

He let me out of the car, waved cheerily, and I went in alone.

It was very quiet. There was no one in the kitchen. I bit my lip, frowning. Presently I heard Mellors' slippers on the stairs, and he appeared at the kitchen door. His face was closed and dark, and he gave only a cursory nod in greeting.

'There you are,' I said, a little too brightly.

'I've put Emily to bed,' he said.

'Gina could have done that.'

'Emily likes a story,' said Mellors.

He did not extend the implied reproach. And though I waited for him to ask where I had been, he did not. He went about his own tasks quietly, as he always did, but every line of his body was tense and withdrawn.

'Did you have a pleasant day?' I asked.

'Usual kind of thing.'

'I've been to visit Duncan's friends,' I said baldly.

He did not reply.

'I didn't plan it. Duncan just turned up, and I couldn't see anything against it.'

His continuing silence drew more and more words from me in explanation, even though the whole matter was so trivial.

'It was a pretty house and there was a kind of English tea party. With wine. You were quite right about the people, you know. They were horribly boring.'

He turned at this, and his anger was unmistakable.

'Boring, were they?'

'Horrid, pushy women and flabby men,' I said. 'I

couldn't come back sooner because I had to wait for
Duncan.'

'*You lying bitch!*'

The violence in his voice stunned me. I could not
move, or say anything more.

'Look at yourself. Look! You must think I'm a complete fool.'

With two steps, he crossed the kitchen, took me by
my shoulders and turned me round to face my own
flushed face in the kitchen mirror.

'*Bored*, were you?'

'But I *did* have to wait for Duncan,' I protested.
'How else could I get back?'

'Don't you think I know you? Don't you think I know
when something excites you?'

I turned now in a blaze of anger of my own.

'How absurd to behave like this over a tea party.'

Against my will, the young German with eyes like
Emily flashed into my mind.

'It's not the visit,' he said. 'It's your under-hand-
edness. You could have told me. You knew where I was
working. Can you think I'd have asked you not to go?
You go where you like. But I didn't know. Gina didn't
know. Emily didn't know. And we didn't know because
you went off *in secret*. Like a guilty schoolgirl.'

'You talk as if I'd been going off to see a lover. It
was just a whim.'

He grunted.

'Nobody in the least interesting was there, or the least interested in me,' I said wildly.

'So you had no fun at all?' he jeered.

'It meant nothing to me. Nothing,' I said, an edge of hysteria in my voice.

He stared at me coldly.

'The idyll's over,' he said at length. 'Foolish of me to think otherwise.'

'Because I visit a few English friends and drink wine in a garden with them?'

'Maybe so.' He nodded.

Now I was completely furious.

'Sometimes you really are stupid.'

He laughed at that.

'Am I?' he mocked me. 'I suppose you think something is bound to be right if you say so.'

I would have liked to break one of the plates on the table across his head. Instead I rushed at him and tried to beat at him with my hands. He held me at arms' length without much difficulty, until the fury died out of me and I collapsed against him, exhausted and in tears.

'Fly at me, would you?' he said queerly. He seemed pleased. 'There's some life in it yet, then.'

Seven

A few days later, I was walking downhill into the woods of the Bellaggri estate. Now that Gina looked after Emily most afternoons, I was free to make my way through the olive groves alone, admiring the splashes of wild poppy and the hummingbird moths that hovered among the brightly coloured bindweed. I was free, but also lonely. There was a heavy scent of flowers on the air, and the narcotic drone of cicadas rising in my ears. Halfway down the hill, there was Gina's family house and from it came the crowing of a cock and the noise of Gina's younger sister beating linen in the garden.

At the hill top I could see the house Hughie and his friends had rented for the summer. The house was much further away than it appeared, since the landscape dipped down through the dense woods before turning up again towards Raddo-in-Chianti. There were no fences, no hedges, and the woods were almost pathless.

Lost in my solitary thoughts, I suddenly came face

to face with a short, blue-eyed man, who inquired brusquely what I was doing on his property.

'*Your* property?' I realized that I must be talking to the Count Bellaggri himself. I had never met him before. 'I'm sorry. I am the wife of your gamekeeper,' I explained. 'We live in your house over there. I have never been told to keep out of the woods.'

'The wife of my gamekeeper?'

His eyes ran over my fair English face, flushed now with exercise but still most unlike the tanned and leathery faces of the local peasant women.

'Mellors' wife,' I said.

He registered my dress which, though simple, had a kind of elegance, and the Englishness of my voice. My Italian was fluent enough now, but my accent remained unmistakable.

'I remember now. You are Hilda's sister. Isn't that so?'

I confessed that I was, a little uneasily.

'You remind me of her.' His hot, blue eyes went over me speculatively. 'Do you find much entertainment here?'

'I like to walk,' I said, turning away. 'If you do not object to it.'

'Please do. Why not?' He was clearly intrigued by me. 'I hope your little house isn't too constraining?'

'It's charming.'

His eyebrows rose at that. I guessed he knew something of my story, as well as my background.

He looked amused by my reticence. Amused by me altogether, I thought. As his eyes went over me, I drew myself up with uncertainty. I knew the Bellaggri family had owned estates in Tuscany since the twelfth century, and I felt in him all the arrogance of an ancient lineage I could not match. Truly, I thought, I am more a bourgeois than an aristocrat, after all. My title came only through my marriage to Clifford.

'You must call on us. At the house,' he said at last, gesturing over his shoulder towards his palazzo.

You can imagine I did not mention the encounter to Mellors. And when, soon after this, a heavy white envelope arrived with an invitation to a party at the Count's palace, I gave no indication of how such a thing could have come about, and showed no intention of accepting.

'You aren't interested?' he inquired, pleased but surprised.

'Not in the least.'

The reminder of Bellaggri's friendship with Hilda was far from welcome. I wanted no connection between my present life and the one I'd left behind. Mellors put a hand over mine in a gesture of tenderness. From the other side of the breakfast table, Emily said, 'Can I go out and play with the *ragazzi*?'

By *ragazzi* she meant Gina's children. I frowned at the easy Italian idiom. It was convenient, but it was far from appropriate that Emily should play so often with the family.

'It's time Emily went to school,' I said to Mellors. 'Don't you think?'

Mellors shrugged, and beckoned the child round to sit on his knee. Emily went eagerly, and threw her arms around his neck. I remembered the cool, though indulgent, relationship I had had with my own father.

'Who's my darling girl?' asked Mellors.

And Emily gave me a little triumphant smile as she ran off.

'You spoil her,' I told Mellors, a little piqued by that evidence of childish rivalry.

'Nonsense. It's the ordinary warmth the English have lost. The Italians know what children need.'

'I have been thinking,' I continued however. 'She must go away to school.'

'Away? Where?'

'Florence. There is a good school there. An English school.'

'She seems happy enough here.'

'You don't want her properly educated?'

'I want her to know things that'll be useful to her,' he said slowly.

'It's a school for the children of diplomats. She'll meet nice children, learn good manners.'

'And learn to despise her own father,' said Mellors, 'I should think.'

For the moment I left the matter there, seeing the darkness in his face.

Emily, too, had no wish to go away from home.

'*Why* do I have to go away to school?'

'To learn. And to meet children your own age,' I said brightly.

'Daddy can teach me everything,' said Emily.

'Oh, but he hasn't the time,' I said. 'And then he doesn't know *everything*.'

The girl flashed me an angry look.

'Happen he knows all ah want to know,' she said, in a reasonable parody of Mellors' occasional Midlands dialect.

I was not pleased by her pertness.

'Where did you learn to talk like that?'

The little girl nodded sagely. She had an instinct that she had done something irritating, and was taking advantage of it.

'Ah can talk like this when ah want,' she said.

'Well, I hope you won't *want*, when you get to school.'

Mellors had come in unseen as I said this, and was not best pleased to hear the sharpness in my voice.

'Leave the girl alone. She doesn't want to turn into a lady, that's all.'

Emily flashed him a pleased smile.

'She's going to be a spunky good 'un,' he said.

'You *can't* want her to grow up in ignorance.'

'I don't know as I care,' said Mellors. 'She's my little girl, aren't you?'

Emily beamed with pleasure.

'I climbed to the top of Monte Ellici yesterday,' she said eagerly. 'But I couldn't see any wild boar.'

'Well, they're shy,' he said. 'They're used to being hunted. That's why you can't see them.'

Let me not pretend. I was infuriated by an intimacy which excluded me even while I was trying to do my best for my child.

'She'll grow up without an idea in her head,' I exclaimed.

'Ideas aren't good for women,' he said slowly.

'All right for young *men*, though, are they?'

Mellors looked up resentfully, knowing I had Bernardo in mind.

'Boys have to make their own way,' he said.

Unlike Hilda, I had never been much concerned with rights for women, but I was incensed at this. Emily, however, continued to stare up at Mellors in adoration. He was the god of her world, and Mellors basked in her admiration like a lizard in the sun.

'Girls have to marry,' I said, rather lamely.

'Do they?'

Mellors smiled as if he would have liked to keep Emily for himself. For ever. I lowered my eyes, and said no more.

When Emily had gone to bed and we were eating

his favourite Tuscan bean soup and drinking a glass of rough Chianti, I took the matter up again.

'Emily will have to have a life of her own one day,' I insisted.

'Aye, well, she'll grow up soon enough,' he agreed sombrely. 'And learn the wrong we did her. She's a child now, but when she gets to be curious she'll think the less of us. Let me have what I can.'

'I never heard such *selfishness*,' I exclaimed. 'The girl has something to learn, certainly. For that she must go to school.'

'And the fees?'

'I shall pay the fees,' I said. 'What else?'

He drew in his breath sharply, and I knew he was angered by the casual reference to my income.

'I'm still the man in this family,' he said.

Little as I wanted to quarrel, I was incensed by his overbearing assertion.

'You can be the man every *other* way.'

'And what does that mean? If you know.'

A little colour came into my face. The last few weeks he had fallen heavily asleep at my side almost as soon as he got into bed, as if completely exhausted by his working day. I had made no attempt to wake him.

'Men make *decisions*,' I said, in a conciliatory tone. 'That's all I mean. I want you to make the important decisions of our life.'

'Except for this, which is too important to be left to me.'

'Let's not argue about it now,' I said, moving towards him, smiling. 'Let us speak of something else. It's late. Let's sleep on it and think tomorrow.'

He watched me narrowly.

'And what will you tell the school about her parentage?' he asked. 'You don't want the child a laughing stock.'

'I shall tell them we are married. She will not be Lady Chatterley's daughter, she will be Mrs Mellors' child.'

'And I suppose that will silence the rumours?'

'No one knows anything about us here,' I exclaimed.

'*Don't* they?' he mocked me. 'Well, once you mingle with the English abroad, Connie, they soon will. I don't mind for us. Not any more. It's the girl I'm thinking about.'

'So am I.'

There was a sadness in his face. I wanted to caress him; his face, his shoulders, his thighs; to see the drowse of desire beginning in him; but as I put out my hand to him, he thrust my fingers away as if he were angry with me.

'Don't do that,' he said. 'I used to feel my own desire first and then you responded. Not now. You stir me up. You use me.'

I tried to ignore his words and came closer to him,

so that I could put my hand below his work shirt, and feel the lean body beneath. I could feel the line of his muscles, and the tension at his waist. Under the trousers, his body was already growing for me, and I put a hand to the buckle that secured his trousers, but he pushed my hand away.

'Why don't you wait for me to make demands on you?'

'Your body already desires me,' I said.

'That is mechanical. Nothing more. The Catholics know,' he said. 'That is why they keep women pure. Until they marry. That's the whole point of purity. It's obscene to have a woman use a man. For her own pleasure.'

I pulled back my hand as if he had burnt me.

'Go to bed,' he said to me, wearily.

The rejection made me so angry that I went upstairs without another word and flung myself across the bed without any thought of sleep. I felt his behaviour as an insult. Below me I could hear him taking the dishes into the kitchen: the tidy habits of his army days persisting, even though we had a servant to do our chores. For some reason the peaceable clinking of dishes, his voice raised in a pleasant humming, compounded my fury. Without wondering what I intended, my bare feet took me downstairs. I could see him silhouetted against the kitchen window, washing the heavy pottery. A week before, feeling rash and happy,

I had bought six plates of Tuscan pottery with thick red and blue strokes, which formed the pattern of a painted cockerel. They stood, neatly stacked, on the scrubbed kitchen table. Now Mellors' sexual snub had roused a wave of irrational fury that included all the chosen prettiness of our domestic life together. I took the top plate off the pile, meaning to throw it against the far wall; a childish act, certainly, and destructive, but not an aggressive one. My only intention was to signal my rage and humiliation. I wanted the smash of broken pottery; just that, and no more.

I'd aimed to the right of his figure. As he moved towards me, the plate caught him a glancing blow on the shoulder before shattering on the tiled floor. The noise was deafening. In the silence afterwards I could hear a night bird very clearly and distinctly. I hoped Emily would not wake and be frightened.

For a moment, Mellors looked completely astonished; almost stunned by my gesture. He was only slightly hurt. But his eyes flickered wickedly and he strode across the kitchen in a flash, to seize my arm in a sharp grip.

'You bitch. You stupid bitch.'

I mumbled something about not aiming at him, but if he heard my words, he did not accept the excuse. Instead he slapped me round the face, as deliberately as a man might discipline a child in some household where children are hit with routine severity. I could feel a trickle of blood at my lips. Then I dropped to a chair in my misery, my face burning, and began to sob. How could I have put my life into the hands of a man who treated me so wickedly? Never in my life had a man so much as lifted a hand against me. In the houses of the poor, I knew, women were sometimes battered by drunken men, but I had never imagined a similar fate for myself.

'Oh *very* nice,' he said. 'Very charming. Sob away.'

Even as I wept, my mind began forming plans of escape. I must get through the night, I told myself. Then I could take Emily and a few suitcases and leave in the morning. There would be no problem. A train from Florence. I could send a telegram to my father. He would meet us off the boat. I should never have taken up with such a brute.

He watched me as I cried, offering no further violence, but far from sympathetic.

'How can you be so cruel?' I cried, between gasps and tears.

'Cruel?' He seemed bewildered by the accusation.

'To strike me like a dog,' I said.

The words brought on a new paroxysm of tears. The misery of it made me weak.

'You're the one who began throwing plates,' he pointed out, calm himself, but in no way apologetic.

'It still wasn't right to hit me. You hurt me. I can

feel my lip swelling. Maybe where *you've* lived, it's all right to retaliate by hitting a woman.'

I realized as soon as I'd spoken that my words were hardly calculated to please him, but he took them quietly enough.

'Where *I've* lived? I see what you mean. So it is.' He nodded. 'And you should have thought of that before you took up with me, Lady Chatterley.'

'I only meant . . .' I began.

He shook his head.

'I know what you meant right enough.'

I made a desperate effort to explain myself.

'*Try to understand.* It was what happened before. What you said to me. You rejected me.'

To my annoyance, I had begun to apologize to him. He still looked at me fiercely.

'So I did. A man has to have that much freedom.'

'Your *eyes.* They're so black and bitter. When you look at me like that I feel so lonely,' I cried.

'*Lonely,* are you? Don't you think I feel that?'

'No,' I cried. 'I don't think so. You have Bernardo and all those men in the café to talk with, and you have no idea, no idea at all, what it's like to live in this house waiting for you to come back. And then . . .'

I stopped.

'You foolish woman,' he said. 'Do you want everything in my life to turn around you? That would really finish us.'

A great fatigue came over me. Suddenly I wanted nothing but to curl up in a warm bed and sleep for a long time.

'I don't understand,' I said at last. '*How* are you lonely?'

'I try to work out how or where to fit,' he said simply. 'Do the best I can. But I can't and I don't. As for the child and her schooling, if that's what worries you, we'll come to some agreement.'

I wanted him to put his arms around me. I wanted to hold him so we could comfort one another. But it was not what he needed.

'I'll have a walk outside, now. Go to bed.'

As I watched him go through the door, a great desolation filled my spirit.

I woke just before dawn the next morning with a pain like a stone in my chest as I remembered our quarrel. He had not yet come to bed. The light was beginning: grey and misty behind the olive trees. I shivered with the thought of the day. Should I pack my clothes? Was I really going to leave him? I went instead to see where he was. He had fallen asleep in one of the large square chairs downstairs, still holding a book in his hand, his face open and defenceless as a child. He did not stir as I approached.

'Come to bed,' I whispered.

He nodded, and I urged him to stand.

'It's not yet time for work. Come to bed.'

He leant against me, and we went upstairs together.

He woke fully, an hour later, and entered me at once with all the eagerness and passion of a young lover, so that for that next day at least I forgave him everything.

Over schooling, we compromised. Mellors agreed to English schooling for Emily, and I saw there was sense in his anxiety there should be no mention of the name Chatterley. What other hope was there for the child but such concealment? Yet it made me uneasy.

Eight

That autumn term, I drove Emily to Florence myself, borrowing a car from Duncan's friend Hughie. It was a longer drive than I had expected and I was lost once or twice on the narrow Tuscan roads.

The Plaidy School was close to the Duomo, and it was difficult to find anywhere to park the car; but when that had been arranged, Emily and I presented ourselves at the school entrance in the Via Santa Margherita de' Cerchi and were admitted to a cool and pleasant house furnished austerely in English washable covers. The first person we met was an old schoolfriend of mine from finishing school days in Switzerland.

'*How* is Clifford?' she asked, when we had embraced.

'I'm married to someone else now,' I said quickly.

My friend's delight at seeing me, and inspecting my pretty child, seemed untainted by any scandalous interest; a few questions elicited that her husband had been posted for the last ten years to Singapore. Nevertheless, the question confirmed Mellors' common sense.

For all Emily's supposed reluctance to leave home, she was interested enough in the new environment, and eagerly agreed to the music lessons I proposed for her. She and my friend's daughter sized one another up cautiously. Whatever my own feelings, Emily seemed happy to have an acquaintance in the school.

Looking at my watch, I decided I had time to go for a short walk around the Piazza della Signoria before going to the hotel. As I began to walk in that direction, a little disconsolately – for I was far from certain my obstinate wish to educate the child at an English school had been sensible – I was surprised to hear my name called. Turning, I saw Kurt Lehmann, the young German I had met briefly at Hughie's house on my visit with Duncan. He was standing beside a dark blue brougham with large rubber wheels and red shafts, gleaming all over with varnish, glass and chromium.

'Can this belong to you?' I asked him, astonished at such evidence of prosperity.

He laughed at the idea.

'Of course not. I was sent on an errand.'

'By whom?'

'The family I am staying with in Florence. Are you staying here a few days?'

'A night only.'

'You seem upset . . .'

'It's nothing. I've left my daughter at a kind of boarding school for the first time.'

There was no need, I reflected, to explain any other source of anxiety.

'And you feel you have lost her.' He seemed to understand some of my feelings at once.

'I'm afraid she will resent and blame me.'

'Did you blame your *own* mother then for sending you away to school?'

'My situation was a bit different,' I said ruefully, without offering any further explanation. 'In any case, I can't remember her. It was my father who was the important presence in my childhood. Do you have parents in Germany?'

He looked at me with his wide, dark eyes, and I was reminded again of the child left behind at the school.

'I don't know *where* they are exactly,' he said.

'Shall we have a coffee?' I suggested, taking the initiative rather to my own surprise.

'I know a good place,' he agreed. 'Just through here.'

As I followed him into a narrow lane, I felt my mood changing. It was as if I had suddenly become aware of the clear yellow light enveloping the city.

'Florence is so beautiful,' I said.

'Naturally. Most of Florence was built during the Renaissance,' he agreed.

'This feels medieval,' I argued.

'I suppose Dante might recognize the little alleys,' he said. 'Though he could never have seen the Duomo.

Brunelleschi built the dome, of course. The largest of his time. Have you climbed the 463 steps?'

I told him I had done so many years ago.

'I'm glad you aren't going to insist that we are living through a new Italian Renaissance nowadays,' he continued.

'I suppose it's always bankers and princes who make art possible. Nothing very moral about beauty,' I remarked.

We were walking past Ghiberti's doors at the eastern end of the Baptistry, the golden gates of paradise as Michelangelo called them, and stopped for a few moments to look.

'Yes. The earlier ages had their own despots,' he agreed. 'And their republics weren't particularly benevolent. Did you know that when the French invaded Tuscany, Savonarola claimed it was God's punishment for obscene books? You can see the spot in this very square where they executed him.'

'If you know so much about Florentine cruelties, why have you chosen to come here?' I asked.

'I didn't have an enormous choice,' he said ruefully. 'It was rather a speedy decision. I came with the one suitcase of a refugee. And there were friends.'

'Will you look for a place in a laboratory now?'

'Not here.' He shook his head.

'Where do you stay?' I asked him, wondering if he stayed with Duncan's friends.

'The owners of the carriage,' he smiled, 'have been very kind. I, too, have a sort of family here. The Bassani. Perhaps you have heard of them?'

I had not.

'They are an old Sephardi family. They live in a villa in the north of the city. Their park is like a protected paradise, though I don't know for how much longer.'

'Jews aren't badly treated here, are they?'

'Not yet. Indeed, some of them profess great loyalty to Mussolini.' He laughed. 'It is their old habit to try and conform to the society in which they live. Some even join the Party.'

I must admit I found this casual mention of Jewishness more alarming than a possible attachment to the Fascist Party, which I saw entirely through Mellors' eyes. I had known an artist or two who had Jewish blood in Hilda's London circle, but they were more evasive about their heritage.

'How Jewish are they? The Bassani?'

'*Racially*, do you mean?' he teased me.

'I don't know what I mean,' I said, confused, colour flooding my face.

By this time, we had found a café with a green awning and several empty, shining white tables. We ordered two large coffees with the cream spinning on top and chocolate grated into the white foam. The sun had come out and lit the side of the square where we were sitting.

'Are you enjoying your stay in Italy?' he asked politely. 'Have you seen much of Tuscany?'

'On foot,' I said slowly. 'Not much chance to use a car.'

'Have you seen San Gimignano? They call it the city of beautiful towers. Perhaps your daughter Emily would enjoy a visit?'

'Marvellous frescoes,' I agreed. 'Do you know Memmo di Filippucci's "Wedding Scene"? His painting of a bed, with a lady in it?'

He looked at me with a strange expression. For a moment I felt a pang of sensuality, and wondered if he shared it. Then I realized his expression was a kind of puzzlement.

'Perhaps you had some education in art history yourself?'

'A little. When I was younger,' I admitted uneasily.

'Where was that?'

'Dresden,' I said. 'Nothing very serious.'

He nodded.

'Just a little finishing off for a young lady?'

I bit my lip at that. The blood had come up into my face.

'Tell me about yourself,' he said.

I had no lies prepared for such a casual meeting. What to invent?

'My father is a painter,' I said.

'Well known?'

I hesitated, and he saw as much.

'Yes,' I said, confusedly.

A pause fell between us.

'And your husband?' he inquired. 'Mr Mellors, isn't it?'

'He works for the Count,' I said shortly. 'In his stables for the most part, though he also helps oversee some of his game.'

Perhaps I waited for his comment, but he only nodded, as if what I said confirmed his judgement.

'And your own family? Are they all scientists?' I asked, a little wildly.

'On my father's side, yes. My mother is a pianist.'

'They didn't leave when you did?'

'No,' he said quietly. 'They arrested my father as a Socialist agitator. He is in a holding camp with many others.'

'And your mother?'

'I don't know,' he said.

At this I made a little exclamation of incredulity, and he gave me a tired smile.

'You see, my dear Mrs Mellors, there are some problems of which you can have absolutely no conception.'

While this was plainly true, I found it strangely easy to talk to him. I thought of the antagonism so often in the words exchanged with Mellors, and puzzled why there was so little difficulty in saying what I thought to Kurt. It must be because there was no sexual connection between us, or because we did not have to live at one another's side.

He had persuaded me to join him in a strega. The hot yellow liquid opened my lips and I began to speak unguardedly.

'Why is all sex such a war?'

'Is it?'

'Yes,' I said. 'Men hate women. I don't understand it. They *dislike* them. Not just because some of us want equal rights: we don't all want equality. It doesn't matter. Even if we simply sit and wait for approval, and try to live quietly, just getting on with our lives. If we live at their sides, it's still a war.'

He didn't seem very convinced by my outburst.

'I don't hate women,' he pointed out. 'I don't think your generalization would stand up to much investigation.'

'Do you mean biological investigation?'

'It must be nonsense, don't you think, just as an observation? The species couldn't survive if men and women hadn't evolved better relations than that. Do women dislike men?'

'No. We need them. Desperately,' I said.

He seemed thoughtful.

'Then you think the war is *all* the fault of the men?' He was teasing me now, and I was sorry to have given away so much. Then he shook his head and admitted, 'I suppose you may be right to wonder if human beings have evolved together satisfactorily as a species. They are certainly pretty aggressive, especially in herds. The aggression isn't something men direct only towards women, though, is it?'

'It may be we deserve it,' I continued, lost in the track of my own thoughts: remembering Clifford guiltily; thinking of my treachery to him. 'Perhaps we are all betrayers.'

'No,' he soothed me. 'Women obey their instincts, like all animals.'

And so we talked. There was no doubting it; for all he was so different from anyone I had ever met, I was drawn to him. I would have liked to stroke his brown arm, where the little golden hairs glinted so charmingly. I certainly hoped there was no outward sign of these feelings: I had no wish to embarrass him. Nevertheless, as he took me to the Piazza della Signoria I felt that, for the first time since I had arrived in Italy, I was enjoying the country as it should be enjoyed.

Not long after establishing Emily at her school, a letter came from Venice to announce Hilda planned an autumn visit to Tuscany. She would be staying, she said, with the Bellaggri family. Mindful that Mellors disliked to be surprised, I showed him the note and waited for his comments. None came. Another letter followed with all manner of scurrilous gossip which I read in secret with avidity. Clifford was off on a cruise with his housekeeper, Mrs Bolton. My father had taken up with an opera singer. Giorgio was in New York.

'And what news of you, dear sister?' Hilda added in a postscript. 'Still locked in monogamous fidelity? No regrets, no ennui?'

That second letter I committed to the flames of the fire of pine cones.

When Hilda arrived at our house wearing a green poplin dress with a light coat over her arm, Mellors was out at a political meeting with Bernardo. Hilda, whose eyes had never been in the least myopic, produced a lorgnette to examine the cottage. She looked, I thought, rather like a slimmer version of my mother when she was young; she scrutinized the chestnut-roof and poked curiously into the pantry.

'*Do* you have electricity here?' she asked, as I poured her a glass of wine.

'Well, the refrigerator can't be used at the same time as the iron,' I said, pausing and determined to answer all her questions precisely. 'We make wood fires in the winter.'

'Do you have hot water at least?'

'Sometimes we don't have water of any kind,' I said.

Hilda stared at me with an odd resentment.

'But you're happy?'

'Yes,' I said. 'On the whole.'

'You are still passionate lovers? After all these years

together? Do I believe you, I wonder? Duncan writes from time to time,' said Hilda, knowingly.

'I hardly *see* Duncan,' I said irritably, 'so I can't imagine what you are hinting at. And his friends have no charm.'

'None of them?'

I frowned.

'I rarely see them. So I can't say.'

'And where is Mellors this evening?'

'He is at a meeting. Something political. He says he needs to sort out his ideas.'

'I see,' said Hilda.

'He doesn't usually stay late,' I said, sounding more defensive than I intended.

Even as I spoke, Mellors pushed open the door and saw our visitor. Hilda smiled at him.

'I've come to bring you an invitation,' she said brightly.

Mellors stared at her with a certain suspicion.

'From your employer,' Hilda explained.

Mellors' eyes narrowed.

'He didn't mention it to me when he came to take his horse yesterday afternoon.'

'Oh, but this is a *formal* invitation. Look. I insisted you be asked in the same way as his other guests.'

Mellors took the envelope and opened it. Inside was a gold-edged card.

'There is a party. You will both come, won't you?'

She could see that Mellors had no interest in the card, and, moreover, resented Hilda's presence. 'Oh, but you won't be so mean,' she coaxed him. 'For Connie's sake.'

Mellors said, indifferently, 'She can go if she wants. Why are we invited?'

'Oh, the Bellaggri family is feudal. Almost paternal. They like to offer their faithful servants supper and wine occasionally.'

'And have them mingling with their guests?'

'Not the *maids*, I don't suppose,' laughed Hilda. 'And certainly not the people in the kitchens. They'll be too busy. But surely you'll accept? It's expected.'

'We were invited once before,' said Mellors. 'But we didn't go. It didn't matter.'

He turned away and I tried to catch Hilda's eye. She seemed reluctant to meet my gaze and, when she did, I could see she meant well enough. I was far more alarmed than pleased, however, and I could see that Mellors, too, was calculating how much she would have needed to explain to have Bellaggri renew his invitation.

'It's of no interest to me. I have been to far too many parties,' I said, distantly.

I thought Hilda quite unbelievably tactless. Or malicious. Her very arrival in this part of the world made my concealment less complete. Did she need warning that we did not want our story brought into

148

the open? I hoped she had enough sense at least to be silent about that.

'Connie looks quite depleted,' said Hilda. 'She needs entertainment. Duncan said she was looking well, but I don't think men see *anything*.'

'Perhaps I was feeling better then,' I said, as coolly as I could.

Hilda's eyebrows rose knowingly as she stood up to leave.

'Too much domestic virtue. You'll dwindle to nothing.'

After saying goodbye to her, I picked up the gold-edged invitation again, thoughtfully.

'Perhaps I *do* need some diversion. After all, I don't have a pupil or political rallies to amuse me.'

'You will persist in seeing my interest in politics as a kind of boy scouts game,' he said irritably.

'Well, and *isn't* it?' I was delighted by the image. 'All the marching and the flags.'

'No. People are learning how to join together here, trying to make a better society, and I want to be part of that.'

'And do you really think there's any *hope* of it?'

'I want to think so. Some dignity for working men. Something to believe in.'

I was depressed by this admission of an emotional need I could not satisfy.

'About this party—' I frowned, returning to the point. 'We *could* go, couldn't we?'

'*You* can go,' he said.

'Not without you,' I pleaded. 'The invitation comes to both of us. I don't want to go without you.'

'You insist on me coming?'

'It's not a question exactly of insisting. More a matter of propriety. Since you, after all . . .' I hesitated, 'are the only real connection we have to the Bellaggri household.'

This was the right thing to say and, after a moment's hesitation, he agreed with me.

'All right. We'll go if you like. Let's see how these people enjoy themselves. While they can.'

There was something ominous in that, but I did not explore what he meant; I was so glad to hear he would come.

As I thought of a ball at the Bellaggri palace, I realized I should need something to wear. So I decided to combine my visit to watch Emily perform in her mid-term play with a rare shopping trip.

The atmosphere of the school, even the hum of English voices in the Great Hall, reminded me not altogether pleasantly of my own early days at boarding school, and I found my heart banging nervously for Emily when she stepped on to the stage. A moment later, I realized I need not worry. Her voice was clear, and she seemed far less nervous than I was. Afterwards, she introduced me to some of the girls in her class, and though I guessed she was not yet sure of her position among them, she was remarkably offhand. The teachers seemed to be right: she had adjusted very well to her new life.

For myself, the following day I found it strangely intoxicating to shop in Florence. I was tempted by inappropriate gloves and shoes, scarves in subtle colours. As I looked at myself in the mirrors of the most elegant shops, I felt myself growing taller by the moment. At length, I selected an extraordinary dress that brought out the redness of my hair.

'You look like a princess,' approved the sales girl.

The dress was rather more costly than I intended, not to mention my other purchases, but my father had sent me a double birthday present in sterling only a few weeks earlier, to make up for one he'd forgotten to send the previous year, and there was no great pressure on my allowance apart from the school fees. As I left the shop, I felt a beautiful, confident woman.

It was only as Mellors and I dressed for the party together that I became aware of the enormity of the change I had effected. He watched me stonily, and as I turned for his approval, he said:

'We make an incongruous couple.'

I stared at him. Mellors had one good suit in

charcoal grey, bought more than ten years earlier when he was an officer in India; it had been a sensible purchase at the time, and even now it looked hardly worn; it still fitted him and looked well enough on his straight figure. I thought he looked rather distinguished as we set out together.

'Men don't need showy plumage,' I smiled.

The Bellaggri gardens were lit with candles like a fairyland. In the fading light of the autumn evening I made out an orchard of fruit trees. There was a long white-clothed table on the terrace, with a lawn going down to wild ferns, dark trunks of poplars, twinkling beeches and cedars of Lebanon. There were already many people gathered on the lawn: the women brilliantly clad in orange and emerald dresses, cut away to expose their legs; the men in formal clothes. On the terrace, a feast had been set out for the guests: caviare in silver bowls of ice, cold fresh salmon, little vol-au-vents stuffed with minced chicken. On rubber-wheeled trolleys, servants were bringing wine in carafes, and other drinks of water and raspberry juice, with slices of lemon and grapes.

It was a shock to be in the presence of so many people. And perhaps because of my delicate high heels I walked differently. I certainly felt different from the person who waited every day at home for Mellors to return. Perhaps I was no more than Mrs Mellors in a good dress. Yet, even as I told myself as much, I was enjoying the glances I attracted, my sense that this was a community of people happy to welcome me among them. I knew Mellors felt less at home. And even as we moved about the room together, something else had begun to disturb me: it was as if Mellors had begun to shrink in relation to the pressing crowds around me. I had become so used to seeing him as the central, most powerful figure in my world, that even to find him the same size as other people was very strange. I felt I must comfort and reassure him that he belonged, and yet could not do so because it was so plainly far from the case. With part of myself I longed to be home again with him in our own quiet stone house. Yet no one knew my story, I told myself, except possibly the Count. There was no reason to be anxious, even though I had shed the invisibility worn so carefully since coming to Tuscany. In such a mix of emotions I drank more wine than I usually did.

The light went quite suddenly, as it always did in Tuscany, and the party drifted through the French windows into a long Renaissance ballroom, with a cascade of chandeliers overhead and old paintings of Bellaggri ancestors on the walls. The terrace remained alight with candles, and some of the guests preferred to remain outdoors in the evening coolness. The windows were open to the terrace, and evening scents followed us. Without undue alarm, I saw the Count and his wife approaching. The Countess Bellaggri was a splendid creature with fine, coppery hair unfashionably loose on her shoulders, marvellous legs and a very white skin. For a moment our hosts stood before us to exchange civilities.

'And do you play tennis?' the Count inquired, looking directly at me.

'Not often,' I smiled.

'We have a splendid tennis court which gets far too little use,' he said regretfully. 'I should have been happy to have you make some use of it. Plain earth, I'm afraid, but we keep it even.' Then, smiling, he moved away.

I became conscious that Mellors had been holding himself stiffly at my side, as if about to go before a firing squad.

'He didn't even *look* at me,' he muttered now. 'But that's all right. I don't want his friendship.'

'It means nothing,' I said.

Of course he felt out of place, for all his bearing. I could see he was angry with himself for coming. His wry expression caught at my heart. Yet he looked not so much embarrassed as disgusted, as he stood in the charm and dazzle of the ballroom. Perhaps he was remembering his friends in the field and their sunburnt backs.

'We'll go soon,' I said, 'if you're hating it.'

He did not reply.

Nobody came to speak to us for a time. Waiters filled our glasses, offered us delicacies, went on their way. I would have liked to have made something of the occasion for him; to introduce him to some of the people who stood about, but I knew no one. And the splendour was something for which the English country balls I remembered had given me little preparation. I might be at ease myself, but I could not give Mellors an entry to it. With that in mind, I looked around for Hilda as the only possible link to the bustle of people who seemed to know each other so well and were talking eagerly to one another in a language I could barely understand.

Across the room stood a tall, black-haired woman, with hair unfashionably and magnificently wild and a superb bosom, talking with enormous animation to a pale emaciated gentleman in his forties. There was something hypnotic in the glitter of the woman; the diamonds at her throat, and the silk of her dress shot through with golden thread. Yet she was not altogether a beauty. Her teeth as she smiled were set too far apart for that.

Close to her, I recognized the bearded face of Hughie, Duncan's friend. With relief, without thinking, I smiled and beckoned; he came over at once, though he was uncertain who I was. He stared for a moment at Mellors, as if trying to place him. Seeing as much, I introduced him as my husband, and was rather annoyed when Mellors made a point of adding, as he shook hands: 'I look after the Count's horses.'

Hughie smiled doubtfully at this, and then turned back to report some news about an art exhibition opening in Venice. I answered civilly, racking my brains for some topic which would include Mellors. I was angry with him for making his social rank so explicit, and with myself too, for insisting on his presence in such a place.

Partly to distract Mellors from his own disgruntled mood, I asked Hughie about the glittering black-haired woman and her pale companion.

'Oh, he is the local nark for OVAF,' he said. 'And that is Beatrice. She is Bellaggri's sister.'

Seeing I didn't understand the initials, he explained: 'The organization for putting down opposition to Fascism. They say he tortures people he doesn't like.'

'I'm sure the Bellaggri family would have nothing to do with someone so sinister,' I said, shocked and not sure if he was teasing.

Hughie gave a bark of laughter.

'Beatrice is a law unto herself. And let me tell you, she has to do with someone far more alarming. She lives in Rome, you know. It is common knowledge she is much favoured.'

I remember staring without understanding what he meant.

'How does she maintain that constant laugh?' wondered Mellors, with distaste and much less overawed. 'She must be either manic-depressive or—'

'High on cocaine,' finished Hughie. 'They say she is mad.'

'She is certainly spectacular,' I agreed.

'And are you enjoying the splendours of Tuscany?' Hughie asked Mellors.

'The peasant's dream,' said Mellors, with a certain bitterness. 'And these people still have it all.'

He was far from at ease, but, addressed now for the first time, spoke frankly, as he always did.

'It's a very enjoyable party,' I said, my eyes on Hilda and the sinister friend of Beatrice Bellaggri, who were now approaching together.

'Darling!' said Hilda. 'This is Fiero Pucci. He doesn't shake hands. Fascists don't.'

Hughie said, 'I hope you won't insist on the Roman salute.'

Pucci took my hand and bent over it graciously.

'Enchanting,' he said.

But Hughie was looking from Hilda to myself.

'Are you old friends or perhaps relations?' he asked uncertainly.

'We're *sisters*,' said Hilda, without a moment's pause for thought.

I bit my lip. Hilda seemed to have no tact or sense. And Mellors gave a hard, dry laugh.

'I see.' Hughie nodded, as if he felt some responsibility to conceal the anomalies of the situation now exposed. He was plainly bewildered to imagine what could have brought a sister of Hilda's to live with a man who looked after the Count's horses. The very conjecture was an embarrassment. Only Pucci seemed unaware of what had been revealed.

'You English,' he said, with an expansive gesture. 'Once you were our allies. Perhaps again.'

Mellors seemed perfectly composed, though his eyes flashed with dislike of the situation. He addressed himself to Pucci.

'Do you think your new government will change anything much?'

'Oh, yes,' said Pucci, nodding his head. 'Already we change a lot.'

As Hilda and Pucci drifted away, Hughie gave an exaggerated sigh of relief.

'Isn't he a monster?' he inquired, turning to politics with some relief.

'I don't know,' said Mellors. 'I suppose *you* think of yourself as a Socialist?'

'Yes, I do. Moderately.'

'Isn't Mussolini also a kind of Socialist?'

Hughie laughed. 'Don't you believe it! He made a deal with the war profiteers long ago. He may have threatened to hang them from the lamp-posts once, but he took their money soon enough once he got into power.'

'Aren't you pleased, though,' I asked, 'that the Bolsheviks have been kept out?'

Hughie shrugged.

'A Party to smash the Bolshevik menace is usually as bad, or worse.'

'Mussolini has a lot of popular support,' said Mellors uncertainly. 'I know that.'

'A lot of working men have fallen under the clubs of his Blackshirts, all the same.'

'And a lot marched on Rome with him,' said Mellors.

'As for the march on Rome, I can tell you why the Fascists marched when they did – it was because Italy was recovering. In a few months' time it would have been too late.'

Mellors shook his head.

'Ask yourself,' said Hughie. 'How do you rule a country when the best minds of the people don't want you to? Easy – you eliminate the opposition. What else? Matteotti was beaten, stabbed, mutilated and burned.'

'You speak very freely,' said Mellors. 'If the Fascists are as ruthless as you say.'

'Well, here in the Bellaggri house—' Hughie stopped.

'I have heard about the Bellaggri family,' said Mellors. 'For all their claim to aristocracy, there is something askew in their family tree, isn't there? You know what I mean – they say the Countess had a large dowry, a fat cheque, and jewels, too.'

'Where did you hear all that?' asked Hughie.

At the far end of the room, a small four-piece band, with a saxophone and clarinet, had set up their instruments. One of the players was a negro.

'This American rubbish! Even here,' said Mellors.

The band began a sentimental song from a recent film, and people glided on to the floor. Then the simple, dreamy tune was broken open by a riff from the saxophone. After a moment's surprise, the dancers responded gaily, if awkwardly, to the syncopation. I was exhilarated. It was a long time since I heard anything so cheerful.

But Mellors had never enjoyed this kind of dancing. For him, dance music – which he remembered no doubt from the days at his local Palais – was no more than an excuse to hold a woman in a bear hug, and move slowly with her held up against his belly. He did not truly approve of that either but he was deeply offended by this new jazzy dancing, in which the woman made all the movements and was given all the chance of display, while the bewildered man stood still, offering little more than a supporting hand.

He said something of this and, as he spoke, I could not help feeling some application was intended to my own sexual behaviour.

'Don't be such a *puritan*,' I said sharply.

The euphoria of the music rose in me; if this dancing *was* sexual, a special kind of corrupt female sexuality, then I was attracted towards it. I watched Hilda dancing energetically, impudently. She had always danced with more verve than I did. It looked enviable.

'Shall we try at least?' I whispered to Mellors.

He looked at me as if I had proposed something obscene.

'Not my style,' he said, cuttingly.

So I gazed about, reluctant to abandon the pleasure, wondering who could share it with me. Hughie was too straight-limbed and English to be able to do it well, I knew. But a young Italian man was at my elbow in a moment, seeing my lit face and the way the music ran up and down my body. He bowed and asked for the dance and, though I found my eyes moving towards Mellors for his consent, I had already nodded acceptance. Truly my glance at Mellors for approval irritated me. Hilda was right: I *had* dwindled since living with him. Why should I *not* dance? There was nothing immoral in it.

'I think I will,' I said, handing my wrap to Mellors, my eyes lowered.

He made no comment.

The Italian danced well, and I responded easily to the grace of his body and the sinuous way he threw me a little distance before winding me back towards him. The music had gone to my head, and I began to invent steps of my own as another song enfolded me. I could feel the heavy beat in every one of my gestures. My partner was at a distance; I could feel his admiration.

In that attention I was once again a sexual being. Yet I was not dancing for my partner: I was dancing for Mellors; not to provoke him, exactly, but to exhibit my skill and my joy. In its silk, my body showed the line of waist and breasts as I let the music shape my steps. 'Bravo,' someone called. Mellors seemed to be smiling, but his eyes were angry, as if he hated me for the display. He turned and left the circle. At once all the pleasure went out of my performance. I continued till the music ended, out of politeness, but my thanks to my partner were perfunctory. I had to find Mellors. No one else mattered.

So I circled the floor, avoiding Hilda and Pucci and Hughie, and then looked on to the terrace, presuming Mellors had gone out into the dark gardens. I knew he wanted to escape. He could always become his own separate thing. I hated him for that, but there was nothing I could do about it.

At last I found him. Not on the terrace but in a conservatory at the side of the house, where he stood alone, looking up at the skilfully husbanded tropical fruit. In the darkness, I made out an odd smell: a mixture of wood and citrus fruits. On the shelves at the side of the glasshouse were carefully arranged large, round yellow fruit – grapefruit, I supposed, put there to ripen.

'There you are!' I said, my body filled with the relief of his presence.

He did not seem particularly glad to see me.

'This stupid world,' he said. 'I have no time for it.'

'But you don't think the less of me for the dancing?' I could not help asking.

'You do what you like,' he said.

His face was closed to me.

Under the sheets that night, he lay on his back looking up at the ceiling. I put a hand out to him, unhappily. For all his unfairness, I could not bear the animosity between us.

'Do you think—?' I began.

'Spare me your voice,' he said. 'I don't want to hear your rubbish.'

I bit my lip, and my eyes prickled with tears. He continued to lie on his back, and I could feel his eyes were open.

'I don't say it's your fault,' he said. 'A woman and a man can't relate only as if they live on an island. Society places them; and that changes things between them. Bound to. And that's bad for us, Connie.'

'It need not be,' I cried. 'Haven't we proved it not so?'

'No. The whole of society would have to change for what I've just said not to be true. Maybe that's what I'm hoping for.'

I wanted to hope with him, but his voice gave me little chance.

'I want to be with you, not anyone else. I hate Hughie's high voice and patronizing manner as much as you do,' I said.

'Hughie?' He fell silent for a moment. 'He doesn't have much to recommend him, certainly. Not intelligence. A confidence maybe, but that just comes from schooling, and families that have taught him his place is to be on top. Of course he and his lot are certain of everything. As long as the world bowls along as it usually does, they have no problem understanding and controlling it. But let something happen to surprise them,' he finished with sudden viciousness.

'What then?' I asked.

'Then their inflexibility will be a disadvantage,' he said, with a rather gleeful chuckle.

I joined in the laughter, a little uncertainly as I felt the malice in it.

'As for you, Connie, you're part of the same crew.'

'No, I'm *not*,' I protested. 'How unfair. Why must you drive me from you into the group you're attacking, when I only want to be on your side?'

He laughed at me.

'No real men would dance like that,' he said presently. 'It's obscene. It's for homosexuals.'

'I don't think—'

'You can see it in their faces, the men. What they

want. It makes me feel ill. They're like insects.'

'You don't have to be afraid of that.'

'Did I say afraid? Anyway, it won't go on much longer, their arrogance,' he repeated. 'They won't be able to lord it over people better than they are for ever.'

'Does Bernardo say that?' I asked, with a flicker of anger at the implied threat. 'Or his friends? But perhaps they're equally unjust; perhaps they're even a good deal *wickeder* than the people you want to put down?'

He lifted himself on one arm.

'You think you know better, do you? Really? Thought it all out, have you, with your usual penetrating intelligence? Well, we'll have to see.'

The sarcasm hurt, but I was scared, too.

'Is there going to be violence?'

'Without violence there never is any change.'

He rolled over then, as if the thought he had just allowed himself had given him a measure of relief.

Sleep was impossible for me. I rose from my bed and stood looking out at the Tuscan moonlight which lit the rim of the valley in which we lived. The sweet night air came in through the open window. I could hear a night bird calling, and guessed at the scurry of a rabbit in the olive groves.

To go to the Bellaggri party had certainly been a mistake. Why had I even thought to enter a world so alien? Alien to myself, as well as to Mellors, though I was seemingly so much more acceptable there. Now there was a distance between us much greater than anything his passion for local politics could have made. I looked at the blue light behind the cypress and felt tears of loneliness come into my eyes. Was there to be no more tenderness between us? I stumbled back to bed and after a long time fell asleep.

A few hours later, I woke to watch him dressing. Keeping my eyes closed, I was aware that he was looking at me, and that I presented a rather pathetic figure as I lay huddled under the clothes, curled up as I was, pitiful and a little defenceless.

'Are you going?' I asked him sleepily.

'You wanted me last night, didn't you?' he said, baring his teeth. 'Oh yes, I know that. I know you did. And that was supposed to be enough to placate me? To make up for everything a man needs in his own house?'

'But what *is* it you need from me, my dearest love?' I cried, ready to give him anything in the world.

'Respect!' he cried. 'To be properly valued and looked up to. And that's impossible. You *couldn't* look up to me, could you?'

I tried to protest.

'Don't pretend. Whatever you say will be a lie. I know,' he said.

The injustice of that reproach went into me. Was this all he understood, after all that had once held us together? I wanted to say something cutting and could think of nothing. Instead, I felt the tears coming to my eyes. Angrily, I jumped out of bed, to hide my unhappiness.

'Let me go then,' I said. 'If that's what you feel.'

He was standing in the doorway and put across an arm to bar my way.

'What's that?'

'Let me go, if that's all you know about me. There's no sense prolonging this.'

But he wouldn't let me through.

'What are you babbling about?'

'If you still loved me, you couldn't speak to me as you do. It's over. I must get away.'

I could not make him let me pass.

'You've got so used to talking to me like you do,' I said sharply. 'You don't realize how it hurts.'

'You aren't going anywhere,' he said.

'Do you plan to lock me in?'

'I will if I feel like it,' he said slowly, his arm across the door and his face as closed and stubborn as an animal.

The blood rose in my head. It was unthinkable to be imprisoned in my own bedroom.

'You swine!' I shrieked at him.

He turned, astonished.

'You humiliating swine!'

Then I began to sob breathlessly, hardly able to

control the shaking of my limbs. As I watched, he turned away with a little laugh.

On the mahogany dressing table by the window stood a silver-backed hairbrush and a matching hand-mirror that had once belonged to my mother. It was his laugh that cracked something in me. My head was pounding with furious blood as I picked up the mirror and flung it at him, but, hearing a noise, he turned his head and it missed, crashing on the floor instead. We stared at one another, both astonished.

'That time you wanted to kill me,' he said quietly.

Certainly I could have hurt him very badly. My blood had cooled now, and I was appalled at what I had nearly done.

'Come here,' he said.

I went towards him, ashamed and a little afraid. He put his hands on my shoulders and then tipped my chin up to look into my eyes, while I tried to keep them lowered, overcome with the knowledge of a savagery I had not known I possessed. I wondered if he would kiss my lips. Perhaps we would find a sweet resolution of our differences, as we had so often in the past. But he did not caress me. Only searched in my eyes for something he evidently could not find.

'Go downstairs,' he said. 'Make a pot of tea.'

Nine

For a week after the party at the Bellaggri palazzo, we lived with a coldness between us. We went to bed at different times; Mellors woke early and left our bed stealthily. A new groom had been employed in the stables and Mellors was required to work high up the stony hills in the landscape of the wild boars. When he came down in the evenings he went to meet Bernardo and his friends as soon as he had washed. He knew I was lonely, but he didn't care. Since he had decided I could not value him as he wanted to be valued, he felt no obligation to make me happy. I could sit and wait, or go and see my English friends, as I pleased.

And I knew how he felt. And why. I watched him stride through the white and dusty pathways where the grass had been burnt by the sun. As he swished at the stones with his stick, I saw the hatred in him.

It wasn't exactly me he hated. Even now, if he saw my naked flesh as I towelled myself thoughtfully after a bath, I knew I seemed tender and vulnerable, that I stirred his protective feelings. But clothed, he saw me only as part of a group that dismissed him as a human being. They didn't know him, or care to find out about him. He imagined I could see no more than they could. Now, as the days passed and the silence grew between us, he took a certain pleasure in my bewilderment: he could see that I did not know what to do about his antagonism.

One night, when the moonlight came in through our open bedroom window, he undressed quietly while looking out at the olive groves and turned to find me sitting up in bed. I was weeping without restraint.

'Can nothing put it right, then? Tell me,' I sobbed.

His mood changed at the sound of my voice, and he came to the bed at once to put his arms round me. He could feel my tears on his face, and he stroked my hair. Yet, even as he soothed me and felt me clinging to him desperately, I knew there was a part of his brain that was cold and distrustful, as if he feared I might trick him into submission.

I could not stop sobbing even in his arms.

'I thought you didn't want me any more,' I said.

The black anger went out of his blood as he felt my body shaking. He stroked my arms and the back of my neck and I felt a sleepy happiness relaxing my limbs.

'Lie still,' he said awkwardly. 'We'll sleep. Be still.'

And gradually I was calm, and the sense of our bodies stilling themselves into peace ran through all my being. We lay back together, and he put his head quietly against my breasts.

'My love,' I whispered. 'My love.'

He lay against me, his face buried in my flesh. But did he need me? He showed no desire for me. Lying together we could both feel the sweet drowse of sleep which had eluded us for hours some nights without this embrace. He seemed to want the warmth and softness of my body. Yet he evinced no sexual desire.

'Don't you want me? *Don't* you?'

'Be still,' he soothed me.

'Don't you love me any more?'

He didn't answer at first.

'I could die like this. With my face against your breasts.'

I held him close.

'We mustn't quarrel again,' I said, my voice choking. 'Never. Promise me.'

There was no resurgence of sexual desire. His love seemed more like the love of a child for his mother. We both felt that peaceful bond. So how could we enjoy sex together? He lay against me in that happiness, and presently we were both asleep.

In the morning I woke first and, as he came to consciousness, he found me looking down at him tenderly where he lay in the crook of my arm. He didn't like that, and pulled away roughly.

'I'm not your *baby*,' he said.

'I didn't suppose you were.' I smiled at him.

He accepted my kiss and the hand stroking his head, but I could tell it made him feel less than manly, as if I had enchanted him into forgetting all his legitimate rage.

The sharp light of early morning as I came down to the kitchen suggested it was going to be another brilliant winter day.

'What are you doing up so early today?' he chided me.

'I have to collect Emily from Florence,' I reminded him. 'I've arranged a car.'

Wanting to please him, I found his favourite jam, and offered to make fresh tea.

'*Stop* it,' he said at length. 'You aren't my mother.'

I was brought up short by that, remembering his wish not to be nursed like a child against my breast, the drab, hardworking woman I had once met in the woods near Wragby, and the contempt with which Mellors had treated her.

'Indeed I am not,' I said quietly.

I had wrapped a housecoat of pale green silk around myself and once again, with my nakedness hidden, felt estranged from him, and a little put out by the comparison.

'I always thought you rather disliked your mother?'

'I did,' he said shortly. 'It was a poor best she did, for all her talk of slaving for the family.'

'But weren't you upset when your father shouted at her?' I asked.

'It was nothing to me.' He shrugged. 'I hated him anyway, because he used to hit me with a strap.'

I was disturbed at the recollection of the violence in his own background. I've read that people often repeat the patterns of their own childhood, and for the first time I applied the theory to my own case. Perhaps that was why a loving peace could not last between us. It wasn't all my doing, as he seemed to believe. It wasn't only because society pressed in on us either: another antagonism was always waiting to trouble us, as if he could never throw off his own childhood experience.

Mellors was uneasy at the thought of Emily's return. He had not seen the child during the school term and anticipated the changes in her with foreboding.

'We shall have to think of something for Emily to do during the holidays,' I said.

Emily was formidably composed. In her Panama hat and white blouse she looked a stranger; a golden-haired, sweet-faced child with a direct blue gaze.

'Why didn't you come and see me in the school play?' she asked her father. 'You could have. I know you could.'

'Nay,' he said, tousling her hair. 'I let your mother go. She knows how to talk to the old biddies, and I'd just annoy them for you.'

Emily frowned. Her mother was acceptable to teachers and parents alike. She knew that.

'*Why* would you?'

'I say what I think,' he said, his face closing. 'Don't worry about it.'

And the girl ran off to give Gina a warm kiss.

Later that night, as I helped Emily get ready for bed – brushing her long hair in the mirror – she asked me: 'Were you ever married before?'

I stared at her pert little face.

'Why do you ask?' I said, carefully resuming the long, soothing strokes.

'Julia said her mother was married before,' she said, 'so I wondered.'

'Who was she married to?' I asked brightly.

'I don't know. Someone else,' said Emily impatiently. 'You aren't answering. Were you?'

'Yes,' I admitted, remembering there was a girl in the school whose mother had been told as much.

'*Goodness*,' said Emily, seemingly impressed and

for the moment satisfied. 'Was he as handsome as Daddy?'

'He wasn't,' I said, smiling.

How to describe those first years when Emily was making a new life away from us? I missed her desperately. And Mellors and I did not fall back easily into our old intimacy. With time on my hands, I remembered I had once been interested in the history of art, and began to take some pleasure in going round the countryside exploring the treasures of the Renaissance. Once or twice I made common cause with Duncan on my visits to Florence. More often I explored on my own; relishing the jewelled blues of Mary's dress in Piero della Francesca's 'Madonna del Parto', Da Vinci's 'Annunciation' in the Uffizi and Botticelli's sweet-faced Madonna in the Galleria dell'Accademia. Mellors had no time for such wandering. And Emily, though she was growing up as intelligently alert as I could have hoped, was free only in the holidays.

It was Mellors' idea to take Emily to see the Palio at Siena and when he suggested it, I remembered Kurt Lehmann saying it was necessary to know someone with a balcony over the Piazza del Campo. I wondered how to arrange it.

'No need to bother with that. People stand in the

centre of the square,' said Mellors over breakfast. 'That's where the excitement is.'

'And the child?'

'I can hold Emily on my shoulders.'

'I shall see *perfectly* well,' said Emily impatiently.

These days her voice was cool and free, and she was often critical of me.

Mellors smiled at the child with a little flash of triumph in his eyes.

'I don't think you realize how *hot* it will be,' I exclaimed. 'Or the press of people.'

'The *people* manage very well,' he mocked me. 'And so shall we, my lady.'

I was too stung by the wilful separation he made between us to argue further, but in the outcome another opportunity presented itself: Giuseppe, the local baker, hearing Mellors tell of his plans, invited us to join his party in an apartment overlooking the Campo.

'Because you are English,' he said simply. 'And for the *bambina*. So she remembers well her time in Italy.'

Mellors accepted the invitation, though Bernardo warned him darkly that Giuseppe was known to be a Communist.

'His Sienese friends must be quite rich, though,' I remarked when I heard the plan.

Mellors stared at me resentfully, disliking the assurance in my tone.

'Why do you assume so?'

'I guess it,' I said, flushing. 'Because they have an apartment on the Campo. Isn't it rather surprising if Giuseppe really is a Communist?'

'I don't care about politics at that level,' said Mellors. 'It's no more than housekeeping, when it comes down to it. I want to show Emily something of ancient, primitive Italy. She spends too much of her young life with dried-up old spinsters who are dreaming of days in the colonies.'

It was hardly worth entering an argument about Emily's teachers: Emily was progressing excellently with her studies and I had no wish to bring her schooling into question.

August 1936 was particularly hot and dry; there were several days without water. Mellors had to bring containers of the precious liquid in a cart from the reservoir. On the morning of the Palio the light was dazzling. We all rose early to be ready for Giuseppe, who was taking us to Siena in his car. I made Emily wear a broad-brimmed hat against the blaze of the sun, and all the way there the white dust of the twisting roads tasted harshly in my mouth.

We left the car some distance from the Campo; in the parish of the Ostrich, as Giuseppe explained: 'It won't *win*. But they are very patriotic.'

Walking in the direction of the Duomo, there was

noise and excitement everywhere. Silk flags hung from every awning and window in the narrow streets: Dragon and Giraffe, Panther and Hedgehog.

'The *contrade*,' Giuseppe explained. 'The competing parishes.'

The heat made me feel a little dizzy. The pink stone of Siena seemed to throb against an unrelenting blue sky. I remembered my last visit long ago, as a tourist with Hilda, and found myself saying wistfully to Emily: 'There's a lovely marble fountain of clear water on the Piazza del Campo.'

'Where could water come from?' asked the child, suspiciously.

I shook my head: 'I don't know.'

'There's an aqueduct,' said Giuseppe, falling into Italian. 'Since the Middle Ages. But we won't be going into the square. Not unless you want to die of heat and noise.'

The noise of the milling crowds in the narrow streets was more than enough, and I thought back to the days of a quieter visit, to the coolness of the Duomo with its marble floor and black and white pillars, and was overcome with nostalgia for my adolescence. I steadied Emily's sunhat on her head. We were still many streets away from the centre of Siena.

'Some day we'll come and see the Duomo,' I told Emily.

But the child was giving all her attention to Giuseppe, in imitation of her father.

'Tell me what happens in the race,' she was asking.

'First they draw straws, little girl,' said Giuseppe indulgently. 'Then the horses are blessed. Look!'

He pointed to a horse which at that very moment was being led out of the door of a small church, surrounded by men in brilliant coloured silks.

'You see,' said Giuseppe, pointing to a pile of horse manure still steaming next to the church. 'That's supposed to be lucky.'

At last we walked through the Piazza San Giovanni.

'Look at the sun symbol on the side of the Duomo,' Giuseppe was saying. 'St Bernardino of Siena. He wanted the Sienese to live as one people under the risen Christ.'

'And give up their dragons and giraffes?'

'Yes. They didn't, naturally. Now, my friend's house is on the Via di Città. We shall see from there. And if you are bored with the horses, there will be cool white wine, signora. And ice cream for the *bambina.*'

'Your friends are very hospitable,' said Mellors.

The apartment that belonged to Giuseppe's friends was very surprising. It had high ceilings, long windows, and art nouveau furniture in reddish wood. Over a huge fireplace with a curved mouth hung a portrait of a magnificent woman with black hair, a fan in her hand, and a milky white dress. Many people, some well-dressed, stood about with glasses in their hands. Our host, Signor Mirelli, a tired old man in a formal suit, would have been perfectly at home in the Bellaggri household.

'Come in, come in,' he welcomed Mellors. 'We have a lot of foreigners here. And the English are always welcome.'

I stared up at the painting.

'A poetess who lived in Venice in the seventeenth century, now probably forgotten,' said Signor Mirelli, seeing my interest.

'Is she a relative?' I asked.

'Of sorts,' he said.

The room was filling up with new arrivals but as Mellors took off Emily's straw hat and they became aware of the serious little girl, people made way enthusiastically for the child to be brought up to the balcony window. From there, she and Mellors could see pink-tiled roofs, the high bell tower of the Palazzo Pubblico, and the huge crowd gathered in the fan-shaped piazza. Outside the windows were the beat of the drums and the roar of the crowd as bareback jockeys in hard hats rode by in their brilliant colours. Emily squealed with delight as flags were thrown as high as the balcony. When a traditional drummer in black and brown with a medieval brown hat came by, she called out: 'His stockings don't match.'

And the Italians laughed with pleasure. The Italians *do* love children more than the English, I thought. And

Mellors, too, as he looked out on the thousands of people gathered in the centre of the square, was relishing the spectacle. Knights in armour, who must have been close to death in the heat, rode by, gleaming in blue and gold metal. He savoured all the pageantry.

Even if Mellors had wanted to take refuge inside the room, he would not have left Emily pressed up eagerly against the edge of the balcony. And perhaps he felt some resentment that, as so often, I left the hard work of parenting to him. I don't know. I knew what I ought to do, but I could not make myself press forward to join them. I accepted a glass of cool white wine and sat down at the further side of the room. I was glad I had chosen to wear a new dress from Florence. I looked well in it. But what, after all, was the race to me? Or to most of these people?

I asked the question politely and curiously of Signor Mirelli.

'Tradition, I suppose. It's been going on since the thirteenth century,' he said courteously. And then, as he turned away to talk to his other guests, I recognized Kurt Lehmann.

His presence was so unexpected that I could hardly bring myself to smile, though the shock was like a pleasurable shot of adrenaline to my system, making everything in the room suddenly vivid. He looked unsurprised to see me, I could not but observe, and soon came over.

'Tuscany is very small.' He smiled. 'And Giuseppe and I meet often. I hoped you would be here.'

I repeated my question about the Palio, my thoughts racing as I tried to imagine what Giuseppe the baker, the owner of this elegant apartment and Kurt Lehmann could have in common. My political innocence at this time was almost complete. Sometimes I read a copy of *The Times*, but not often, and, though I knew the Italian regime was Fascist, and that Bernardo supported it, I had no very clear idea where anyone else might stand.

'Siena is a frozen city. Nothing changes here. People are loyal to the old customs. Tonight there will be celebrations and fights.'

'Let's hope it stays quiet, at least in Siena,' said Signor Mirelli.

The implication that things were far from quiet elsewhere was not lost on me.

'Is there some news?' I hazarded.

Kurt nodded to our host.

'You are asking the right man.'

Signor Mirelli gave an apologetic shrug and explained to me: 'I used to be the editor of a newspaper here.'

'Until last week,' said Kurt.

Seeing I looked bewildered, Signor Mirelli added, 'I decided to publish a few stories from the north. It was unwise.'

'He means Germany,' said Kurt. 'Signor Mirelli

doesn't say as much but it was also rather brave of him.'

'It's Rome, only Rome,' said Mirelli impatiently. 'Always they want to keep their hands on Tuscan affairs. To interfere.'

'My friends the Bassani also have a touching faith that Tuscany is very far from Rome,' said Kurt ironically. 'And very different from Rome, naturally. Let's hope so, but I doubt it.' He saw I could not follow the conversation, and added, as if by way of explanation, 'Have you seen the statue by the Museo dell'Opera del Duomo? The wolf that suckles a child? Is that a myth for a gentle people? Only when I came to the Palio did I understand Italy.'

I should have been troubled by what he was saying, but instead my face warmed and relaxed in response to him. His eyes were as dark as I remembered. I no longer felt remote from the occasion: all the confusion was transfigured in his presence.

As Mirelli moved away to greet other arrivals, I asked, 'What are these events in Germany our host reported in his paper?'

'Round-ups. Arrests. Thousands of them.' He smiled wryly. 'Of course there are so many new crimes, the police can hardly keep up.'

I remembered his parents were still in Germany, and, as I asked after them, a muscle twitched under the skin of his left cheek.

'My father is dead,' he said.

'I'm so *sorry*. How?' I faltered.

'A heart attack. In Dachau. You could say he, too, was unwise. Took part in an obstacle race.'

I was completely bewildered by this, and he saw as much.

'The guards arranged the race for the prisoners. My poor father was never very athletic.'

'Then why did he take part?'

'The guards insisted. And they had machine guns.'

He gave a grimace that was not exactly a smile.

'But that's *murder*,' I cried.

'Not in Germany. Not under Hitler.'

I thought about this for a moment.

'But do people in the rest of the world know things like this are going on?'

'Perhaps they don't believe it. Perhaps they know and don't care.'

'And perhaps they are afraid to know,' said Signor Mirelli, who had returned to our side. 'Because then they might have to do something about it. Which could be dangerous.'

'I can't believe *that*,' I said, wondering how much Mellors knew about such things: he was so involved with Bernardo and the young Party enthusiasts in the village.

'Have you heard about the Bellaggri family?' Mirelli asked Kurt.

'Why? Has something happened to the Count?' I cried.

But I had no chance to hear more about the Count's fortunes just then as I could hear Mellors' voice from the window, as if he spoke from another world:

'Connie! Come and look! The Palio is going by.'

At his side, Emily, too, called out, and I roused myself to move towards them, though I did not know what I was being asked to look for. Kurt followed me and a space was made for us at the stone balustrade.

'There it is,' said Kurt. 'Drawn by white oxen. It's a white banner and a silver plate.'

'What happens if your district wins?' asked Mellors.

'You give parties,' said Kurt.

'And if you lose?'

'Whatever happens in Siena you give parties.'

The race began several times as the horses, forced to the starting rope, jostled, pranced and set off down the course. They were brought back again and again.

'It will be over in a blink once it starts,' said Kurt. 'This is the important part.'

I could feel him standing next to me, although our bodies did not touch. I refused to admit the sexual quality of my interest, in part because he was so handsome and I was older than he was: I did not want to be exposed, betrayed, snubbed. But in any case, for all our recent dissension, I felt altogether bound to Mellors. I had no interest in a casual flirtation. What would my life be worth if, after all that had happened, I was overcome with desire for another man? My discomfort made it difficult to talk normally.

'Some people in the centre of the square are being helped to an ambulance,' I observed.

I felt ill in the sunlight, and had to shade my eyes against the glare. The heat was intolerable, though there were four fans in the ceiling of the apartment. I hated the race, I decided. To gallop on cobbles would hurt the horses' feet. They must break a leg if they fell. As I watched, a jockey took a fall from a restless horse. Sickened, I turned away.

'Where are you going, Mother?' asked Emily impatiently.

'I must sit down,' I said.

Mellors looked at me with a glint in his eyes, and for a moment I wondered if he suspected the effect the young German had upon me.

'A bit too *strenuous* for you, is it, milady?' he asked.

'Why does he call you milady?' asked Kurt, who had followed me. I did not reply.

After the race, there was a meal of *minestra di riso in brodo e fegatini*, a *polpettone* of turkey in jelly, a salami of tongue with black olives and spinach stalks in oil, and chocolate cake with walnuts and pine seeds. The Dragon, it seemed, had taken the prize, and that pleased the assembled guests.

Kurt Lehmann prepared to leave.

'Are you travelling back to Florence?' he asked me.

I shook my head. Mellors, at the other side of the room, was waiting impatiently.

'We'll meet again, I'm sure,' I said swiftly.

I hardly knew what I meant by that, but he nodded slowly and we shook a polite farewell.

Mellors was not, in the ordinary sense of the word, much given to jealousy; but he was hypersensitive in other matters, and had watched my conversation with Kurt Lehmann with close attention. He did not comment on my preoccupation, however, being in the grip of another excitement of his own.

Outside in the streets, in the darkness, as we left, groups of young men swirled round each other: drunk, hot, hostile. One group baited another, and it was easy to imagine the baiting could turn to violence. Mellors was excited by the drama of their antagonism.

'Look at their beauty and confidence,' he said. 'And yet these youngsters are as poor as the English in their mill towns. *Now* do you understand what has to be changed? In England? It isn't just economics. It's a matter of the spirit.'

'You are an optimist, I think,' said Giuseppe, kindly but without much respect for the point of view.

We were getting into his car as he said this, and I saw the darkness come into Mellors' face as he helped Emily into the back seat and carefully took his own.

'You think I am mistaken?'

'Of course.'

'You have been to England then?' inquired Mellors.

'Not to England, no, but—'

'Yet you are quite sure I am mistaken?'

Giuseppe guided the car gently between the crowds of passers-by.

'What Mellors means,' I began, aware that Giuseppe was put out by the tone of Mellors' voice and realizing it was a long, winding drive back to the village.

'Be quiet, Connie,' said Mellors. 'Giuseppe hasn't understood what I am saying. I'll explain.'

'About violence there is nothing to explain,' said Giuseppe.

'There's a relation between maleness and what society needs to be healthy,' said Mellors.

'I don't know about maleness, but violence is violence, Signor Mellors,' said Giuseppe. 'People are hurt. Heads are broken.'

We were on the open road by now, and Mellors began to expound his views on maleness at length. As the quiet road ran between the wheels, there were fewer and fewer remarks from the driver. Soon I could make out nothing more than the quiet music of Mellors' voice in Italian: calm, reasonable and persistently flowing. Emily had fallen asleep at my side. But my wish to sleep was thwarted by thoughts of Kurt Lehmann. And guilt, too, for what these thoughts revealed to me.

When we arrived at our stone house, I could see that the conversation had ended badly. Giuseppe was stiff and perfunctory as I got out of the car. As if to make up for whatever had been said, I tried to be particularly effusive. Mellors' own gratitude was no more than formal. He carried the child in his arms and so had an excuse for going straight into the house. I turned back to Giuseppe with an inquiry in my face.

'Sometimes he is wrong. You should tell him,' Giuseppe remarked, patting his forehead with one finger to indicate someone whose brains are on the turn.

'About politics, no one is right.' I laughed.

But the incident troubled me.

Even though we had come back tired, I knew Mellors would make love to me that night and when he came to bed his body was alert and ready. I welcomed him. But it was difficult to find my own satisfaction: he would not rub my body as I needed, and I had to push and grind myself against him, struggling until my body was running with sweat to find release. When, after an enormous effort, my body convulsed with pleasure, I felt an overwhelming relief. It *was* still possible, then. I could still find pleasure with Mellors. I buried my face in his neck and kissed his flesh.

After a moment I became aware that he was quite unresponsive to my show of affection, that his muscles were taut as if he were angry. I lifted myself up to look in his face.

'What is it?'

'You *had* to wait, didn't you?'

'Didn't you want me to come?'

'Yes, of course. But not like that, with me inside, passive and just something you *used*. You've gone dead in there.'

For a moment the words stunned me with their violence. Then I remembered what he'd said of his wife, Bertha Coutts, long ago, when explaining how they had come to separate and why he found her so repulsive. He had spoken of her with the same disgust, but I'd accepted what he said then without question, as if she were part of a quite different species, not a woman like myself. Yet what did I know of her or her version of things? I'd heard she was a heavy drinker. I'd never felt much warmth towards her. I imagined her without the least sensitivity, with gross appetites and a brutish nature. To have the same words used of me as he had once used of her was something of a shock. I'd always imagined her as middle-aged and common, bloated and blotched with sexual rapacity. It came to me now that I was already much the age Bertha had been when she went rampaging about the village. She had gone off with another man, I knew; but I was hardly in a position to take a moral line over that.

I remembered how, a little while after I had gone off to Venice, pregnant, and wondering what to do, Bertha had broken into Mellors' cottage and lain there in his bed, naked, until he returned, hoping to woo him back; while she was there, her discovery of some of my property precipitated our scandal, but I'd never resented that. I had taken her arrival in the cottage as some evidence that the poor woman loved Mellors. Perhaps she did. Now, in the shock of Mellors' accusation, I wondered about her more closely, how she had come to behave as she did.

'Don't you want me to have my own pleasure?' I pleaded.

'If you could have it sweetly, like you used to, of course. You were a *real* woman once. You used to be soft as a fig down there. Now you push your prow of bone at me like a beak.'

The accusation went home. He was right. I had no sensation left except for the very tip of me, the very outside top tip of my sexual parts. He had called Bertha an old trull; perhaps, in my selfish desperation, I had become as much one as she had been. 'Perhaps it happens to all women,' I whispered, following my own thoughts. He almost persuaded me I was ageing out of womanhood altogether, though there were no signs of it yet in my face and body.

I remembered once asking Mellors how he first came to take up with Bertha. He'd explained that whereas the local women were priggish, she seemed in love

with the sexual act itself. He'd liked her well enough
for that when they began together. Perhaps it had been
rather with her as with me in those early days? Until
she had begun to clutch herself so desperately to find
her satisfaction. 'The devil to bring off,' he had said
of her. But wasn't I rather the same now? Writhing
against his thighs.

Did it happen to all women? I didn't know. I felt the
shame of it enter me as if it were a criticism of my
whole sex. And the unfairness of that shame.

'It's something that happens to women when they
start to look down on a man.'

'But I *don't* look down on you,' I protested.

His eyes wrinkled and his mouth made a new, bitter
movement against me.

'How would you describe it, then?'

I hesitated.

'My lady,' he jeered.

'I can see you are sometimes unhappy here. Emily
sees it, too. That's why you lose your temper with
people. Like Giuseppe.'

His face darkened.

'If I lost my temper with you, you might see a difference,' he said. 'And I saw well enough which side you
took when I was arguing with Giuseppe.'

'I wasn't following the argument: I was asleep in the car,' I cried.

'*Were* you? I supposed not.'

But he seemed mollified. Then he rolled over and away from me.

In my loneliness, I remembered the young German and the pleasure of that thought suffused my body, easily, readily. Perhaps I'm a whore after all, I wondered, sickened by the evidence of my own depravity.

'Whatever else you get up to,' he said, as if he had uncannily intuited the source of that quiver of my body, 'don't let it interfere with Emily. That school is bad enough. They teach her rules. And she judges me by them.'

It cannot have been many days later that a letter from Clifford found me. He was travelling to Venice. He had no intention of calling on us, of course, but if I would care to meet him, he was staying on the Lido. He was unhappy about Emily. In England, people were worried about Italy, and he would like to talk about my plans.

Ten

Emily was up early every morning that summer, and sometimes she and Mellors had breakfast together. They easily re-established their old intimacy. If I joined them, they looked up in surprise, as if I were an interloper. And the harder I tried to enter the conversation, the more Mellors' eyes glittered with amusement.

Emily was growing into an unusually assured child; her blue eyes were as fierce as her father's, and she was equally persistent in her questioning. I remember once she asked him where he had served in the army, and why he had left it.

'A lot of girls in my school have fathers in the army,' she explained. 'And some of them served in the war.'

'Well, I didn't see much fighting,' he said.

'Some were in India like you.'

'Listen,' he said after a time. 'I don't come from their lot, Emily. I'm from the Midlands poor. Mining families. You have to know that.'

She absorbed the information slowly.

'You were an officer, though, weren't you?'

'For a time,' he said roughly.

'You didn't go down the mines yourself?'

'No, but there are those of my family who did.'

'I don't care about that,' she said loftily.

I could see her questions made him uneasy. He wasn't going to pretend to her. He had too much pride for that. But there were answers she would not like to be given; answers that he feared would make her think less of him. I admired her composure, even as I could see that between us we risked turning her into a woman far too mature for her own good.

'Take me with you today!' Emily pleaded with her father one morning, while I silently poured the tea.

'It's too far,' he said. 'And you're too big to carry.'

'I could take a pony.'

'The country is too tricky for that,' he said.

'We could visit San Gimignano,' I suggested. 'See the paintings.'

Emily made a little expression of disgust.

'You *promised* we could go to the sea,' she reminded me. 'Can't we have a day at La Spezia? I swim well now.'

'Must it be the sea?' I wondered.

'Yes. It's much more exciting.'

'I don't know. The bus is so hot.'

'Your mother,' said Mellors to Emily in a conspiratorial whisper, 'doesn't believe in getting too *sweaty*.'

195

Emily wrinkled her nose at the word, and then laughed. I bit my lip.

'I just try to be sensible,' I said.

'Yes. Your mother is *very* sensible. She always knows the right thing to do. Don't you, my lady? Anything that doesn't put you out too much.'

There was an ugly, jeering note in his voice.

'That's a little unfair!' I began, and saw his head swivel towards me at a new angle, rather as a horse turns its head and lays back its ears in an evil mood.

'Not *fair*?' he mocked.

I set down my cup in its saucer, shakily.

'And what is *fair*? Tell me that,' he demanded. 'Your rich friends going to the sea in their carriages, I suppose?'

'But I didn't say—'

'You didn't say, because you don't *see*,' he said trenchantly. I could see his eagerness for a confrontation, and lowered my eyes.

When Emily had run off to play, I put out a hand to Mellors' bare arm, but he flinched away from me.

'*Why* do you want to set the child against me?' I asked gently, though I was hurt by his reluctance to be touched.

'You imagine that.'

'No,' I said. 'You ridicule my words every time I open my mouth.'

'Are you trying to tell me how I'm supposed to talk now?' he demanded.

I saw the redness in his eyes and the tension in the set of his jaw.

'I'm not reproaching you,' I began.

'You do nothing else,' he said.

Now my blood began to beat angrily in my chest. 'You have everything upside down,' I said despairingly. 'It is you who are always blaming me, usually for things that are not my fault.'

'What I say must be changed on the way in,' he said, in a kind of honest bewilderment. 'You find harm in everything.'

I was nonplussed for a moment at that.

'Perhaps I *do* misunderstand. Maybe there's *nothing* wrong with what you say to me. Maybe it's your manner, just *how* you say things.'

'My *manner*, is it?' Now his eyes crackled with blackness. 'I'll behave as I like in my own house.'

'Yours?' I said sharply.

'A man's house is his own, isn't it?'

'But it's my house too, surely?' I cried. 'And you don't let me exist here. If I can't speak to my own child at the breakfast table, what place is there in the world for me?'

He gave a bark of laughter.

'Don't talk to me about having a place in the world.'

*

That Sunday, Mellors offered to take Emily to La Spezia himself. And he arranged it so they would only need a lift to the bus stop from Giuseppe. He had worked out times and changes. He packed sandwiches for himself and the child. They left soon after dawn.

That summer of 1936, it was I who had no place, whatever he might imagine.

Alone, I went out into the fields in the first grey light. I slept a little while in the hammock Mellors had thrown between two trees. When I woke, I felt bored and miserable. The weekend before, when Mellors had been particularly busy and Emily had an invitation to visit one of her schoolfriends for two days, I had taken myself off to see Hughie and his wife. It had been a mistake. Did I have in mind another meeting with Kurt Lehmann? I admit I would have been glad to find him there. But mainly I wanted company. And Mellors had not voiced any objection aloud. However, his mouth folded into a line when I mentioned my plan over breakfast.

Kurt Lehmann had not been among the guests who lay about in striped chairs on the browning grass or fanned themselves in the shade.

'He may be in Switzerland,' Hughie told me when I brought myself casually to inquire about Lehmann. He had come to sit at my feet as I absorbed that information, and seemed to register my interest with malicious curiosity. 'We're all going home soon, anyway.'

'Why is that?'

'The balloon's beginning to go up,' he said.

I stared at him.

'You must have heard something of it, even in your little love-nest. There's civil war in Spain,' he explained. 'Europe seems to be taking sides, and England and Italy aren't on the same one.'

'Things are never as simple as Hughie thinks,' said Cynthia. 'Not when you go into them. There'll be right and wrong on both sides.'

'But *we're* going back, all the same,' said Hughie firmly. 'None of my business, of course, but what about you? Passports in order, and all that?'

'My husband's work keeps us here,' I said.

'They say Bellaggri's in trouble. Gone to Rome for questioning.'

'Lost his protection,' said Cynthia disdainfully.

'I know nothing about it,' I said.

For a moment I wondered where Bellaggri stood in such a confrontation.

'The summer's over,' said Hughie.

The words sank into me. I went and sat a little apart from the young people around me, whose conversation seemed meaningless. I had no desire to meet new people. The effort of finding out about any of them seemed too much trouble. When it was a little cooler, I went home.

Now, for all the failure of that excursion, I felt almost lonely enough to try again. But I shook off the temptation: would Hughie and Cynthia even be there if I crossed the hills to visit them? Resolutely I went to take a long, slow bath in the new tub, relishing the scented soap I had bought recently in Florence. As I sat in the water, I smelled my soapy fingers and thought more about the shape of my own life than European politics.

At length I got out of the bath and looked at myself for a long time in the full-length baroque mirror. For all my closeness to forty, my body had kept its youth: still white and full at the thighs, curving sweetly into my waist. I sighed. What was the use of being beautiful and young if there was no man to love you? Mellors had loved me once, and stroked my full white curves with desire. Now his love brought me little pleasure, and was altogether lacking in the tenderness I had once so relished. My life was softened with neither kiss nor caress. As a person he had no time for me. I must turn away from him, I told myself. I must learn not to care that he no longer valued me. Perhaps Hilda had made a better choice of a way to live, even though I had once despised it.

'I *don't* want to live as you do,' I'd once said to her. 'One man after another. What do any of them matter? Do you even remember their names?'

Now Hilda's laughter mocked me: 'At least I won't simply waste away like a downtrodden skivvy.'

Yet who could I turn towards? I knew so few people. The thought of Duncan's mildness and lack of passion repelled me.

After a long while, I dressed and went to my writing desk in the window overlooking the olive groves, and began to compose a short note to Kurt at his Florence address. The tone was impossibly difficult to get right, and I crunched up the page and threw it into the wastepaper basket. It was then I became aware of a low, green car coming down the white path.

Staring, I made out two people sitting in the front of the car. Kurt was in the driving seat, and there was a luscious, dark-haired young woman at his side. An instantaneous jealousy stabbed me as I walked down the stairs to greet the visitors. As usual in Tuscany, the outer door of the house stood open, and I met the two of them in the hallway.

'I hope you don't mind us calling,' said Kurt.

'I wish we had more visitors. Do come in,' I said.

My voice was a little strained, because seeing him had revived many of the confusing thoughts that bothered me while I was trying to compose the note. And the presence of the young woman made me self-conscious. The girl would be no more than eighteen, I thought enviously. And her hair was so black and thick; her face so vivacious in expression.

'My sister Elsa has joined me from France,' Kurt said.

At this, I revived wonderfully.

'Your *sister*?' I kissed the bright young face in relief. 'How marvellous to meet you!'

Now I smiled at Elsa in eager welcome. And my words seemed to pour out as if released from somewhere pent up for a long time deep inside me.

'I'm so glad of the company. There is no one else here. Do come inside.'

'I'm afraid my sister doesn't speak very good English,' said Kurt.

His sister gave a rueful smile.

'I just came here. Tuscany very pretty,' she said, and laughed. 'I mean, this part.'

'Pretty, but I prefer the cities,' Kurt said to me. 'You must get very bored in the countryside.'

'I don't even *think* of the city,' I said. 'I think of home. Of England.'

Until that moment I had not known how much: suddenly, my homesickness was overwhelming. 'Do you know, I found a shop in Florence the other day that sold Oxford marmalade,' I marvelled. 'I didn't even know how much I longed for it until I saw the jar.' I laughed suddenly, remembering the excitement of the purchases. 'And I have a *treat* to share. In the same shop, I bought a bottle of Pimm's. There's ice, for once, and fresh mint in the garden. Would you enjoy an English drink for a change?'

'Anything English,' said Kurt. 'Though I don't know the drink. We think very much of England, my sister and I.'

'We plan to go there,' said Elsa, in her low growl of a voice.

I was astonished at the idea of these two exotic creatures in an English landscape.

'Politics?' I guessed, remembering what Hughie had said.

'For a long time now England has been the only hope for Europe,' said Kurt.

I was astonished to hear it, Mellors having so very different an opinion.

'I thought England was finished,' I said doubtfully. 'Isn't there a desperate slump?'

'Everywhere,' Kurt agreed. 'But your people are still so decent. And, of course, for us it is no longer a question of idealism. You have an empire. You are still strong. You can stand up against the monsters.'

We all went into the kitchen so that I could find the ingredients to prepare the drink. As Kurt stood behind me, watching me slice the cucumber and lemon, he said quietly, 'Hughie said you were asking after me.'

I felt a sudden pang of anxiety at the way Hughie's leering face might have mentioned the inquiry.

'Yes,' I admitted. 'I wondered what had become of you. That's all.'

'You never wrote to me,' he reminded me.

'I thought of it,' I confessed, 'but somehow—' I stopped.

How could I admit how uncertain I was about what he wanted from me? Now that he stood close to me again, his dark eyes looking directly at me, his admiration was unmistakable. I floated on it. I was intoxicated by it. And what else could his arrival signify but his own interest? I looked up at him, and my lips relaxed into a bold smile for the first time in months.

When I'd poured the drink, both Lehmanns sipped and pronounced it delicious. In the glow of alcohol, our conversation opened out generally, though Elsa still said very little.

'What is this rumour about Count Bellaggri?' I asked.

Kurt seemed well aware of the situation.

'You must know his sister Beatrice used to be one of Mussolini's mistresses?'

I *didn't* know, and said so, remembering the wildness of the woman and her high, persistent laughter.

'Well, now she is out of favour. Not dangerous for her, but it means the local OVAF are allowed to take more interest in the Count.'

'I somehow expected he was a supporter of the government,' I said hesitantly.

'At the beginning, yes. An enthusiast. But his wife is from a Jewish family.'

'I thought there were no laws against Jews in Italy?' I cried.

'Not yet. But the two dictators are getting friendlier by the minute. It's natural for the Fascists to be curious about Bellaggri's allegiance.'

'And what form does that curiosity take?' I asked.

'He has been invited to Rome. For questioning. I expect it will be like Galileo.' Seeing I did not follow the reference, he added, 'They will only have to show him the instruments. By the way, have you heard the news about Signor Mirelli?'

I frowned.

'The man who put his apartment at our disposal in Siena,' he reminded me. 'I'm afraid he's dead.'

I let out a little exclamation of horror.

'How on earth? He didn't seem ill.'

'An accident in the streets of Siena, they say. A hit-and-run motorist.'

For the first time I felt a little shiver of fear.

'If you come to Florence, you can find us at the Bassanis',' said Kurt, 'but we shall be leaving Italy soon.'

They showed no signs of wanting to be on their way that afternoon, however, and soon I was offering them cold salami and salad.

Even as we gossiped together into the early evening, another drama was being played out on the shores of the Mediterranean, though I did not hear about it until much later.

Eleven

Mellors and Emily took the bus to La Spezia with families of Italians travelling with their children for a Sunday at the beach. Emily was never put out by the crush: sitting on the wooden slatted benches, she swung her legs and chattered to her father.

I know La Spezia well, and can imagine them sniffing the seaweed and listening to the call of seabirds. Everything delighted Emily, though to Mellors' eye it was little more than a seaside town, with a few tourists in white jackets and Panama hats. Emily loved the pretty boats.

They undressed on the beach that belonged to the Hotel Excelsior. That was where they took off their shoes and changed into costumes, bundling their shirts and shorts into the bag that had held the towels. There was a red flag over the beach, which flew, puzzlingly, at half mast, and Mellors went off to find someone who knew where it was safe to swim, even though there were plenty of bathers in the sea.

Nobody could tell him, though a large man with

shoulders tanned to a walnut brown told him the flag had been there for two weeks.

I know the sea at La Spezia. The water is calm, still and green. The sea shines on the surface like silver. For a while, Mellors and Emily stood close to the shore in the shallow water. Then they both began to walk out together along the edge of the sea. At last they found a little shelf that dipped down and let them get their shoulders underneath the water so they could swim.

Emily swam as playfully as a little frog, her chin well out of the water. Mellors kept a little further out than she was to make sure she was safe. The sea was very clear, and he could see the shells on the white seabed.

They were level with the Hotel Excelsior when the current captured them. It reached Mellors first. One moment he was floating along, his fingers almost able to touch the sand beneath them, and the next they were both being sucked outwards together, away from the shore. Emily was closer to the shelf than he was, and was swimming strongly. She would be all right, he told himself. There were men coming to pull her clear. She would be all right. He wasn't so sure about himself.

Safe on the shore, Emily looked back and saw him battling. Mellors always swam with one shoulder up in an ungainly sidestroke, his mouth twisted sideways the better to breathe. To the girl it must have looked then as if he was losing ground, as if he were being swept further out, and she screamed like a wild creature. She pushed away the hands of her rescuers to run to him as he rose out of the sea. Then she held him round the legs, sobbing with terror, her face blubbery with tears and her whole body shaking convulsively while he held her in his arms. I know all this because she woke so often in the weeks that followed and when I went to her I listened to the same story again and again. I know he spoke to her gently, as he would have spoken to a frightened animal. 'What's this about? We're safe now, aren't we? Be still.'

Afterwards Emily couldn't explain to either of us why she continued to sob. But I understood, when he told me about it. She had seen him fighting in the sea, and had seen his arm come up again and again. She was crying because he had been powerless. Because no one had helped him. Because he seemed so gallant, and in danger. And because she loved him.

'That was just silly to scream like that. We were never in much danger,' Mellors tried to soothe her for days afterwards.

I know, too, that all the way home, he was very quiet, blaming himself for what might have been the outcome. But, once home, there was something else that must have hurt him even more than the thought of his own stupidity: his knowledge of the child's raw need of him. And the way that bound him to me. It was like a curse, for him, that love he felt for his daughter. It meant he could not escape. Bertha Coutts, too, had given him a daughter, but the child had not touched his heart; she had been a creature of his own village, and he had treated her with easy contempt. He had left her behind without pain, and only rarely remembered to send her a card. But Emily he admired, loved, and needed in his turn.

'She is the best part of me,' he said to me soon after La Spezia. 'The only thing that has turned out just as I would have wanted.'

I knew the truth of that, even though it meant acknowledging the limits of his love for me.

He didn't talk about any of that when he returned to find us all chattering in the kitchen an hour or so after dark.

'Entertaining, are we?' he asked, dazed in the electric light after the walk from the bus stop.

I introduced Kurt's sister and Mellors nodded courteously enough.

'The child's exhausted,' he said flatly.

Kurt stood at once.

'No reason to go,' said Mellors politely. 'But I'll put the child to bed.'

Did I suddenly remember the scrunched-up letter in the basket of our bedroom? Perhaps. I heard Mellors walking across the floor above our heads, then going to the bathroom. When he returned, he looked brisk and energetic.

'I know you, don't I?' he asked Kurt.

'Yes. I'm a friend of Giuseppe.'

'A Communist, are you?'

'Not exactly.'

'There are too many hidden Communists in Italy,' said Mellors.

Kurt seemed in two minds whether to continue the conversation.

'Do you admire what is being done by the present government, then?' he asked.

'The peasants are better off,' said Mellors shortly.

'And the castor oil, for those who don't agree?'

'Lies and propaganda,' said Mellors.

Elsa heard the tone of the words and frowned, looking at her brother for guidance.

'We should go, perhaps?' she suggested.

Her dark beauty took Mellors' attention for a moment.

'You are guests in this country,' he said thoughtfully. 'You shouldn't make trouble here.'

'People like us can't avoid trouble,' laughed Kurt. Then he shook his head. 'I'm disappointed to find you so impressed. We think of England as the home of fair play.'

'As to *that* . . .' shrugged Mellors, sceptically.

'What about poison gas in Abyssinia?' Kurt inquired.

Mellors frowned.

'There is nothing about poison gas in the Italian papers. It is probably an invention of the English press. Those swine talk about humanity, but all *they* really mean is profit, profit, profit. The English want to keep Italy out of Africa.'

'Of course,' said Kurt, mildly.

He saw that Mellors was unlikely to be moved from his position, and rose once again to go.

'Hughie's friends were talking last Saturday about children gassed in Africa,' I said incautiously.

Mellors' eyes swivelled angrily towards me. He had almost forgotten my presence. Now to find me entering the argument and appearing to take the side of the young German infuriated him.

'And what do you know about such matters?' His eyes glinted evilly. 'You *can't* and you *don't* know anything for yourself; you just repeat what is told you. I suppose one must expect women to mouth what they're told, but at least have some modesty.'

Kurt's eyebrows rose at the violence of Mellors' reaction, and his eyes met mine with a question in them. My candid gaze dropped before his, and soon Kurt and Elsa left for Florence.

As soon as they had gone, Mellors said to me, 'He's a Jew, isn't he? You can always tell.'

I flushed. 'What have you got against Jews?'

'Did I say I had anything against them? I liked him,

actually. But they always see everything from their own point of view. As if theirs was the only suffering that had any validity.'

These days, Emily liked to read in bed herself, but sometimes I brought my own favourite childhood books to entertain her with at bedtime. It was a way of getting close to her, and she did not protest. Since her experience at La Spezia, she had clung to me a little anxiously, and I was glad to be given a chance to talk about her life at school, her friends, her plans. Just before returning to school she told me she wanted to go off to Switzerland for a skiing holiday at Christmas with the English family of her best friend Julia. And then she became very serious.

'Is Daddy angry with you?'

'Of course not,' I said steadily.

'Julia's Mummy and Daddy don't speak any more. Don't live in the same house,' the child confided.

'It happens sometimes,' I said.

'Julia says she has to choose where she spends her summer holidays.'

'That must be horrid.'

'She's supposed to be going with her mother,' said Emily. 'But we're going to Switzerland with her father. It's all arranged.'

I soothed her as I brushed her hair, but her childish

softness smote me as I felt her vulnerability binding me into the situation.

There was no Indian summer that year. When the grapes were in, there was rain and wind, and Gina made a huge fire of pine cones. Mellors returned from the woods and sat in front of it with his feet bare, while I brought him a bowl of golden *ribollita*. He had developed a hard, dry cough, which he refused to take to a doctor.

'Stop fretting. I always had bronchitis as a child. The army checked there was nothing wrong with me,' he said.

I could see he was thinner. His neck and shoulders, which had once turned so finely, looked almost gaunt as he towelled his wet hair. There was grey at his temples.

'But the war was so long ago,' I murmured, thinking of all the beauty and strength he had when I first saw him, and how unbearable it was he should be frail.

'I'm not really ill,' he insisted.

He had to spend two days in bed, nevertheless, though he refused to let a doctor visit him.

The first morning of his illness, I went up to see if there was anything he wanted. He was fast asleep. His temperature was high, and he had kicked away the sheets. I could see him lying unclothed on the bed.

For several moments I stood looking at the line of his back from his shoulders to the narrow hips. He was muscled and shapely as a dancer. When his legs shifted I was filled with the desire to kiss and caress his exposed body, to put my mouth against his most intimate flesh, to taste the salt in his skin. But I remained motionless. He was altogether separate from me. I told myself that it was because he was ill and sleeping, but I knew it was far more. I did not dare approach him with desire.

Twelve

Once Emily was back at school in Florence, I tried to face up to my painful situation. Mellors no longer loved me. Even the child could see as much. His face was hard and closed, and he no longer showed any kindness towards me. When I remembered the tenderness of our early years together, when my helplessness so amused him, I was overwhelmed by sadness. He went about his daily work, and we no longer talked to one another more than was strictly necessary. He brushed aside any attempt I made to talk about what was happening in the village.

One day, when I went to buy bread from Giuseppe's, I found metal shutters down over the windows of his shop. Nobody could tell me what had happened, or indeed where I could buy bread.

'Is Giuseppe ill?' I asked one of the women I knew.

But the woman turned away, her face hidden in her black shawl. No one knew anything. At an upstairs window I made out figures moving behind the glass, but I could recognize none of them; I rang the bell several times, loudly, but no one came to answer me.

Puzzled, I went on to the grocer. There, standing in cleanly pressed new uniform, I recognized the figure of Bernardo.

'So, you've joined the army?' I asked him as cordially as I could manage. 'I wondered why you don't come to our house to take English lessons any more.'

'Good afternoon to you, Signora Mellors. Too busy for lessons now,' he said.

I was struck by the shine of his buttons and the insignia on his sleeve.

The woman who ran the grocer's also seemed impressed, and had made up a basket of fruit, which she pressed on Bernardo to take back to his mother. Something in the way she pressed him seemed more placatory than generous; she looked almost afraid of him. He accepted her offering with a patronizing smile.

'We are taking Tuscany in hand,' he informed me. 'And I am in charge of the crack-down.'

'Your English is very idiomatic,' I smiled.

'Villains and traitors are everywhere,' he said, shaking his head.

I had been going to ask about Giuseppe's closed shop, but changed my mind. Something alarming was clearly going on.

I had just come out into the brilliant sun of the little square, and was debating with myself where I could find news of Giuseppe when a young boy I recognized from the Bellaggri olive groves staggered down the steps from the adjoining house. He was unwashed, and his lips were bloody. To my horror, he fell to his knees at my feet and began to speak in a flood of Italian I could not follow. There were teeth gone from the front of his mouth, and seeing I could not understand what he was saying, he began to weep and to repeat one word again and again.

'Please,' he was saying. 'Please.'

I bent to listen to him, but I could make out nothing more. Then I became aware that Bernardo had come up to us, and the boy flinched away on the cobbles.

'He needs help,' I exclaimed. 'He's hurt.'

'Yes, he needs help,' Bernardo said almost jovially. And he gave a signal for the other two uniformed men at the corner of the square to approach. He nodded at them, and they lifted the boy bodily and threw him into the back of the truck.

The noise of the thin, struggling body thrown against metal made the sound of stage thunder. I listened to his screams as the truck pulled away.

'Good afternoon to you, Signora Mellors,' said Bernardo, as if nothing had happened.

My limbs felt as if the muscles had been paralysed by a nerve poison. Then, with my shopping incomplete and my mind bloodless in its terror, I set off back up the lane that led to our cottage.

To my great relief, I found Mellors at home, and

poured out what I had seen, but he seemed more weary than shocked by my story.

'Yes,' he said. 'Yes. These things are happening. I don't really know what lies behind them.'

'But you know what Bernardo and his Fascist friends are capable of, you can't continue to be caught up with them?'

'Perhaps not,' he said at last.

Something quite different seemed to be worrying him.

'Is something *else* wrong?' I asked him.

He looked at me then, and I saw a blaze of anger in his eyes.

'You tricky, devious bitch,' he said at last. 'Do you remember Giorgio?'

I had to think for a moment before I could recall the young Italian film director who had been Hilda's lover long ago.

'Let me *remind* you,' he said, smiling mirthlessly. 'I had the same problem at first. Just now I met him in the hills above the Bellaggri place. A cousin of the Count. Couldn't remember me at first, couldn't Giorgio, but when he placed me he remembered all he knew about me. Which was that Hilda and you arranged this job.'

I had almost forgotten the deception, and to me it seemed rather unimportant in the light of everything else that was happening around us. Mellors, I could see, felt differently. In his eyes I read a murderous anger which drowned out even the horrible events I had been describing. Of course I saw it from his point of view: Hilda and I had conspired together to deceive him, and he had fallen for it. I could not deny the charge, but it hardly seemed weighty in comparison with Bernardo's complicity in the events I had witnessed. I tried to say as much.

'Don't try and distract me, you treacherous bitch. Your underhand fixing brought me here. You've taken six years out of my life with a trick. You brought me here. All the mistakes I've made here go back to that one error. All your fault. And mine for listening to you. I'd like to smash you in the face.'

The injustice of this took my breath away. Was I responsible for the opinions Giorgio had played upon? Had I led him to Bernardo and his thugs? And I remembered the situation in which Hilda and I had concocted our plot.

'It wasn't so calculating,' I said. 'You and I both needed to escape. Didn't we?'

'Are you saying you *didn't* arrange it?'

'No, I'm not,' I said. 'Just trying to explain how the arrangement came about.'

'You tricked me. You and your smart-arse sister. Between you. I don't suppose it was your plan. You aren't so ingenious, are you? But you'll follow if someone leads.'

If I was afraid of him, I was determined not to show it.

'It wasn't an important lie,' I tried to say.

'Like *all* women's lies, I suppose.' He nodded, his throat rasping.

'Can't you understand why I did it?'

'And I thought you were so wonderful to follow me abroad,' he said. 'You rotten, cheating, lying bitch . . .'

He lunged at me as if only violence could complete the sentence. For me, it was not so much this physical threat as his words, that seemed to go to the heart of my allegiance. I dodged his fist and whirled away from him in a blind, staggering movement, quite lacking in any grace or control. And one of my ankles seemed to give beneath me as I turned. In a moment I had fallen clumsily and he was bending over me.

'Marvellous,' he said. 'You look wonderfully comic.'

'And your face is cruel,' I wanted to say, but bit the words back because his expression frightened me.

'Let me up,' I begged instead.

He smiled. 'And what if I don't choose to?' There was a peculiar stillness in his face. 'Lady Chatterley,' he said, amused by the absurdity of my posture.

'You need not bait me with that,' I cried. 'I've never taken any particular pleasure in that title.'

'Then it's very ungrateful of you,' he said. 'It opens doors for you. Where would you be without it? If you were stripped of it? What kind of presence do you think you'd have if you travelled somewhere anonymously?'

'Presence?' I stammered.

'Just as a woman?'

The words hurt me at my very centre, and he saw as much.

'You don't have Hilda's looks. Or her intelligence, do you?'

'You want to hurt me,' I said.

'Nothing could,' he replied. 'You're too smug.'

I wanted to throw something at the vivid, mocking face, with the brilliant blue eyes.

'And you?' I shouted furiously, my control breaking. 'How can you criticize me for not loving you? What love do I get from you?'

'Exactly,' he said sadly. 'That's what I mean.'

The left side of my face began to throb where it had caught the table. I could feel my eye swelling. I felt a little sick.

'Let me up,' I said again.

He made no move to prevent me. That night I had no idea where he slept.

Kurt came to see me soon after this episode. It was a cold afternoon. The air was bright, but the sun had a silvery pallor and the green of the leaves darkened in it. There were a few trees with bare branches, the occasional pile of brown leaves at their bole. We walked back down the hill together, absorbed in conversation. Through the windbreak of cypress trees, I could make out the cart that brought our groceries making its way back up the track that led to the main road.

'We've been walking a long time,' he said. 'Are you cold?'

I shook my head and huddled more deeply into my fur coat.

'When are you leaving?' I asked.

'I should have left long ago,' he said quietly. 'Things change for the worse all the time. The Bellaggri family are going to America now. Did you know that?'

I shook my head. Somewhere at the very edge of my mind I made out that, if it were true, it might put Mellors out of a job. But my thoughts were focused elsewhere.

With the head of his black stick, he struck at the rocks as we passed.

'And Mussolini is off visiting his friend Hitler in Germany. I expect he will be impressed.'

'They say he despises Hitler.'

He laughed. 'He is pragmatic. He will think what is best for himself. As most people do.'

And I wondered: What is best for me? I knew the answer. To let this moment go and say nothing.

We paused at the rim of the valley. The cottage was clearly visible now, but Kurt seemed to have something else he wanted to say.

'I have some friends with a house on the lake, in Geneva. But I have to find work, and that won't be easy.'

He put a hand up to my face. 'How did you come by that bruise?'

I had almost forgotten my quarrel with Mellors about Giorgio's revelation.

'I fell over,' I said, without too much dishonesty.

'Are you quite happy? You and Mellors?' he asked me. 'You seem very different creatures.'

'You don't know anything about him,' I said loyally. But I could not dodge the shrewd stare. 'We were happy *once*. More happy than any two people I have ever known, but . . .'

Suddenly I burst into tears. I had never talked to anyone about the course our love had taken. Aside from Hilda, who had always seemed to be comparing her own life with mine, no one even asked me any longer. Duncan had gone back to England. There seemed to be no one who cared whether I lived wretchedly or happily. The note of sympathy in Kurt's voice released me from the silent endurance in which I had been living, and everything began to pour out of me. Our quarrels. Mellors' resentments. The way he felt I had betrayed him. He listened to it all, and then said, simply: 'Leave him, Connie. It will get worse, not better.'

'What about our daughter? She idolizes him.'

'As she grows up, she will be glad you left. Be rational. You must.'

'I *can't*,' I said.

He gave me a thin-lipped, ironic smile. And the blood came up in his face as he stopped and took my hands.

'You must know why I'm asking you. That it's not just casual curiosity. My plans are all uncertain, but I'm finding it hard to leave you.'

'Oh, no, my dear—' I tried to stop him.

'Let me tell you.'

'Please, don't say anything,' I whispered.

But I did not pull my hands away and we stood for a long while looking into one another's eyes.

'The Bassanis have left, you know. For France,' he said, as if he remembered our intention to meet in Florence. 'My sister is going to Paris. I don't know what I shall do yet.'

Then I let him kiss me gently on the cheek; a child's kiss.

That night I dreamed I was lying with Kurt in the double bed of my own cottage. And suddenly I found myself wondering where Mellors could have found to sleep. That question bothered me so much that, for all the delicious tangle of legs my mind had thrown up to delight me, I had to get up and look. All over our stone house I went in my dream; even into Emily's room, now empty; looking through the window at the white, full moon. But he was nowhere. I went out into the garden. The night was white and cold and I was frightened and called out, 'Darling! Where are you? You'll catch cold.'

When I woke, I knew, however drawn I might be to Kurt, I had pledged my life to Mellors. And I was not yet free of him.

A little later that same week, Mellors set off, as he usually did, to go down to the café for vin santo. I felt nervous, after what I had seen a few days before. In the sharp autumn air I could taste burning wood; there were a few cries of night birds, otherwise silence. I thought about Kurt's open vulnerable face, and wondered if he was still in Tuscany. I also remembered a letter I had received from Clifford in England earlier that week:

Dear Connie,

You will be surprised at hearing again from me. You didn't reply to my last letter, so I'll come to the point at once. I'm worried about Emily. I know what you'll say, and it's true the child has little to do with me, but bear with my interference. You know we have friends at the Embassy in Rome. Things may well be turning nasty in Europe again. Would you consider sending the child to school in England? I'd pay, of course, and stay at a distance if that's what you'd like. But do think of it.

Your own situation cannot be easy. Some people who met you in Siena thought you looked as if the sun were something of a fatigue to you. You were always a fair-skinned Northern European type, and I can imagine that is the case. But *if*, I only say *if*, mark you, if it's more; if you're unhappy, if you need a friend, I'm still here, my dear. And always will be.

I had thrown the letter away from me in disgust when it first arrived. How could he pretend to friendship when he had refused to let me have a married life in England by blocking a divorce? Still, even though I had no intention of writing back, the affection in his words brought tears to my eyes. I was so very alone. At one point in the evening I heard what sounded like the noise of a rowdy party echoing across the quiet valley. It was only as I decided to go upstairs that I heard Mellors returning.

At once I was aware that something was very wrong: he looked white and sweaty.

'What is it?' I asked, frightened by his expression. 'Has there been some other horror?'

'Yes. There's been a battle in the town square.'

'Were you involved?'

He hesitated. 'I saw it. That was enough.'

'What did you see?'

'Some people had been hiding Giuseppe in their flat. Since the Fascists closed his shop.'

'Why was he hiding?'

'He was in trouble, of course,' said Mellors impatiently. 'And he and his friends were being taken into custody.'

'By the police?'

'Yes. But there were people turned up who have nothing to do with the village at all. From as far away as Siena or Florence. I don't know. Armed with sticks.'

'Were the police armed?'

'No. Probably they hadn't expected resistance. But Bernardo's men had guns. Someone was killed. Not Giuseppe. He was taken away in a van.'

I remembered the young boy with blood on his face, being taken away at Bernardo's order.

'You won't try and justify such behaviour, will you?' I said.

He did not reply. He was shaking – with something between fear and excitement – and I went to put my arms around him. He pulled me to him in a desperate, clutching moment. The face against mine was wet. It chilled something in me even as I soothed him, stroked his hair and his face, kissed the veins at the side of his forehead.

'Your friend Lehmann has been hurt,' he said presently. 'I believe he has been taken to hospital.'

It seemed to be something I guessed even before he spoke.

'*Badly* hurt?'

'I don't know. He was taken off.'

'Couldn't you do something to help him?' I cried out.

'I couldn't help anyone.'

It must have worried him more than he let himself know. In my imagination I could see Kurt's scared face and the uplifted truncheon of the young Fascist who had felled him.

'These things happen,' he said thickly.

We went upstairs together, and lay with our arms wound tightly round each other as if we had never been enemies. After only a few moments, I could feel his body stiffening with desire, but I felt nothing. He mounted me quickly and I felt his thrusting body remotely. It seemed as if the violence had quickened something impersonal and male in him, and that it had nothing to do with me: his simple male thrusting came from a blind bit of himself, indifferent to me. My role was only to lie still and contain his passion; I waited for it to be over without impatience. I felt like a mother roused from sleep in the night to feed a child, only anxious to have the feeding over and done with.

'There,' he said, satisfied.

Was that the kind of loving he wanted, I wondered, my thoughts racing. He was soon noisily asleep. I held him in my arms, listening to his breath with a remote tenderness. And at the first light of dawn I was dressed and ready.

'I must go to the hospital,' I said.

At first, the hospital staff of the Convent of the Sacred Heart in Orvieto were reluctant to admit that anyone called Kurt Lehmann was a patient. They kept consulting one another in Italian, as if they had received imperfectly understood instructions. In my expensive hat and chic costume, though, I was treated with great civility. Perhaps they had been instructed not to antagonize visiting foreigners.

At length, a pale nun with a heavy chin asked for my name and, for the first time since my arrival in Italy, I deliberately used my old title. It seemed to convince the Sister that I was no journalist or spy, a conclusion that showed no great understanding of the English aristocracy.

Kurt was lying back against the pillows, seemingly asleep. There was a bruise over one cheekbone, and the skin of his lips was broken. I stood looking down at him for a while before his eyes opened.

'Connie,' he exclaimed. 'I don't understand. They said Lady something. I couldn't grasp the name.'

He tried to push himself up against the pillows, as if to appear less undignified.

'I heard you were hurt,' I said, and sat down at his side on the little wicker chair.

'Not badly.' His wrist was strapped up, and he explained he had broken two fingers. 'On my left hand,' he grimaced, 'so it's no great matter. There was a bit of concussion.'

'You might have been killed. Someone was, you know.'

'I've seen worse violence,' he said. His eyes wandered over my clothes. 'How *grand* you look.'

'I thought I might need to bluff my way in.'

'I suppose I'm off limits,' he said ruefully. 'Was there anything about the riot in the newspaper?'

'Nothing I saw. You're lucky not to be in gaol,' I said.

He lay back in the pillows. I could see that his head was still painful.

'Probably you shouldn't have come to see me. They'll remember,' he said.

'*They* won't touch us. We're British citizens.' I felt fairly confident of the truth of what I was saying. 'What will you do now?' I asked and, without thinking, put my hand on his.

A little shock went through us.

'It depends,' he said at last. 'We can't stay in this country. That's clear.'

'Where will you go?'

'I had thought of America, but at the moment that's

quite difficult. We have friends in Switzerland. They might look after me for a time. But then I shall try to go to England,' he said simply. 'If England will have me.'

The light picked up the glints of gold in the hairs on his arm. 'I'm glad you aren't badly hurt,' I said.

A pause fell between us and I rose to leave.

That December Mellors stayed out of the house and away from me as long as he could, walking about the high rocks long after his work demanded it. He no longer went to join Bernardo and his friends; he was usually alone. I knew he couldn't bear to return home. He stayed out until it was dark, often in the rain, not always bothering with the yellow oilcloth he once carried everywhere. I knew he felt as if everything in his life had failed him: both his hopes for Italy and brotherhood, and also his hope in our loving partnership. Sometimes, as I sat in an upstairs window with my hair combed loose, I made out his form sitting on a stone wall at a distance, watching the racing clouds, or looking up at my form, lit by candlelight. He seemed to have a terrible reluctance to enter the house. One night, when he came in, he was chilled to the bone.

'You are soaked through,' I cried, as soon as I saw him.

'Never mind for that,' he said roughly.

He was angry at the chattering of his teeth and, when I tried to bring him closer to the fire, he flung off my hand.

'You're *ill*,' I told him.

And then he broke into a paroxysm of coughing. I got to my feet and he pulled out a handkerchief.

'That's *blood*,' I said, recoiling.

'What of it?'

'Have you brought up blood before?' I put out a hand to feel his forehead. It was burning hot.

'I'll call the doctor,' I cried.

This time he was too ill to protest. The doctor from the next village came quickly enough, but he took his time inspecting his patient, who was now lying in his bed. After he had listened to Mellors' lungs, he took me aside. He looked grave.

'What is it?'

I could see from his face that he had something unpleasant to impart. He shook his head.

'Pneumonia,' he said. 'And maybe worse.'

Mellors tossed and turned restlessly, hearing nothing of what was said. I felt the blood drain from my heart.

'Worse?'

'Signora – has he ever been touched with tuberculosis?'

'He never mentioned it,' I frowned.

'I am pretty sure,' he said. 'I'm sorry. Of course there will be more tests.'

'These days something can be done. Surely?' I cried.

'Keep him in bed. Let him eat as much as he can. Drink milk every day. Build him up. Have you not noticed how thin he is?'

I hung my head.

'His lungs are damaged,' the doctor said quietly.

For several days Mellors' temperature alternated wildly, rising in the evenings to 103°. In his fevers, he yelled abuse at me, and even when he was calm and his temperature was normal, he gave me few friendly words. I brought him iced drinks and tried to tempt him with Gina's cooking. He was sometimes aware of my kindness but the anger he felt against me seemed to connect with every other disappointment in his life. As if I were responsible for them all. In his fevers he confessed that burning hatred. It chilled my blood to hear the accusations. And he always called me Lady Chatterley, as if the words were the outward sound of the damage I had done him, as if it had been the linking of his life to mine which had wrecked the possibility of his own dignity. Of course his words hurt me. And on the darkest nights I felt guiltily there must be something in it: that I had robbed him of his maleness by coming from a class which did not acknowledge what was valuable in him, and saw him only as a creature whose function was to serve. I understood that this was why he could no longer bear to please me but must have me demonstrate my wish to please him. It is so strange. Women don't mind recognizing the men they live with are socially superior. It rather delights them. A woman who'd married a lord would be flattered. But a man can't feel that. Mellors felt demeaned.

Once he inquired about Lehmann. I explained he was out of hospital, that he had gone to Switzerland to stay with friends. But it was as if he were still close enough to read my thoughts. For certainly I often thought of Kurt and his love. Some nights I dreamt of him and woke with a terrible sense of loss.

The sun was bright but the air was as cold as any English day when Emily returned for the Easter holidays. She rushed up to her father's room as soon as the cart brought her down the track to the house. She was now eleven years old, with round blue eyes and straight golden hair: a creature from an elfin world. In the bedroom, she flung her winter velour hat on the straw-seated chair. And then all the force seemed to go out of her as she saw Mellors sitting up in bed, a red dressing gown round his shoulders, a little ginger stubble at his chin and a book in his hands. I greeted her from the windowseat, but she took no notice of me.

'You're back, then,' Mellors said quietly.

'You didn't write and tell me how ill you were,' she complained, not yet approaching. She was frightened by his gaunt face.

'Well, I knew you'd be home for the holidays.'

'Do you lie here all the time? In bed?'

'Nay,' he smiled. 'I'm supposed to rest after lunch, that's all. Don't go fretting yourself about me.'

'What about the horses? How can they manage without you?'

The child approached the bed now, emboldened by his matter-of-fact voice. A shadow crossed his face.

'There's a groom come to take over my job. Last month. He manages well enough.'

'Even for the stallion?'

'He's been sold, I hear. The Count has his own problems.'

Now Emily bounced on to the bed, wanting to throw her arms round her father, but he turned his head aside.

'You know I've got a cold,' he said. 'I don't want you catching it.'

'What about the boars over the hill?'

'I don't know,' he said. 'The Bellaggri family are away. Did you have a good trip back from Florence?'

'Yes.'

She hummed to herself for a moment.

'What's it like out?' he asked.

'All bright and blue.'

Through the window the sharp winter sunlight came in through the glass.

'I'll read now,' he said.

She could see he was tired, but could not help watching him curiously, even when he picked up his book.

'Go downstairs, there's a good girl,' he told her.

'There's no one to talk to down there,' she said.

'I'll come,' I said, from the windowseat.

Her eyes dropped, but she followed me down to the kitchen.

'What has Gina made for supper?' she asked, once we were there.

'All your favourite things,' I said, smiling. 'Are you glad to be home?'

'I don't know,' said Emily. 'Will my father get up tomorrow?'

'Yes,' I said briskly. 'Probably.'

'Can he go out in the cold?'

'If it is sunny. It's good for him, when the air is dry.' I put my arms round my daughter in an enveloping hug.

'It's marvellous to have you back again.'

That night, the child woke from her sleep with a cry of terror. When I went to see her, she explained, 'There's a man with a knife. He's very strong. Daddy's going to be hurt if he tries to stop him.' And then she burst into tears.

'There's nothing here,' I said. 'Look. Nothing. You

have been dreaming.' I drew the curtains, thoughtfully, and went back to sit on the child's bed. 'Dreams don't always mean what we think,' I said, stroking the child's hair. 'We'll sort it out in the morning.'

But I slept little myself that night, listening to Mellors' rasping breath and worrying about my daughter.

It was then I heard from Kurt. His friends had found him a position in Geneva: not one he wanted, but at least he was able to work. And he had not forgotten me. Mellors made no demur when I said I needed a short holiday in the Alps soon after taking Emily back to Florence. He did not press me about the old schoolfriend I claimed to be visiting. And Gina would look after him. When I gave him the address of an hotel in Adelboden, I said, 'I'll come back at once if you need me.'

'You need a break from all this,' he said.

I was not sure if I imagined a sardonic twist to his lips.

It was deep winter in the mountains. As I travelled north on the train over the Austrian slopes, I remembered from summers with Hilda long ago how the Gothic lichens fell wet and dripping over the red sandstone. I remembered water everywhere. Now snow lay in the hollows, ice on the rocks; brilliant and exciting.

I arrived in Murren on the first stage to the high Alps, to meet Kurt, dressed in a polo-necked jumper and a well-cut English overcoat. I marvelled at his composure. My own heart was banging wildly at the sight of him.

'Just let's make sure we get on the right train,' he said. 'Terrible mistake to find ourselves *en route* for Berlin.'

He didn't seem anxious about any other aspect of our meeting.

'Connie, is this case yours?'

There was a coffee wagon on the platform, and he bought two cups of the hot, strong liquid and a split roll with tomato and egg at its core. Before long, the train was running through the mountainside. We had left the warmth of Tuscany for another world. The sun was hot, but the landscape was white. By the time we arrived in Adelboden, two miles above the ordinary world, my nerves were calmer.

Kurt had booked two rooms in a small hotel that looked out on the triangular face of the Breithorn. We left the station in a small sledge, open to the raw wind. I felt we were small and alone in the whiteness. Everywhere, the snow was deep and silent, weighing down the eaves of the houses. Overhead was a pale blue sky. As we drew up at an inn with painted shutters, a golden light glowed from the porch. People approached the open door in skis and snowshoes.

'Not very grand,' said Kurt. 'I thought that was best, really.'

We tramped up the stairs to our rooms. Mine was

small, and walled with brownish wood. There was a hand-bowl and jug for washing.

Kurt shrugged as he saw the facilities. 'The sheets are white and clean. That's what matters.'

We bathed and changed in our separate rooms. Nothing had been said about the terms on which we were meeting. He had neither held my hand nor offered to kiss me. Yet, as I laid out my nightdress across the bed and selected a dress of vivid blue silk, cut low at the back, even as I told myself that I had been right to come, I was afraid too. Not guilty. *Afraid.* Of what Kurt would think of me once we were in bed. I had Mellors' voice in me still, not reproaching me, not jealous of me, but accusing me, nonetheless: of unseemly lust and ugly sexual behaviour. Of being dead in my most intimate parts. How could I regain that confidence I once had so naturally? Could I respond to any man? Or had that lovely readiness left me for ever?

I looked in the mirror to confirm at least the beauty of my blue dress, and it seemed to me that it shone with a brilliant light, almost like the mountainside around us. But the shimmer of the fabric could not reassure me. The glitter was on the surface, and what I feared was some inner inadequacy, hidden in my body.

Kurt caught his breath as he saw me: a catch of breath, a delight I had almost forgotten I could arouse.

There were a few other guests: a German and his young bride, and an English couple in their sixties. The hotel restaurant was little more than a plain, clean room with a wide window which looked out at the mountain. There was a storm beginning. The mountainside was struck blue by lightning. As I watched, I felt I was looking at the whole power of the universe. The blue light illuminated the granite slope.

'I feel superhuman up here,' I said lightly.

'Don't say that,' he said quietly. 'I'm only interested in your humanity.'

Our eyes met and now it was my turn to catch my breath.

'Do you still think you want to make for crabby old England?' I asked him.

He stared at me for a moment in surprise. 'Why does that come to mind?'

'I don't know,' I said.

He watched me, and then nodded. 'There may be an opening. I've heard from Haldane. And some people at the Cavendish.'

'And if it's arranged, will you go?'

'Of course. I can't stay in Switzerland much longer.'

'How do you *bear* it?' I asked him. 'Not knowing from week to week what will become of you?'

I can't remember how he replied, but I know he put a hand on mine, almost as if he sensed something of the turmoil inside me. And so we began to talk freely again and while we did I was able to forget my anxiety about our lovemaking. Perhaps Hilda would have laughed at my apprehensions, but she had never lived alongside an eloquent and bitter man as I had, or taken his words into her so fully.

'Do you want a brandy with coffee?' he asked me.

'I don't think so.'

At my bedroom door, I paused as I turned the key and he waited for an invitation to enter. Once inside my bedroom, he asked coolly: 'Can I help you take off your dress?'

I turned to let him help pull down the long zip, and let the blue silk slip to the floor. His eyes went over me. I felt them like a touch.

'You are beautiful,' he said.

And then I was very afraid. I wanted to say so. All the uncertainties Mellors had wakened in me seemed to root me to the spot. I could hardly lift my arms to welcome him as I wanted. My mouth was dry with desire, but I could only look at him and long to love him as he wanted to be loved. Not to repel him with my eagerness. Not to overwhelm him. I wanted to say: I don't care if you give me pleasure or not. Just take your own. Only tell me what you want and I'll give you that.

He began to take off his clothes. He had a narrow, lithe body; not particularly athletic, but young and strong. Once unclothed, he came towards me, and lifted me easily on to the bed. Then he lay beside me and his hand went over my body, investigating my shape, touching me slowly and knowingly: breasts, nipples, the roundness of my belly and then my thighs. He seemed to be in no hurry as his hot, open mouth met mine in a kiss. I waited for him to snatch at me, to possess me, but he seemed to have all the time in the world, even though I could feel the stiffness of his body filled with desire. He seemed in no hurry to enter me. Instead, he went on stroking and teasing me with his hand, while I arched and gasped in a storm of delight. He smiled to see my pleasure. I had forgotten it was possible for my body to send up such a wild sequence of sensations, each sharper and more delicious than the one before. At length, he lay across me and put his body inside mine with a slow, deliberate gesture, even then in no hurry; he could wait while I came again and again before he collapsed into his own climax.

From my breast flowed an immense yearning. 'How good that was,' I whispered. 'You understood my body.'

'I'd not be pleased to be valued for that,' he said, smiling. 'One body works much like another.'

First his clever fingers had unlocked the deepest source of my sexual response, so that my body streamed for him, and now his words seemed to release me from my fears. I was startled as I thought of Mellors and his insistence on the rights and wrongs of sexual behaviour.

'Isn't there a right and wrong way?'

'There's no secret,' he said, amused. 'The greater part of sexuality is in the head.'

I lifted myself up on to one elbow. '*Is* it? In the head?'

'Suspense, anticipation, delight. And fantasy. But a woman knows how to give herself pleasure with her fingers,' he said, still stroking my body with his hand. I pulled away from him. 'Does it offend you to know as much?'

'I thought only perverse women found that part of their sexual organs so important,' I exclaimed. 'Lesbians, who don't even like a man to be inside them.'

He laughed at me. 'The clitoris is a normal sexual zone.'

He did not ask me where I had received the idea that some caresses were perverse. Instead, he put his hand on the bush of red hair between my legs, and felt delicately for the opening of my flesh.

Afterwards, I said, 'I don't want Mellors to know about this.'

'Of course not.'

'Now or ever,' I said. 'It would hurt him so much.'

For I thought of Mellors now almost as a child whom I had to protect. And, as I told Kurt the intimate side of my story, the shame of sexual unhappiness began to leave me. All thought of treachery had vanished. My life with Mellors now seemed a poor, grey dream. Nothing remained of the happiness of our first years together.

'If only I were free,' I found myself saying.

Married or not, I could never feel free from Mellors now. But Kurt did not press me to commit myself to him. And I stayed only two days, as I had arranged. I had to go back. If for no other reason than for Emily.

When I returned, Mellors asked me nothing. I had steeled myself for his interrogation, but it never came. He did not inquire into the identity of the schoolfriend whose invitation I had obeyed. He must know I have been unfaithful, I thought, a little ashamed, a little sickened at my own duplicity. He must *know*, and that is why he asks nothing. Perhaps he is afraid of what I will say. Or decide.

Our first quarrel after my return was over something altogether different, and left me forgetful of his generosity, and longing to be free of his hurt and hurting words.

Thirteen

It was Mellors' idea that I should agree to meet Clifford in a hotel in Florence soon after I returned from Adelboden.

'I really don't want to see him,' I argued.

'It must be about a divorce.'

'He doesn't say that.'

'He's too cunning to put it in writing.'

'And does it even matter after all this time? A divorce?'

'It will matter to Emily,' he said.

And so I agreed.

For all the sharp wind, it was warm and pleasant in the foyer of the Hotel Excelsior. Clifford had left a message for me to join him at his table. And when I saw him there, I felt a confusion of emotions for the man in his steel chair. He looked ruddy and powerful: his chest and arms even more muscular than I remembered, though the years had brought grey to the hair at his temples. His eyes flashed blue ice as they looked me over intensely.

'You still look amazingly young and beautiful, Connie,' he said. 'I suppose we have to thank Mellors for that.'

I murmured something noncommittal.

'I am a little surprised, I'll be honest with you. The reports I have been getting are rather different.'

'*Reports?* How hideous! Do you have me watched?' I exclaimed.

'Not spied on,' he reproached me. 'But your sister and I sometimes meet. What more natural than to inquire about your welfare?'

I knew very well it was from Hilda he had received his 'reports', which I guessed were no more than gossip from Duncan: my flash of anger came from another source. He had correctly read a sexual glow in my complexion and bearing. But I knew it was Lehmann who had put it there. Not Mellors.

'I wanted to meet Emily,' he said. 'Why didn't you bring her, as I asked?'

'Because she wouldn't know who you are,' I said steadily. 'It would puzzle her.'

'Don't you think she must be told? Who I am and who she is?'

'Who *you* are has nothing to do with who *she* is.'

'You are very selfish,' he said, irritably.

I smiled at the unashamed selfishness of his own disappointment. 'You should think of Emily,' he said presently. 'She could be a very rich woman if she pleased me.'

'I don't want her *assessed* by you,' I said sharply. 'She pleases us, and that's enough.'

'Are your own resources so remarkable?'

'They are adequate.'

It wasn't true. I had already had to write to my father once, to beg the money for the school fees. I had even made myself accept a small sum from Hilda. And though Mellors still received his wages at the end of each month, I knew well enough his salary would not go on for much longer. His work was already being done by other men. Bellaggri was a wealthy man, but he was hardly bound to be a charity. Money was going to be a problem for us soon enough. But admitting as much to Clifford was another matter.

Clifford beckoned a waiter, who had been hovering about the neighbouring table.

'You know what they do in this hotel? A remarkable Gin Sling! The waiter here purports to come from Raffles hotel in Singapore. I was there recently. Exotic. You should travel more, Connie,' he said casually.

'I'll try the cocktail if you recommend it so highly, but I have no great curiosity about the East.'

Clifford smiled at the waiter and ordered the drinks with an air of enjoyment.

'You should. The world is changing, Connie. The East is alive. Don't you read the papers?'

'Not much.'

For a moment I wondered how he had contrived to get on and off ships halfway across the world, but I could see the ferocious energy and willpower in him, unabated; even more fierce than I remembered it.

'Did Mrs Bolton look after you on the trip?'

'Yes.' His face darkened for a moment. 'She was very kind. You live too far away from the world, Connie. It won't be possible for long. If there's a war.'

'Why do you think there will be war?'

'England is re-arming,' he said quietly.

'I suppose it's how our capitalists hope to survive.'

'Something of that.' He nodded. 'I don't know. I'm in two minds. Hilda says the Germans understand what they're doing.'

I thought of Lehmann, and of his father, forced to entertain his guards in an obstacle race.

'Has she been there to see?' I asked, sarcastically.

'Several of her friends *are* there, you know. She likes the country. But that's not the point. If there's going to be a war, you can't be stuck over here, old girl. Now, can you?'

He spoke as if with the voice of reason and I disliked him very much as I thought of Lehmann, and what he'd been saying about the hope he placed in England. I sipped my drink and thought Hilda and Clifford might not represent the England Kurt had in mind.

'You aren't listening to me,' he complained. 'Well, I

don't suppose you were ever very interested in politics. To get back to Emily. Does she get on with Mellors?'

'She loves her father very much.'

'I suppose that's natural. Still, Connie, think about it from my point of view. I am an old man and I want someone to be fond of.'

'Don't you have Mrs Bolton?' I asked him, with a little edge of spite in my voice. As if he were the only one to be lonely; as if his pleasure were the only thing that counted in the world. The selfishness of the man offended me.

'Mrs Bolton?' Once again a little shadow crossed his face. 'Yes. When she was alive there *was* someone I cared for. Not perhaps altogether in the way I wanted. But after you abandoned me, she was at least someone. I can see you haven't heard. She died last February.'

The news astonished me. I thought of the warm, living flesh of the woman whose bold voice had been so ready to advise me.

'I can't imagine her dead,' I said at last.

'Yes.' He smiled awkwardly. 'Funny, isn't it? And I go on somehow. Awkward and only half alive, but somehow I don't drop off.'

'Who looks after you? How do you manage?'

'I have a man to tend me. I hate it, but it seems best. I don't seem to be able – ' he looked amused ' – to make any relationship with a woman that lasts.'

'I'm sorry if you are lonely,' I said formally.

'Hilda says your daughter is clever and pretty.'

'Does she say so?'

'I asked her.'

'What are you after?' I asked directly.

'Adoption,' he said quietly.

My breath was taken away by the impudence of the suggestion. I would have liked to get to my feet and leave him then and there.

'What an *absurd* thought!'

'Is it? Mellors cannot work any more, can he? Your marvellous lover?'

I saw the pain in him. The emptiness, too. And I knew the abyss that lay underneath the sneer on his face. His eyes gleamed more wildly than ever. I even felt a little afraid of him. Yet, for all the paralysis in the chair, he seemed a robust man.

'Mellors is ill,' I agreed. 'I think he is consumptive. He would be all right in the clear mountain air. Where we are it's hot and dusty and aggravates his chest. When he's a little better, we shall travel to Switzerland.'

He gave a bark of laughter.

'What an unlucky wife you are, my dear. So all three of you are living on your allowance.' He whistled. 'I always thought it would come to that, somehow.'

'It's not important. As long as I have enough to keep Emily at a good school. She is happy enough.' Against my will, I remembered the nightmares from which Emily still suffered. 'She's all we have,' I found myself saying. 'How can you even think for a moment I would allow you to take her away from us?'

'Don't you have your great love for one another?' he jeered.

'That's another matter.'

'Does she think you are married?'

'Of course.'

'But you are not,' he said brutally. 'Legally, Emily counts as my daughter, if I choose to make her so.'

'I don't believe that.'

'Your feelings do you credit. But be sensible. You may throw away the world for yourself, but why do so for your daughter?' I drew away from him, desperately. His words seemed irrelevant, outside my own concerns.

'In any case, the estate is entailed on the male line,' I said.

'I can break the entail if I wish,' he replied eagerly. 'I have no particular desire to see all I've worked for go to some far-off relation.'

'But Emily is *no* relation at all,' I pointed out. Then I hesitated. Mellors' hopes that this meeting might be a prelude to discussing divorce seemed remote indeed, but I had promised to inquire, and I lifted my chin and said, bravely, 'Perhaps you have thought better about a divorce?'

Clifford put his head on one side and his eyes gleamed craftily.

'Let me see her. Why not? Then we can discuss it.'

'No,' I said.

I stood up. He looked smaller in his chair now, and I had nothing more I wanted to say to him.

'One thing he is right about,' said Mellors when I recounted this conversation to him. 'As Emily grows up, she will not be pleased with her inheritance.'

'I deny that,' I exclaimed.

'Whatever you say.' He smiled. 'Not everything that is uncomfortable is also untrue.'

There were other troubles. The Count and the Countess had left for America, and there was an uncomfortable question mark over our occupancy of the cottage. The Count's nephew now lived in the Bellaggri palazzo. In the village it was said he found the estate had been run with a reprehensible slackness by the genial Count, and was now determined to put all his affairs into some kind of order. It was also rumoured that he was an enthusiastic supporter of the government. He had no time for the Count's sentimental attachment to things English, which derived, like his command of the English language, from schooldays spent in Great Britain. Bellaggri's nephew was eager to make his own allegiance clear. In July 1937 he gave us notice to quit.

'I suppose we must move off,' said Mellors.

'To Switzerland,' I cried.

'And live on your money?'

'Until you are better.'

'What could I ever find to do in Switzerland?' He smiled bitterly. 'I don't want to depend on you for the rest of my days.'

'If you live in the mountain air, you will get strong,' I said.

Mellors' eyes narrowed. 'Very concerned are you?'

'Of course I am.'

'No other reason, I suppose, why Switzerland seems a good place to go?'

'What do you mean?'

But I knew perfectly well.

There had been one letter from Kurt, which arrived only a week or so after our meeting in the mountains. I took it away to read greedily in secret, wondering if Mellors had noticed the red Swiss stamp. If he did, he made no comment. But, for all my eagerness to open the envelope and pull out the crackling paper, there was nothing in the letter that Mellors might not have read without perfect equanimity. Kurt spoke only of the hopes he had of being accepted in Cambridge. We might never have spent two nights together in our nest on the mountainside. I tried to think that his reticence was only a matter of prudence, but his words chilled me with disappointment.

All I had ever wanted was to love and be loved. That was why I had thrown away my safe position at Clifford's side. That was why I had tried to make a life with Mellors. It was why I had left him for my weekend away with Kurt. But it seemed I was once again to be disappointed.

I don't know what I had been expecting from Kurt's letter. Perhaps some declaration of love; some invitation to follow him wherever his strange refugee life took him. But I had to admit to myself that he had given me no indication of any such desire. What did I know of his intentions towards me? Probably he had none. I was nearly five years older than he was. How could I dream he was planning to throw in his life with mine? He would want children of his own, and perhaps I could have no more. These reflections did not fit me well for the days that followed, as Mellors' illness made him increasingly querulous. Naturally I was well aware of the irony that my lover was living in the very country to which the doctor urged me to take Mellors for his health. Perhaps that knowledge prevented me from trying to speed our departure as I should. At any rate, I did not push for the move. I tried to put Kurt Lehmann out of my mind. It seemed to me that my life had its shape and I could hope for no more than the satisfactions of a good nurse. And I was not always a good nurse.

We had been given a few months' grace to decide where to move; and I tried to explain the situation to Emily when she came home for the summer. She was quite excited at the prospect of change, and was all for moving to Florence at once, but I had to explain that, once Mellors' salary was gone, the three of us could barely afford to live in the countryside with any kind of dignity, and certainly couldn't afford to do so in an expensive tourist town. In any case, Florence was unsuitable for Mellors' lungs.

'Can't we go back to England?' she asked me.

I had been thinking of it myself.

Emily liked to show off what she had been taught in school, and she had been learning about the history of democracy in England. Mellors was impatient with it and mocked her.

'They say what they're paid to say. You don't see. You don't know. If you were in England, you'd see how much democracy was worth. There are millions of poor wretches who can't find enough to feed their families. The whole country has stopped working.'

The child's eyes assessed his words, and their coolness, so like his own, maddened him. 'You haven't been to England yourself for years. How do you know?' she demanded.

'Don't be so bold,' he said. 'They don't know everything, your teachers.'

'More than you do,' she said with a little laugh.

When she was impudent, the resemblance between them was so strong that I caught my breath to recognize it. And Mellors saw it too, half pleased.

'There is nothing of your mother in you,' he said. 'Don't you want to turn into a gentle creature, like she is?'

'And be bossed about by you? No, I don't,' she said.

Then she laughed; a quick, frightened sound, as if she felt she had gone too far. He was standing between her and the door and caught her arm as she made to skip out.

'You little monkey,' he said at last. 'Girls ought to treat their fathers with respect. I could wallop you if I felt like it.'

Her eyes faced him out defiantly. 'Civilized people don't do that!'

'Don't they? Much you know. They kill one another if their blood's up.' But his anger with the girl went as quickly as it had come up in him. Her hand went to feel her arm, which was bruised from his grip.

'And don't go blabbing a whole lot of nonsense. No one's hurt you. Not yet.'

After the child had run off, Mellors tried to straighten the kitchen but the thought of his violent anger with the child had upset him. I could see he was feverish. He had some trouble getting up the stairs to lie down. Once in bed, he looked as helpless as a child under the bedclothes.

When I went up to see him later, I felt my love for him returning. Watching him quarrel with Emily, I had longed for freedom from him so intensely I was close

257

to hating him. Now that hatred was gone as if it had been a poison in my blood. I knew that his body was like my own; that I needed him absolutely.

I put my hand to his forehead. It was dry and burning. 'Shall I get you an iced drink?'

'I don't know,' he said.

It was as if he were refusing to help me by taking any decision of his own, as if forcing me to be fully responsible for him.

'Yes,' I said. 'And an aspirin or two. You have a fever.'

'Do I?'

He coughed and a little fear came into my heart.

I put the limes in a jug and took the ice water from the refrigerator. Strange to think of ice being brought from the hills. Romantic, even. I stirred the glass.

He could not sit up and drink so I held the glass to his lips.

'You're kind,' he said.

He sounded surprised.

'Lie still, my love,' I said, soothingly.

Later, I stood in the window and looked out at the rim of hills. There were so many kinds of tree: Mellors could name them all, and I knew none of them. The moon was coming up behind the crest of the hill and touching all the tips of the trees with silver. There were pools of its light in the garden stone close by the house. A marvellous, silvery blue.

I felt bitterly alone. It was as if I could already anticipate how it would feel if Mellors were to die. I thought of the freedom I had craved, but now there was no pleasure in it. It seemed cold and bleak, like a moon landscape in which my voice would have no sound. How could I live without him? I went back to lie down at his side and he stirred as I lay beside him. His body was still hot, and I could not hold him without feeling my own temperature rise uncomfortably.

'You are so good to me,' he murmured.

A great happiness filled me.

'You love me?' I asked, with a little pathos.

I had doubted it so often in recent months.

'Yes. Go to sleep,' he murmured.

The sweetness of that knowledge ran through my body.

I got up early the next morning, still certain of our love for one another. About ten o'clock I went to see if he would like a cup of English tea, which I had brought back from Florence. I found him sitting up in bed, and my heart lurched uneasily.

'You're better,' I said cheerfully, though something in the blackness of his gaze worried me.

'Am I?' he shrugged. 'Much you know.'

The hostility was back in his voice.

'What is it?'

'I'm thinking of all the mistakes I've made in my life. And how I came to make them. You'll not understand any of it. So don't pretend to be interested.'

'Do you mean *political* mistakes?'

'Everything connects,' he said bitterly. 'You won't believe me, but I see it so clearly. There's an order that mustn't be broken, and if you go against it nothing goes right.'

I bit my lip.

'Who wouldn't want the ordinary man to stand up for himself? The men back home were so lily-livered, letting themselves be put on. But it's all the same. Dress him up in uniform and give him a truncheon, and an ordinary man is as big a bully as anyone else.'

His health remained unpredictable. Some days went by and the thermometer showed nothing abnormal. Then his temperature would fly up again and his whole being would change. The doctor explained that it was a characteristic of the disease, that I must expect violent swings of emotion. I tried to allow for them, but my own moods fluctuated wildly in response. I knew he was trying to explain something to me even when he seemed most unkind.

'You see how it is, Connie. We've been bad for each other. Not our fault. Either of us. But now I can see it.'

'No,' I insisted.

'*Yes.* You'd have found someone else to suit you better. Of course you would. And, as for me, I'd have been better off lonely, going about my old life and never tempted into anything I couldn't handle. At your side I was nothing. Less than nothing. And that's not right. That's not how anyone should have to feel. I'd done something to make sense of my life. Had some dignity until we tried to make a go of things.'

I tried to interrupt, but he wouldn't let me.

'I don't want to hear about your love for me,' he said wearily.

'I only know I exhaust myself trying to make your life better,' I said sharply.

'What good does that do me?'

'You're so unfair!' I exclaimed.

'I'm only trying to understand.'

Did I never think of abandoning my place at Mellor's side? I never aspired to saintliness. Of course I thought of going. But there were many reasons for not leaving him, among them the knowledge of Emily's love. And other, less altruistic hesitations. Where would I have gone? Home to Hilda? My father? Or to pursue Kurt? Yet, for all the selfishness of such thoughts, I was held by something stronger than either my uncertainties or my sense of duty.

When the doctor came, he saw how exhausted I was and warned me: 'Be careful, Signora! If you don't look after yourself, I shall have two patients on my hands. You know this microbe is very powerful. To begin with, let me urge you again – you must sleep in another room.'

'I've always been healthy,' I said. 'I'm not worried about that.'

Yet the note of sympathy in his voice brought tears of self-pity for a moment to my eyes, and I was tempted to confide in him. As I spoke hesitantly of Mellors' sudden rages, and the way I sometimes flew at him in return, he listened unsurprised.

'It is the disease, Signora,' he said simply.

'And where can we go now?' I asked him, explaining that Bellaggri's nephew had given us notice to quit the stone house.

He looked at me with great sadness. 'It will not be easy,' he admitted. 'That cough of his will make him much feared. You know, he would be better in a sanatorium.'

The suggestion pierced my fatigue with a new fear.

'He will not agree to that,' I exclaimed.

So I knew what I must do. I wrote to Bellaggri's nephew, and offered to pay rent on our stone house for another six months. I don't remember now how I found the money to pay him in advance, but I know I had never felt so frighteningly short of money in my whole life.

Over the summer Mellors' health improved and I wanted to believe his recovery was permanent. As the harvest season began that year, I think we both hoped it was possible. He began pottering around again, with his temperature down to normal. Emily went off cheerfully to stay with schoolfriends. The sense of crisis lifted.

Once Mellors felt better, he liked to be out of the house. His greatest pleasure had been the exploration of the landscape around us, and even though his illness had taken away his freedom to walk very far, he usually found a place in the olive groves down the hill from the house, sometimes sketching, sometimes reading. I sat inside to escape the heat.

One day I was surprised to see Bernardo, in full uniform, at our cottage door. His arrival made me nervous, and I dropped the bowl of pins I was holding as I turned up the hem of an old dress.

'Is something wrong?' I asked him.

'What should be wrong, Signora Mellors?' he asked me blandly.

I tried to conceal the hostility I felt for him, standing there with his legs so confidently apart, so full of his own authority.

'I came to inquire about your husband. I have not seen him for some months.'

'He is quite well today,' I said.

He stuck his thumbs in the thick leather belt at his waist. 'Good. Good. I was wondering whether you might like to come to the fiesta today, in the next village.'

'Today?' I was surprised.

'I have a car here,' he said. 'It would be no effort

for him. No need to dress. There will be wine and folk music, and food, of course.'

'A Fascist celebration,' I said, dully. 'I don't know, Bernardo. I'm very busy today.'

I could not overcome my memory of the young boy on his knees at my feet, being lifted bodily to be thrown into a van.

'A folk festival,' he corrected me. 'Traditional. Nothing to do with politics.'

I tried to put aside my own feelings, or at least keep the expression of them from my face.

'Even if you don't want to come yourself, perhaps your husband might enjoy the change of scenery?'

I could see that perhaps he might, and Bernardo went down to the olive grove to ask him. I was in two minds about letting Mellors go off without me, though I was glad to think of him having some entertainment.

But Bernardo returned almost at once, saying that Mellors had refused. When I heard the noise of his truck going back up the dust path, I went to the olive groves to call Mellors for lunch, and he was sitting motionless and disconsolate. From the village across the hills I could hear the sound of music from the fiesta.

'You should have gone, perhaps,' I told him, thinking how little gaiety there was in his life, and how he had enjoyed the village celebrations in the past when he had many friends among the field workers.

'I couldn't go strutting in with Bernardo,' he pointed out sourly. 'I know what they think of him.'

'Did you make an excuse?'

'No,' he said shortly.

The music seemed to be blown towards us enticingly.

'But you'd have *liked* to go in some ways, wouldn't you?' I asked him.

'Aye,' he said. 'There's a friendliness over there.'

And not with me, he intended me to understand, but I did not take offence at it. Instead, I went to have a word with Gina, and after about half an hour a young man from her father's terrace came down the hill on an old cart with the offer of a lift to the fiesta.

'Bernardo may be surprised to see you there,' I warned.

'I shan't care for that,' he said.

The afternoon hours flew by as I sat drinking coffee in the sunlight in front of the house. The landscape was blooming. On the pale olive trees there was a burden of fruit. The grapes were ripe on the vines. The season made itself felt in my own body as a kind of restlessness.

As I walked in the silence, I could not help thinking about the oppressive presence Mellors had become, how much I had learnt to wait on his will, his whim as it had become; to respond when he called, to accept him whenever he appeared, to listen to his words, trying as far as I could to return the answers that would keep him happy and friendly. How his voice invaded me. How he confronted me daily with an image of my own uselessness. That morning I did not have to consider the justice or otherwise of the image. I was free, I told myself. I could taste the freedom in the sunshine; left alone, the sunshine in the air reached me intensely. I could smell herbs; see the light through the trees and the flicker on the leaves, like the paint in an Impressionist painting. My spirit seemed to expand in his absence. I could hear the birds again: larks and thrushes. The chirp of their freedom was like my own. My very limbs felt lighter. I heard myself humming as I cleared my light lunch from the table.

About four o'clock it occurred to me that I had no idea when to expect Mellors' return. Gina had prepared a casserole of the kind he most liked the day before, and I did not know when to set it in the oven. When I lifted the lid and tasted the aromatic sauce with its tomatoes and basil and garlic, it seemed delicious. I felt hungry; more than I had for days. So I decided to set it going: I could eat some myself, keeping his portion warm for his return.

Saying as much, even to myself, changed my mood. For the first time I asked myself whether he had found difficulties getting home. Or whether he might have been involved in some incident with Bernardo. I chided myself for the little clutch of fear at my heart. Surely

Mellors would laugh at me, at the thought that he needed any kind of protection.

For a time I sat on the terrace, watching the hillside flickering; the olives, cypress and ash piled up like a crater with the red sun at its rim. Yet, as the light went, my mood remained one of unease. Perhaps Mellors had gone off on his own in an excess of impatience? He might have fallen somewhere, broken his ankle. How would I know? People had such accidents: they lay in the woods unheard and hurt. The pain of the thought filled me. Earlier that day I had been imagining nothing sweeter than to be free of him. Now the thought of that freedom made me frantic with terror. What was I without him? He was part of me. He was essentially my own body. *Where was he?*

My fear then changed tack. Perhaps he had simply walked away from me altogether. After all, there was precious little to value in our life together now. Perhaps he was never coming back. Perhaps I would never see him again. I felt my eyes prickle with tears at the thought, and my own sentimentality angered me. What indeed *was* there for me to lose? He had stopped making love to me. He did not love me. What *did* he offer that I should have this terrible pain at the thought of his disappearance for ever from my life?

I turned off the stove. I ate part of the food. But the savour had gone from it. The hunger I had felt earlier had left me. My stomach had no room now for anything more than foreboding. And the Tuscan moonlight, when it came, stilled the soft hills with the knowledge of death and separation.

Some time after ten, I began to sob with the abandon of a wild creature. It was no longer that I thought of him lost in the woods; I thought of myself alone as a child without protection in a world that seemed bleak and solitary without him. Even as I broke down and wept, the tears hotly coursing down my cheeks, I heard the noise of a truck. At once I leapt to the window. Outside I could see him climbing down from the high seat of our neighbour's truck.

I watched him getting down and relief flooded my body. My very limbs, which had been coursing with anxious sweat, seemed to relax as I saw him lower himself slowly to the white earth gleaming in the moonlight. His illness was more than usually plain. In a way it was shocking to see how old and frail he looked. I had not observed him closely, as if he were a stranger, for a long time. As he walked the few steps to the front door, I was filled with my old tenderness for him.

I rushed to the door and flung my arms round him. He looked remote and surprised, perhaps remembering my usual manner, but it didn't matter. He was ill, but he was there. I hadn't lost him. I could look after him. The sweetness of having someone to love filled me. There was nothing sweeter, I felt, in the whole vocabulary of sensation. He looked surprised at my emotion. Even sceptical, I thought, trying to read his expression.

How unhappy I had been away from him. What nonsense to think that I wanted to leave him, that anyone could replace the sweetness of our connection. I got into bed at his side. I could smell his familiar flesh. I put an arm round him.

'Let's sleep,' he said.

It was enough, I thought, just to be at his side again, in the warmth of him. I could feel my senses sliding towards sleep with a great peacefulness.

'Do you know,' I said drowsily, 'I think this is how I should like to die. Here, with you, I wouldn't be frightened.'

For answer I felt the kiss of his lips on my forehead.

At the time, it seemed that we had reached a wonderful place, that nothing could ever drive us apart again.

Fourteen

All through that winter Mellors was never without a scratchy chest and a fierce cough, but when spring came he lay out in the sun, his face grey, his wasted body covered with rugs. He weighed no more than ninety-seven pounds, and would eat almost nothing. In the sunlight, his bearded face was lined with pain. I felt very frightened; even more when one morning after an examination, I waylaid the doctor in the garden. His face was very grave.

'You didn't take my warning, Signora Mellors. The Alps are what he needs. One lung is badly affected. He is breathing very quickly and shallowly.'

I hesitated. 'I hear there is a cure of phosphorus and arsenic. Do you think it is any good?'

'Quack remedy,' said the doctor grimly. 'Short of handcuffing him and taking him by force to a sanatorium, I can't see what to do.'

'And would there be hope then?'

'Not much,' he admitted. 'But it would give him a chance.'

Mellors, however, refused to listen to this opinion.

'What is there to hold us here?' I begged, regretting my own stupid inertia of the last few months.

'Nothing,' he agreed, with an edge of bitterness. 'The life is squeezed out of things everywhere. But if I leave, I'll go back to England. I dreamed of it again last night. The green of it. The fields and woods. I won't go to Switzerland. I hate those white Alps.'

I was dismayed at the thought. 'England would be worse than here. I heard from Hilda. It is a particularly wet spring.'

'Then I'll wait. I have an enemy living in my chest, wherever I am,' he said. 'He's sure to win.'

For all his pessimism, he rarely grumbled. He spent a good deal of time reading: books in Italian for the most part. I don't remember now from whom he borrowed them. Once I inquired what kind of books they were.

'History books,' he told me, with a flicker of his old, wolfish grin.

They were of no use to me, and I showed no further curiosity.

Some time after this conversation, I had a visit from a friend of Hughie Williams: Trevor Bunting, an Oxford Professor of History, who was travelling back from Rome. I hardly remembered meeting him, but I was happy enough to make him tea and listen to his advice. We spoke of the common sense of leaving Italy. But it was with Mellors he had most of his conversation.

'I know what is killing me. I know more than the doctors,' Mellors said. 'It's Europe, that disgusting old bitch of a dead culture, with its stupid pecking orders and puffed-up mediocrity. Decaying and bound to die. That's what's dragging me down.'

As I listened to them argue, I was mainly grateful that Mellors' anger was for once turned away from me; I could not share what the two men said; I was too weary. I broke in once to encourage Mellors not to speak of himself with such despair.

'You'll be better soon.'

But he shrugged my words away, and returned to his conversation with Trevor Bunting. They exchanged many ideas I did not understand, and which I had not known Mellors cared about.

After he had left, Mellors was very silent. He asked me what I had thought of Bunting. I said he seemed a pleasant enough man, and he burst out laughing at the inadequacy of my description.

'What did you really think to him?'

'I don't know,' I said slowly. 'You seemed to respect him. Did you not like him?'

He looked at me again, angrily. 'You see? And you think you know me! Of *course* I liked him. But how would you describe him?'

'Oh, don't question me so,' I broke out. 'Whatever I say will be wrong.'

'Do you think he has any wisdom, for instance?'

'Yes,' I said wonderingly. 'He knows a great deal and balances it carefully.'

'If I had been to a university,' he said slowly, 'that might have been the kind of man I would have been.'

'*You?*' I was astonished. I had only ever heard Mellors speak passionately of the truths of the body.

'You see?' He was saddened by my surprise. 'Of course I have been nothing in my life. Nothing to what I could have been. And that's one sadness, Connie, you don't have to face, whatever else you may regret.'

Some nights I lay at his side, my healthy body against his frail one, and felt he was falling away from me; that he was slipping through my fingers.

'Things will be better for you when I'm gone, Connie,' he said sometimes.

'No.' I denied it.

'I don't grudge you that.'

These days he conserved his energy and we quarrelled less.

If cards came from Switzerland, he made no comment. Whatever he guessed, he asked no question. I felt it as an enormous generosity. It was his way of giving me permission to do what I wanted, if only I knew what it was. Kurt did not write often. Sometimes I wrote pathetic fragments of letters, as if to reassure myself of the reality of the experience, but did not send them.

It was several months before there was a real letter from Kurt. This time, for all the coolness of his tone, I made out his eagerness for contact. It was unmistakable, though I could tell something prevented him from being altogether candid. I wrote back a note as cool as his own. I knew now that Kurt and I had not seen the last of one another and perhaps that knowledge made me less patient. Mellors saw the change in my manner at once.

'Just a respite then, was it?' he said to me.

I pretended not to know what he meant, but my mirror showed a woman just turned forty who would find it difficult to dwindle into being no more than a nurse.

'Would you mind if I visited my Swiss friend for the weekend?' I asked.

Mellors agreed at once.

When I returned, he was a little querulous: Gina, who had been employed to sleep in the house overnight in my absence, was too sound a sleeper to come to his call.

When Emily came home for Easter and learned from Gina that I had taken a weekend away, she was furious. She took her indignation to her father, but though he made nothing of the matter, I did not know how to disperse her antagonism.

She demanded, 'How could you go *away*? How *could* you leave him, when you see how ill he is?'

Her voice these days had the edge of her expensive school.

'You're young,' I said lamely. 'You'll understand one day. Your father understands.'

'What *could* be so important? Who is this *friend* you visit?' She was shouting at me.

I tried to go briskly about my business. It was Mellors who understood how to quieten his daughter.

'Your mother needs a rest, too, silly girl. She has to nurse me all the time when you aren't here.'

'And *does* she? Is she kind?'

'I depend on her for everything,' he said. 'Now you're here, we can let her go off for a few days, can't we?'

And so I went off into the alpine brilliance once more to see Kurt, who was in a desperation of his own, applying for visas, and only brought to take full notice of me when I lay in his bed in the evening starlight.

One day, soon after my return, Emily came out of her father's room looking so pale and tearful that I stopped to ask what troubled her. She stared at me as if she hardly knew who I was.

'He told me all about it,' she said. 'He said I'd find out anyway when we got back to England, and he wanted to explain.'

'*What* did he explain?' I asked, my heart sinking.

'How he used to work on your estate. How you left your husband for him. Everything.'

I was furious with Mellors for not consulting me beforehand. It was, after all, my history as well as his. But I recognized he had made his own decision, and that it was part of a separateness he was trying to endure. And I couldn't be angry with Emily.

'I'm glad he told you,' I said, after a pause. 'There is something else I suppose I must tell you as well. I don't want to shock you. But you will need to know. I was never married to your father.' I looked into my daughter's round eyes, and regretted the brutality of my words. 'Darling—'

For a moment the girl seemed almost to suffocate with the knowledge.

'But Mellors *is* my father?'

'Yes,' I said.

'Then it doesn't matter to me,' said Emily. 'Whatever people say. You'll have to explain what it means.'

I tried to do so.

I was not away in the mountains when Mellors died. I have always been grateful for that, and that it was not Emily who found him, lying with his head and arms over the side of the bed. I sent Gina rushing for the doctor, and put ice on Mellors' chest as I'd been instructed, but could do little more.

Mellors spoke again to me only once. I'm not sure of his words. Sometimes I think it was to say our love had mattered more than anything else to him. Sometimes I know that wasn't quite it, not quite, but he meant some good thing, I know that. And I saw a blessing in his eyes, for all the torment we had been to one another.

It was Easter 1938. I arranged a simple funeral. There were few local friends. Hughie had left for England the year before. The Count was in America. I had no more help than the doctor could provide. I wrote to Mellors' mother in Derbyshire, and a sister with whom he'd sometimes been in correspondence. I wrote to his daughter by Bertha Coutts. The letters were formal and matter of fact, expressed no feelings and gave no news of any intentions of my own. I had no intentions. A great numbness filled me. In due course letters came back, which I opened but hardly read.

I had not written to Kurt. I could not even let myself think of Kurt. Emily refused to go back to school, and hung around the house looking almost plain in her grief. I tried to put my mind to her health, but I did not know how to break through her anguished withdrawal. There were other matters to consider.

At breakfast one morning I determined to try to reach her. 'We must leave Italy,' I said, and she continued to look sullen.

'Why?'

'We are too alone here,' I said. 'And we have friends in England.'

Emily shrugged. 'Whatever you say. It doesn't make any difference.'

'I know how you feel,' I said. 'I'm unhappy too.'

She glared at me, as if she couldn't believe it.

'Don't you think I loved him?' I asked her.

She made an odd little grimace. 'He *said* you did. I suppose so. It doesn't bring him back, though, does it?'

'Even so, we don't have to be enemies,' I cried. 'He wouldn't want that.'

I put out my arms and, after a moment's hesitation, she came to me for comfort, and I held her close.

Fifteen

Whatever nostalgia I had been feeling in Italy as I thought of England was rapidly dispelled as Emily and I waited for a taxi outside Victoria Station on a miserably wet evening in late September 1938. No one had come to meet us at the station. Emily, who had fallen asleep on the train from Dover, was shivering with fatigue. She stared around in mute bewilderment at the knobbly, mackintoshed crowds bustling on their journey home.

'You will like Aunt Hilda's house,' I comforted her.

She did not reply, but she allowed me to take her hand as we got into the taxi.

The news vendors, I remember, were shouting the last stages of the Munich crisis.

The cabbie had a face as broad and red as an apple, and had opened his glass panel the better to talk to us when the street lights were suddenly extinguished.

'What's happening?' I asked.

'Blackout,' he told me. 'They'd have it in the West

End, too, but the theatres object. What do you reckon to this Hitler, then? Bombing women and kiddies.'

The streets shone with the rain, and there was a pandemonium of hooting as we reached the traffic lights which no longer functioned on Kensington High Street.

'Seen it on the newsreels, the bombing. In Spain and all. I don't know what's coming over the world, meself. Come back from abroad, have you?' he asked me, as he carried the cases to Hilda's front door. As I gave him the coins for the fare, he added with a degree of self-importance, 'Course, I'm a member of the ARP meself.'

I had no idea what he meant.

'Air-raid precautions,' he told me. 'Where've you been living, then?'

I told him I'd been abroad for some years.

'Best country in the world, this is,' he told me, beaming.

I wanted to agree with him, but I couldn't yet feel it was so.

'Darling!' Hilda opened the door herself, having seen us approach. 'What a horrible night. I do hope you'll forgive me not meeting you at the station, but I was waiting for the *most* important phone call.' She embraced me and looked down at Emily, who returned her gaze steadily, throwing back her head to free her forehead of her mane of long, reddish hair. 'How intelligent she looks,' said Hilda, a little uneasily. 'And grown up.'

Emily gave a flickering smile. 'I *should* be grown up at twelve,' she said.

As she spoke, the electricity supply came on again, and I blinked in the brilliance of the hallway. There was a heap of small cardboard boxes on the hall table, a sight so uncharacteristically dingy that I couldn't help asking what they might be.

'Gas masks,' said Hilda, with a mocking groan. 'Isn't it absurd? I went to some trouble to get one for Emily, but it's all nonsense. Just leave all your stuff here and I'll have someone deal with your things. Come into the warmth.'

Emily and I followed her along the corridor to the sitting room I remembered so well.

'Poor Connie. What a rotten business. I won't ask you what you think you're going to do next,' she said to me, 'because I shouldn't think you have the slightest idea. At least you're both home.'

As I looked around, I remembered how things had always been: the bland comfort, the idleness and the emptiness I had run away from to live with Mellors all those years ago. Now I found myself thrown back into it. Except that I now had Emily to care for.

'What was your phone call?' I asked.

'Oh, that was Ronald. He's a very important politician and, do you know, I think we might even get married.'

Hilda was looking quite beautiful. Her hair was waved to the shape of her head, her eyebrows plucked to a thin line, and her long skirt made her look as elegant as a pencil.

The room was just as I remembered it, except for a pile of black material carefully folded on one of the square armchairs. Hilda saw my curious glance and groaned again.

'So tedious, all this. Because Ronald says there isn't going to be a war, and he knows everybody who matters. He's going to be an earl, you know. When his father pops off. Honestly, you must come to one of his parties. He's absolutely in the swim.'

'I'm not sure I'm up to swimming,' I said wryly.

'Oh, Connie, you've been living too long in a village. You'll be so glad to be back, once you're used to it. Father's very pleased, by the way.'

'He never came to see us in Italy,' I said.

The tea arrived on a trolley, with pretty green and gold china cups to drink from. I saw Emily marvelling at the daintiness of the handles.

'Ronald says you mustn't believe all the nonsense whipped up by the press. Still, I've bought in mounds of sugar. Do you remember how short of things we were last time?' Then Emily gave an enchanting little yawn, and Hilda said, 'Ovaltine and bed? I'll get one of the maids to show you to your room.'

Emily nodded, and smiled for almost the first time.

'She's very lovely, isn't she?' said Hilda when Emily had gone off. 'Though there's something rather formidable about her.'

'She looks like Mellors,' I said flatly. 'And she has something of his character, too, so don't try and bully her.'

'I never bully anyone,' said Hilda, her thin eyebrows rising in an incredulous line. 'Poor Connie, what a life you must have had. Now, tell me everything.'

'Nothing to tell,' I said, with an edge of ill temper. 'I've come back, as I told you I would. Now Mellors is gone there's nothing to hold me in Italy.'

'Well, it's an ill wind,' said Hilda, without much attempt at diplomacy.

Supper began with a thin asparagus soup which smelled of nothing much and tasted watery to me after so many years of Tuscan cookery. My appetite failed me at the first mouthful, but I was glad of the glass of wine. It emboldened me to ask if there were any letters for me. I had written to Kurt, giving him Hilda's address. With a little nod towards the sideboard, Hilda said there were one or two. I had to conceal my impatience, but after I had toyed with the roast of lamb, I got up as casually as I could to see what they might be. I snatched at once at the one in Kurt's writing, even though I could feel Hilda watching me.

'I see you have some other attachment,' she probed inquisitively.

'Not exactly an attachment,' I said ruefully, trying to conceal my disappointment at the contents of Kurt's letter: he had written to say he had heard both of Mellors' death and my departure, but did not yet know when he would get to England. If he did, he would contact me, but at the moment things looked uncertain.

Hilda was following her own thoughts: 'You really do have a knack of meeting men,' she said. 'Do you know, after I broke up with Giorgio, I was quite desolate. There was absolutely no one for almost a year. I don't know *how* you do it. I think it must be something in your passivity. Men like that, don't they?'

I said I had not thought about it.

'Until I met Ronald, I couldn't find *anyone* suitable. But then, I don't suppose this new man of yours is remotely suitable.'

'No,' I said, 'I don't suppose you would think so.'

'Honestly!' She shook her head at me. 'Well, is he glamorous? Do tell, Connie. There's no gossip at all at the moment. All people want to talk about is the war.'

'I like him,' I said. 'I shouldn't think you'd find him glamorous.'

She seemed to lose interest in the matter.

'You'll go and see Clifford, of course?' she said. 'He's been very ill, you know.'

I said I was sorry to hear that, but I had no intention of going to see him.

'His kidneys,' she said. 'It's quite serious. Don't be stubborn, will you, Connie? He seems very keen that Emily should take his name. Which I think is decent of him, don't you? When you arrange a new school, you must make it clear she is a Chatterley. For her sake.'

'Emily wouldn't like that. She was very attached to her father,' I said firmly.

'Do be sensible,' said Hilda. 'I imagine you want to send her to a decent school?'

'She can go to a day school for the moment,' I said. 'Maybe St Paul's. She'd never agree to changing her name, whatever you say.'

'I've never heard of anything so absurd,' Hilda said, glaring at me. 'There's no reason for it. You've forgotten what England is like. Father will have to talk to you. He sends his apologies, by the way. He wanted to be here to greet you, but he's in Scotland.'

'Is he quite well?' I asked.

'Seemingly. A good constitution, for all his vices.'

The fine English Stilton was the only food which seemed to have any savour in the whole meal, and I ate it thoughtfully.

'How are your finances?' Hilda asked presently.

'I pay my way,' I said.

'Good Lord, I should *hope* you might do rather better than that. You must let Ronald help you with your investments. He's very canny.'

'Did you say he is in the House of Commons?' I asked, not because I was particularly interested, but to distract Hilda from her investigation of my affairs.

'No. Should be, of course. But most important decisions are made behind the scenes, aren't they? That's where his influence counts.'

I saw a good deal of Hilda's Ronald in the next weeks. He was a handsome man, with a little moustache, marvellous suits, and a smooth manner. He became very interested in me when he heard I had just come back from Italy.

'*Did* you get a chance to meet Mussolini?'

I said I had not.

'Wonderful man,' he said. 'Such energy. Power. Eloquence. If this country had a man of his stature, we'd never have had a slump.'

Ronald had a very fine house in the Cotswolds, and the first weekend after we met he invited all three of us to stay with him.

'No shooting,' he said. 'Nothing to do. Just a quiet, restful weekend with a few friends.'

Hilda accepted with fulsome delight but, after a

little thought, I refused politely. I had not missed the boldness in his eyes when he described the comforts we should enjoy and decided that Hilda was being a little optimistic about his marital intentions. He was unmistakably a man who loved women, and expected to seduce them. If I had any doubt that he had me in view as a casual addition to his retinue, his hand as he caressed my shoulder on leaving the very first time we met would have confirmed my suspicions.

'He's a friend of Mosley,' said Hilda, who seemed to have observed none of this.

I had to have the significance of that explained to me. 'I thought *you* were a Socialist?' I asked her, unwilling to raise the question of Ronald's flirtatious ways.

'So was *he*,' she pointed out.

I thought Hilda looked rather tired.

Sixteen

I was lost. I was drifting numbly. I could hardly have said what I thought about or what I remembered. There were things to arrange for Emily, so I arranged them. Nothing else mattered. It was as if I had stopped having any inner life of my own.

Some time in October, Ronald renewed his invitation to spend a weekend in the Cotswolds, and Hilda urged me to accept.

'Why *not*? So beautiful. Can't wait to get out of London myself. Ronnie says it will be good for you to get some country air. And good for Emily, too.'

My suspicion of the motives that lay behind Ronald's concern for my welfare seemed so implausible in Hilda's alert presence that I found it difficult to reply.

'There'll be some very interesting house guests,' she promised me. 'Politicians. They're campaigning for the pro-Chamberlain candidate in the Oxford by-election.'

'Whoever they are, they won't be interested in me,' I said.

The thought of Ronald's nearness to Oxford, however, decided me to accept. I knew Emily would enjoy a look at the colleges whose spires filled her school books. And so the following week Ronald sent a splendid Daimler to collect us just after lunch. A fully uniformed chauffeur tucked us into the back seat under blankets because it was an unseasonably cold day. There was white frost as we left London, a pale sun low in the sky, and long shadows over the fields. In the hollows where the sheep huddled, there were little patches of shining ice.

Ronald's house lay behind a long dry-stone wall. We approached through an iron gateway, along a landscaped drive of oaks and beech trees. It was a pretty seventeenth-century manor house, built in yellow Cotswold stone and covered in creeper. Servants appeared as soon as the car stopped, to take away our baggage from the boot and help us up the steps into the entrance.

Several guests had arrived before us and, through an open doorway to a room on the left, they could be seen talking with some excitement. I took Emily's hand in case she was nervous, but she seemed mainly fascinated by the curios she could see around her: Japanese armour, Persian lamps, musical instruments. Later, when we were shown to our rooms in the west wing, she was much taken with the antique toys in her room.

'Will you be all right, sleeping here on your own?'

I asked her doubtfully, although we had been given adjoining rooms.

She came in to inspect my four-poster bed, seemingly unperturbed.

'Don't worry so much about me,' she said.

I stared out of the window at a garden of carefully tended winter roses.

Then Hilda came and urged us downstairs to join the others. Ronald himself had not yet returned from the hustings, but there was already a buzz of something like celebration among the other guests, some of whom were military men. Hilda easily took on the role of hostess, leading me around and introducing me to one red-faced gentleman after another, until at last she looked at her watch and arranged for a kindly woman servant to take Emily off for supper and bed. I hoped Emily would not be frightened in her room so far from the rest of the party, and made a mental note to join her as soon as it was polite to do so.

When Ronald returned, it was time to go in for dinner. He and Hilda were sitting at opposite ends of the table, and I was not altogether surprised to find myself seated at his right hand. At my other side sat a ponderous gentleman with a red face, who talked through most of the meal about the dangers of warmongering, and the people who were plotting to bring the country to ruin. I was less alarmed by his earnest words, however, than by Ronald's intermittent attentions, which were accompanied by caressing gestures. At one point he put his hand on my knee and tried to slide his finger along my leg. I removed his hand firmly, but he seemed in no way put out by the rejection.

Some time after the sweets were served, the results of the by-election came through. The Conservative Ronald was supporting had won a handsome victory against the Independent anti-Munich candidate. A huge cry of delight went up from the assembled guests and I politely joined in the applause, though I was more concerned to escape from Ronald's persistent attentions than with the result of the election. After the meal ended, I pleaded fatigue and went up to my room.

Emily was sleeping sweetly, holding her favourite teddy bear. So I went to my own room and wondered whether I had any chance of falling asleep myself. An invisible hand had turned back the bedclothes of the monstrous bed, unpacked my nightdress and tucked it close to a welcome hot-water bottle. I shivered, and determined to get in beside it. I *did* think of turning the key in the lock before getting into bed, but it seemed an absurd vanity. Why should Ronald pay me a visit when I had given him so little encouragement?

The hot-water bottle must have helped me to drop off, although I had not expected to fall asleep easily. I woke a little after two o'clock in the cold moonlight,

to make out a dark shape sitting on my bed. It was
Ronald.

'Don't worry,' he reassured me.

I clutched the bedclothes more tightly around
myself.

'What are you doing here?' I demanded.

'Don't be frightened,' he said. 'No one can hear us.'

I could see he was dressed in pyjamas and a dressing
gown, and seemed very much at home.

'I didn't *ask* you to my room,' I said.

'Hilda won't mind,' he said carelessly. 'She's used to
my little adventures. Why shouldn't you enjoy yourself?'

'Please go away.'

'Now do be sensible,' he pleaded. 'You are a woman
of strong desires. *Everyone* knows it. It's what everyone
knows about you. Why be so prudish now?' He seemed
absolutely convinced that I was only inhibited by some
social nicety. 'I can promise you I am as virile a lover
as you will find,' he said. And he began to take off his
pyjama trousers to prove the extent of his excitement.

'Please don't undress. I have no intention of welcom-
ing you into my bed.'

He took no account of that, and began to get in
beside me. So I jumped out myself and stood shivering,
with the bed between us.

'This is ridiculous. You must see I don't want you to
make love to me.'

'You are Juno,' he said, in a kind of rhapsody which

made me wonder whether he was not in fact more
drunk than lustful. 'A creature of Rubens. Let me hold
you.'

I could see he was far from deterred by my refusal.

'If you don't get out of my room,' I said, 'I will
scream and all your guests will certainly hear me.'

'They wouldn't mind what we do,' he assured me.
'And you want it. You know you do. Why are you pretending?'

Then, as if deciding that what I craved was to be
overcome by force, he leapt out of bed to seize me.

'Surely you won't rape me?' I whispered, trying to
release myself from his grip, and affecting a more com-
plaisant manner. 'You don't need to compel women,
I'm certain.'

He smiled at the flattery of this and let me go. I
seized the opportunity to back towards the door opening on the corridor.

'Where are you going?'

'To sleep in my daughter's room,' I said, my voice
shaking as my hand found and turned the door knob.

He sighed. 'If you are determined to be so priggish,
very well. I'll find other company. You disappoint me.'

Saying as much, he stalked out of the room, looking
huffy and proud. Nevertheless, I judged it was wiser to
go into Emily's room. And I lay at her side, shaking
with fear and loathing, until I fell asleep just before

morning, resolved to leave for London as soon as I had shown Oxford to Emily.

The next morning, Emily and I went down to breakfast late. She was delighted with the many hooded silver dishes of bacon, scrambled egg, kippers, porridge and kidneys that stood on the mahogany side-tables, but I could take no pleasure in the display. I felt too squeamish after my encounter with Ronald to face the fatty richness. The coffee, however, was good, the first good coffee I had enjoyed since I had returned to England. Everyone was reading newspapers. Hilda joined us, looking rather complacent, as if she had particularly enjoyed her experiences of the night before. Naturally I made no reference to my own.

To celebrate the election victory, we were invited to a party in Ronald's old college's common room. A number of the other house guests had been invited too, and Ronald had arranged a fleet of cars to take us into Oxford. For my part, I was determined to think only of Emily's pleasure. We looked at stained glass and old stone, green quads and willows hanging over water.

'Can I come here when I'm grown up?' she asked me as we watched the undergraduates sailing past on their bicycles.

It was such a surprising wish that I had to pause for a moment and consider the possibility.

'Girls *can* come here, can't they?' she demanded.

'Some do,' I admitted. 'Not many.'

'I'll be one of them,' she said with conviction.

Tea had been arranged in the library of Ronald's old college, and we made our way there, to be welcomed by porters and flunkeys. There were several speeches, to which I could hardly bring myself to listen. Ronald spoke about English decency and the triumph of morality: that much at least I heard before losing the thread. Stiffly dressed waiters brought round canapés on platters of shining silver. Then the red-faced man I had sat next to the previous evening came up to me.

'Oxford is sensible enough except for the undergraduates,' he told me, beaming.

'Don't you approve of students then?' I asked, smiling.

'Not this generation. They're all on the Left,' he said. 'Irresponsible, most of them. Off to Spain, fighting other people's wars. They'd have us all back in the trenches if they could.'

'Surely they'd be most likely to be the ones in the trenches themselves,' I murmured.

'Ruin the country if they had their way,' he went on, as if I hadn't spoken. 'Wanting to let in hordes of refugees. The scum of Europe. Pouring in to pollute our good English way of life.'

I was incensed.

'All refugees aren't scum,' I pointed out, thinking of Kurt.

'Why else are they refugees?' he argued, warming to

his theme. 'If their own countries don't want them, why should we take them in? The press make up stories about their hardships. Escaped from the prisons, most of them.'

His face grew redder by the minute as he expounded his convictions, and I could see Emily looking up at him with clear, unimpressed eyes. There seemed no point in trying to argue with him, so I moved away. As soon as it was polite to do so, I made our apologies and we left to catch a London train. As we got into the carriage, I was surprised by the vehemence of Emily's words.

'Those people don't care about anyone but themselves.'

'I don't suppose they do,' I said.

'My father would have hated them,' she said, 'but I don't suppose they'd have liked him much, either.'

Then she grinned and looked so much like Mellors that I had to give her a hug there and then.

My father did not come to visit me until the middle of March 1939, when everyone was excited by Hitler's invasion of Czechoslovakia.

I have never forgotten my first hearing of a practice air-raid siren. Emily and I were walking in Hyde Park, where people were digging foundations for a brick shelter. The rising whine stopped everyone in their morning walk and, although it was only pretence, I remember the prickle of fear as we looked up into the skies. In the garden of the flats at the back of Hilda's house, someone was industriously digging an Anderson shelter. Looking outside at the corrugated sections being put into place, Hilda said doubtfully: 'Do you really imagine those sheets of metal could protect anybody? I shall go off to the country.'

My father was older, but far from frail and full of his own certainties. He and Hilda, with whom I was still staying, did not see eye to eye politically.

'Ronnie says Chamberlain is a perfectly safe pair of hands,' said Hilda. 'Even if he has been deceived.'

'Your *Ronnie*,' said my father, 'thinks a safe pair of hands would arrange to give Hitler the key to the City of London.'

'Better than being bombed to bits, even then, isn't it? Ronnie says we'll just lose the British Empire if we try to stand up to Hitler. And he says there are even people in the Royal Family who agree with him.'

'How do you fancy being part of the German Empire?' my father inquired.

'Oh, *don't* be silly! It won't come to that. Hitler has a great admiration for all things British.'

'Unless we get in his way, I suppose,' I said. Both of them turned on me irritably. I wasn't supposed to have views. 'What do you think of Churchill?' I asked my father, nevertheless.

'Never trusted him,' he said. 'Not after Gallipoli. Hopeless, reckless brute. Still, we do need someone with a bit of guts. Don't like the present shower. Or your Ronald, if it comes to that, Hilda, with his Fascist friends.'

'Well, there's no need to be *rude*,' said Hilda. She was rather taken aback. 'No one can say *I'm* not patriotic. I'm training to become an ambulance driver.'

My father had come to London for the opening of a small exhibition of his paintings, and off we all went to a gallery in Cork Street.

'Can't expect many people today,' he said mournfully, taking my arm as we walked round together. 'Who wants art if the world's going up in flames?'

Emily stopped at a painting which showed two women singing at a piano.

'How nice,' she said.

'Well, that is—' My father coughed. 'That is *Sargent*, in fact. My pictures are on the other wall. Still, I suppose it is rather good. Well now,' he said, turning to me, 'you could come back to Scotland, if you like, you know. If you start to find Hilda's place too poky. Or the war worries you.'

'I'm fine,' I said.

'You'll find Clifford very different,' he said, after a pause.

'I've no intention of going to see him.'

'You should. You should. He's been ill, you know.'

'Hilda told me.'

'Very ill,' he said, pointedly.

I saw he was thinking of Emily's future and my freedom, and I could not help laughing at his optimism.

'Too late for all that,' I said.

'Not to go and *see* him, it isn't,' he said. 'No reason not to, is there? You don't want to feel regret afterwards. Nothing worse than regret. Or guilt.'

I wondered if he were thinking of my mother.

'Perhaps I will go and see him,' I agreed. 'But not yet.'

'Don't leave it too late,' advised my father. 'We're all getting older.'

He looked, I could not but observe, as spry as he ever did, although he was well into his seventies.

Soon after this meeting, I at last received the note I had been waiting for. Kurt was in England.

Seventeen

Kurt's brief note had no endearments and gave only the barest account of his life and intentions. Yet, at the thought of him, I was filled with longing. For happiness, I suppose, and a human tenderness that I had not found elsewhere. A wild hope of love alternated with the thought that he might have formed some new attachment and be writing to me only out of courtesy.

To reply to his letter in such emotional uncertainty seemed impossible but, fortunately, at the top of his own scribbled page there was a printed telephone number. He was living in a Cambridge lodging house which belonged to Trinity College.

As I paced the bedroom of Hilda's Kensington house that evening, with his note in my hand, I made up my mind to telephone rather than write, and take my cue from what I could hear in his voice. It took me a long while to summon my courage, and I took a glass or two of sherry to make me bolder.

His landlady answered the phone. 'On the second floor,' she said. 'Sorry.'

I apologized for disturbing her.

'Can't be doing with it,' she said. 'Up and down stairs all day if I'm not careful. And I don't even know if he's in.'

'I'd be very grateful if you would *try* for me,' I said, as winningly as I could.

'Take me a while to get up there,' she grumbled, but then went off to knock on his door.

I waited until I heard the receiver lifted off a table-top. 'Dr Kurt Lehmann here. Hello?'

'It's me. Connie,' I said.

'Connie!' There was a pause. 'Where are you?'

'In London. I had your note. I wanted to know how you are.'

'I'm well enough.' He sounded tired. 'They've found some lab space for me in a cellar underneath the Cavendish. Not quite what I imagined, but everyone has been very kind. How is your daughter?'

'She's settling down slowly. She's at St Paul's. And your sister?'

'She's in New York. How are *you*, Connie?'

There were no clues in his voice. I wondered what he heard in mine. There seemed no point in pretending.

'I've been very lonely,' I said. 'I want to see you.'

I heard his breath sucked in abruptly.

'That's more than I expected. Will you come here then? I can't run off till I have things sorted out.'

'Of course I'll come.' The sudden certainty of

happiness flooded every part of my body. 'Whenever you say.'

'Tomorrow I spend finding somewhere to live. And you couldn't stay here, anyway. The rules about lady visitors are rather strict.'

'I'll take a hotel room,' I said. 'I'll come up on Friday and we'll have the weekend together.'

Emily, who had been finishing her homework in the sitting room so she could listen to the radio, saw my face as I came off the telephone.

'What's happened?' she asked. 'You look as if something has lit you up from inside.'

And she looked too wise for her age, I thought, but I gave her a loving kiss. I didn't know how she would react to the thought of Kurt reappearing in my life. We had grown much closer, in reaction to what she thought were the horrible people around Hilda, but I couldn't be sure.

As I hesitated, she said, 'Oh, I see. It's *Switzerland* again. All right. At least he's probably better than those monsters we met with Aunt Hilda.'

Not for the first time, I wondered if it had been Mellors' way of talking to the child that had turned her so early into an adult.

There is a hotel in Cambridge near the river, where a lawn goes down to a row of willows that hang over the shining water. The ducks are iridescent in the sunshine. That Cambridge day in early spring, Kurt and I stood together and looked at the silver glints on the quiet surface. He looked older than he used to; there was even a touch of grey at the side of his head.

'Anxiety,' he said, when I teased him about it. But we spoke as easily and readily as we always had.

'You've been unhappy, I imagine,' he said. 'But you are still gentle. I've thought about you through all my wanderings. When I thought of England, I thought of you.'

'You've never been out of my mind since I came back here,' I admitted.

'Connie, I want to marry you,' he said, taking my hands.

I laughed.

'I'm afraid I am no more free to do that now than I was while Mellors was alive.'

'I know,' he said. He looked haggard. 'And I'm not a very attractive proposition in any case. I have lab space, but I'm a poor refugee and may not be welcome long. You must have heard the news. It's no longer a conjecture. There will be war now. Everyone knows it. Hitler will take Europe like a piece of cake and his opponents will end up in the camps.'

'Would it help if you were my husband?' I asked him slowly.

'Oh, don't do it for that,' he said impatiently. 'If it

were simply a question of finding an English girl to marry, I think I might be able to do that for myself.'

I knew it was true.

'I want to be your wife,' I said. 'I can think of nothing better.'

And so, against my wish, I went back to Wragby Hall, as I had gone once before when I wanted my freedom to marry Mellors. It seemed a very long time ago, but Wragby Hall looked as dark and forbidding as it had then, and I had no more hope of persuading Clifford to do as I wanted. I resented the power he had over my life. Yet, as I came down the drive and saw the dark, blank windows of the house, I remembered Mrs Bolton's death and thought of Clifford's loneliness with some pity. Now there was no woman to tend him. Only a manservant, who came to the door with a closed face and obeyed his master for salary and without love.

'Sir Clifford is in the library,' he told me.

I don't know what I had expected, but not to see Clifford so diminished. The last time, in Florence, he had seemed absurdly hale, for all his paralysed body. I had even contrasted his health unhappily with Mellors in his last illness. But something had happened to Clifford, as my father hinted. The shoulders and arms, which once gave him such an air of power while he was seated, had shrunk. I felt sorry enough for him to approach his chair closely and even to put a kiss on his forehead.

He seemed pleased to see me, but I soon appreciated that he had his own motives for wanting the meeting.

'You didn't bring Emily.'

'No,' I said.

'I asked you to particularly,' he said.

He seemed not to have the energy to quarrel with me about it.

'I hear you've been ill,' I said.

He gave a bark of laughter. 'Even as with Alexander Pope: "This long disease, my life." Don't pretend you can't see what is happening to me. I wouldn't enjoy that, and even the doctors have stopped offering me optimistic predictions. There's not much they can do for me. But I'm glad to see you. I'm glad you and Emily escaped from Europe in time. Emily is important to me, Connie.'

'I don't know why,' I said, with a prickle of unease.

'Hilda tells me she is a precocious child, already thinking of university.'

'We hope she may win a scholarship.'

'Well,' he said, 'I suppose it's possible. But she won't need to. I shall leave her a good inheritance, Connie.'

I shook my head. 'It's not necessary.'

'She belongs to me,' he said, his voice rising. 'She was conceived during our marriage. There's many a child inherits land on no better grounds. And I want a child of mine to take something from me. I'm still a wealthy man, Connie. Even if my store is depleted.'

305

'Well . . .' I began.

'You'll accept,' he said, his eyes shining. 'You *must* accept.'

'First there's something I want to talk to you about,' I said.

'Oh, Connie. Yes, we must talk. There is so much to put right between us. Have you considered coming back here? It is your home, after all. You are still my wife. The bond is real. Used to be indissoluble. That's how I feel it. Always will.'

'I have come to talk about that bond,' I said, awkwardly.

He listened in silence as I explained my wish to marry Kurt Lehmann.

When I had finished, he said, 'Have you completely lost your mind? Marry a *German*? This year? We shall be at war in a matter of months.'

'Kurt has always opposed Hitler.'

'What on earth do you imagine that has to do with it? It's not a question of politics. We shall be fighting a country, not a man. The same country we fought last time. The blasted Boche. God knows, I don't approve of going to war again, but if we're going to fight we'll have to win. Can't be soft.'

'Kurt will be a valuable asset,' I said. 'He's a good scientist. They know that at the Cavendish. And he has every reason to hate the Nazi regime. His own family have suffered.'

'Good Lord. And not *just* a German,' Clifford went on, as if I had not spoken.

I thought the veins at the side of his head would burst.

'Hilda said something to me about it, but I couldn't take her seriously. Such an alarmist, your sister. Always was. This man is a Jew, if Hilda tells me correctly.'

'Yes.'

'My God, Connie, I have to protect you from your own nature. You seem to have a perverse wish to flout every damn thing you were brought up to believe.'

'I don't remember being brought up to any particular prejudice of that kind,' I said. 'My father always believed in judging people he met by what they could do.'

'*Did* he?' He laughed sourly. 'He was glad enough to see his daughter properly married to a baronet. What does he say about all this? Your father?'

'I haven't talked to him yet,' I said steadily.

'Well, I shall have a word. Maybe he can talk you into some kind of reason. A penniless refugee! What next?'

He shook his head.

'Kurt will have a job,' I objected. 'He will have an income.'

'Connie, Connie, you don't understand, do you? He will be interned as soon as the war starts. Don't you realize that?'

It was something Kurt had also tried to explain was a possibility, but I had refused to believe the government would be so foolish.

'Then they will have to release him. He'll be too useful to keep locked up in a camp.'

'Well, at least I can make marriage out of the question for a time,' said Clifford. 'That's one folly I can prevent, if nothing else. I *don't* consent to a divorce. I *won't*. And nothing you say will convince me to do so.'

'We have not lived together for many years,' I said. 'I will talk to a solicitor. It may be there is something I can do. The law cannot be such an ass as to leave me bound in this way for the rest of my life.'

'You are a fool. Always were,' he said.

'Don't upset yourself,' I said. 'Your blood pressure will go up, and it's bad for you.'

'Much you care about what is good and what is bad for me,' he said heavily.

Eighteen

Kurt had taken the top floors of a pleasant cottage in Panton Street, near his laboratory in Free School Lane, and I went down to stay with him for a week in August, leaving Emily with Hilda. Underneath his flat lived Mrs Mowbray, a large motherly woman in her seventies, who plied him with offers of matches and sugar, and assured him that she had laid in reserves of wafers and communion wine for the local church against possible enemy action. She was too eccentric to ask questions about marital status, and if she wondered about Kurt as a possible spy, she was pleased by my evident Englishness. Together, she and I arranged the heavy curtains that blacked out Kurt's windows, and talked about the threat of Hitler's knock-out blow from the air.

Kurt and I intended to consult a Cambridge solicitor about the chances of my suing for a divorce, but I cannot remember now what stage our discussions reached. Kurt had other legal matters to pursue. There were papers from the Home Office that needed signing; complications about salary payments and National Insurance stamps.

It was a hot, dry month, and we spent what time we had together walking by the willows at the back of Trinity College. It seemed a paradise of grass, trees and water. At night we made one another happy in an attic room painted blueberry, under old, creaking eaves.

And the radio, which Kurt set up in the kitchen, dominated our lives. We listened to the news that Russia had signed a pact with Hitler. We heard that the reservists were being called up in England. And Hilda wrote to tell me that the sirens had gone while she was in Harrods and that she and Emily had been whisked down to a shelter, with silk stockings no one would let her pay for. The war was coming, and everyone seemed to believe that London would be bombed flat. So, at the end of August, I arranged for Emily to join me in Cambridge.

It was with some misgiving I watched to see how she would relate to Kurt. There was a spare room, and for the first few nights she and I shared it, for I had no wish to prejudice any chance of friendship between them by flagrantly occupying Kurt's bedroom. As it happened, Kurt was in the lab when Emily and I heard the news that Hitler had gone into Poland.

The day had been hot and sunny, but that night there was a violent thunderstorm. When Kurt came back from the lab, we had a rather poor meal, and went to our separate beds in the ominous, thundery darkness. It was the first official night of blackout. There were no stars, and I looked out at the torrential rain which marked the end of summer, unable to sleep.

That Sunday morning, we listened continuously to the radio in the kitchen of Kurt's flat. Chamberlain was to broadcast at 11.15. I cannot remember what words we exchanged as we heard Chamberlain's old, tired voice tell us that Great Britain was at war with Germany.

Those first few days of war were confused and panicky. Emily's school had been evacuated, and I decided to make local arrangements in Cambridge. Kurt was preoccupied, and a fellow scientist from the laboratory called on some urgent matter, which took him away for most of the week. The only good development was that Emily showed Kurt no hostility. She seemed disposed, even, to like him. I risked asking her what she felt, and she replied: 'He seems genuine enough.' As she spoke, her sharp blue eyes looked so much like Mellors' that I had an uncanny sense of his presence.

Without street lighting, the darkness on a cloudy night made living in a town much like the country. Emily and I quickly got used to walking with the help of a torch, though there were other hazards, and I had a bad fall over a kerb on Lensfield Road.

I don't know what I expected to happen next, but I certainly did not anticipate the disaster that did. Some time in early January, a policeman came to the door and Kurt was required to pack a few bags and leave for the Isle of Wight. He was being interned as an enemy alien.

There was nothing to be done. For all my indignation, the policeman was inexorable. 'Sorry, love. Nothing to do with me. There's a war on.'

Kurt's lips were hot and dry as we kissed goodbye.

It seemed such a cruel absurdity that we should be separated again. And such an outrageous injustice that Kurt should be suspected of spying for Hitler, that I was sure someone would do something about it. I wrote to my father. I telephoned Hilda, now in Scotland, and asked her to see some of the Members of Parliament she numbered so proudly among her acquaintance. I cast about frantically among my own friends for someone who could help.

Emily and I sat together on those dark evenings and talked of many things. Of Clifford and his wish to see her, which she treated with scorn. Of Kurt and our wish to marry. But, above all, of Mellors, and how much he and I loved one another, for all our quarrelling. She seemed to know as much, and perhaps to have forgiven me. That, at least, soothed my spirit as the winter wore on.

Some time in February, my father telephoned.

'Bad news?' I guessed from the note in his voice.

'I got your number from Hilda. Yes. Very. Clifford is dead.'

I sat down in the seat in Mrs Mowbray's hallway. The lightbulb there had been painted blue: the light was uncanny.

'Poor Clifford,' I said at last. 'He told me it was coming.'

My father said, 'He didn't want much of a fuss. Not with the war preparations. Everything happening again. I don't know if you'll come to the funeral?' He cleared his throat. 'Will you?'

I imagined the country church where he would be buried. I thought of the Chatterley family, who would lift their heads as I took up my seat in the cold and bleakness, and see me only as the wife who had abandoned her husband.

'I don't know if the family would want me there,' I said.

'No,' he agreed. 'Well, think about it. The will's been read, you know. Nothing for you.'

I said that was fair enough, all things considered.

'Something for Emily, though. Pity Clifford never saw her. Wragby Hall goes to the cousin.'

I didn't care. It wasn't important. How could it be? I was free at last. To marry a man I loved. Or would be, if he were not stupidly removed from me to a prison camp as if he were an enemy.

'By the way,' said my father, 'I was talking in the club last night to a man who knows that fellow you've taken up with. What's his name?'

'Lehmann,' I said. 'Kurt Lehmann.'

'Right. Seems he's really quite a whizz as a scientist. Did you know that? Famous for it. Anyway, this man is trying to do something about it.'

'Trying what?'

'To get this fellow out of the camp. You know—'

The hope dried my mouth as I understood.

'Can he?'

'Well, he's a minister of something or other. So, probably. He seemed quite hopeful. Don't say anything yet. Careless talk, you know?'

Yesterday I wrote a long letter to Kurt. It may take some while for him to get it. I wanted him to know how I felt, and that we are free to marry and live like ordinary human beings.

And now I wait for his reply. When I look at Emily, I can see Mellors' intelligence and independence of spirit. I pray for her future; that perhaps she at least will live the life he deserved and which was denied to him. She is my evidence of a great love, even as I look to find happiness elsewhere. In her permission, I feel I have his. If we can just get back together again, Kurt and I, and the war and the world will let us, maybe at last I can enjoy a true marriage.